THE UNPARALLELED SERIES

BOOK ONE

To the dreamers, the weirdos, the happily misunderstood, and those who see the world differently. This is for you.

"If we find ourselves with a desire that nothing in this world can satisfy, the most probable explanation is that we were made for another world."

— C.S. Lewis

CHAPTER ONE

NATALYA

I marveled at the wall covered with images reflecting violent emotions. Graffiti art could scream without making a sound. These artists have something to say, and sometimes the only way to be heard was through silent expression. Occasionally, someone would portray a hopeful illustration. The artists are crazy, and most of them never returned from the wall. They would only paint at night, it was impossible during the day. However, when the sun goes down the monsters come out. I guess creativity was worth the risk. What does it mean to live if there is nothing worth dying for? Especially in this world.

My best friend was worth dying for. She was abducted eight years ago by the monsters. Since then, I have sabotaged any human connection I could make. It was by choice I faced this godforsaken world alone, out of fear of loving someone, only for them to disappear or die. I had no confirmation that Eve was dead. Regardless, I couldn't protect her, and that guilt was constantly kicking me in the gut.

I finally pulled myself away from the wall. If I procrastinated any longer, I would be late for school. I dragged my feet along the dusty path and looked up to the sky, my eyes soaking in the sickening orange haze. Underneath it was the fourth dimension, also known as the Dead Land. Trees were stripped of their leaves and the air was draped with curtains of dust. Little pink houses trailed up and down the poor suburb in organized rows. The only inhabitants are children, ages seven to seventeen, with no memory of where they came from.

We are all victims of starvation and hopelessness. The artists are the ones who are brave enough to speak out about it. They delivered warnings in silent messages to the newcomers. The first message I saw when I opened my eyes in this dimension read THE MONSTERS LIVE OVER THE WALL.

That was the moment I was introduced to fear. It was an unshakable sensation. In the first minutes of being aware of life, I discovered the threat of it being taken away. Awakening in this world was like being a newly born infant, except already knowing the horrors that existed without an ounce of innocence or comfort.

I remember studying the wall until I found a list of names. My eyes trailed through the scribbles until I came across a series of letters that emptied the air from my lungs, Natalya Wells. I knew that name belonged to me.

UNPARALLELED

"All the names are on the wall except for mine."

I turned quickly to find the only glimmer of hope this place had to offer, Eve. Seven-year-olds arrive in pairs and my other half intrigued me with her red hair and navy eyes. We were instantly tied together like a knot. She told me stories about the monsters over the wall, who have blood-filled eyes and skin like tormented leather. I learned about Ascendants, the beautiful immortal people that ruled this land. These manipulative beings also created a new race of warriors, with elaborate decorations traveling down their skin that protected them from their enemies. Eve didn't tell me their name or their exact purpose. She told me she couldn't say anything else about them because she would get in trouble.

I entered the cement cave we had for a school and sat down in a desk toward the back. I was not in the mood for physics today. I twisted a piece of chalk in my hand as the rest of the kids came in. School was a choice, there were no adults to tell us what to do. The teacher was here for class and would disappear after. Eve said the teachers lived over the wall and they simply observed us and reported their findings to Ascendants. A new one would come every year. Everything Eve told me was top secret. I wondered how she knew everything, and why doesn't everyone else know? All I know is they took her for a reason, so I better keep my mouth shut.

"Isaac Newton explained how the motion of planets and the falling of an apple are all subject to the same force, gravity," Mr. Barnes stated with excitement. "What makes an apple fall from a tree is also keeping the planets in line within the solar system. This is all basic physics. From our first day of class, we have discussed Albert Einstein's theory of general relativity."

I forced myself to pay attention. Einstein lived thousands upon thousands of years ago in a world before the dimensions even existed. And yet students were still sitting in uncomfortable desks learning about his discoveries.

"Natalya Wells, let's talk." Mr. Barnes said loud enough that the children outside the school could hear.

I hated being called out. "Yes?" my voice wasn't naturally loud or clear, nevertheless, my classmates turned. I didn't speak often, but when I did it was with unyielding confidence.

"What is general relativity?" he bellowed at me.

"When massive bodies take up physical space, they create dips, making smaller objects fall into those bends, something called spacetime." I recited.

"Very good." He nodded at me. "Now what about quantum mechanics?"

I frowned. "Do you want me to teach the class?" The words rolled off my tongue before I could stop them.

My classmates looked away. No one crossed me, and they had a good reason not to. Fear was ingrained as my first memory and so I abused it. Instead of being afraid, I became someone to be feared. I heard whispers fly, saying that everyone should avoid me because I would kill them if they looked at me dirty. When Eve was taken, I refused to take shelter with anyone else. The perception of me as such a violent individual was irony at its best. I've never killed anyone, but many kids in this dimension have. What differentiated me from the rest was how I carried myself. My emerald eyes would leer at anyone coming close to me. I built my body to be strong and I was a natural loner. How people speak about you can invade your mind if you define yourself by their words alone. Words can be prisons, but your actions and thoughts are the keys that will unlock any door. The refusal to care equals freedom.

Mr. Barnes grinned. "Then you must know the answer."

I relaxed, out of all the teachers who have come and gone, I liked him the best. I remember Alda, the teacher Eve and I had together, she looked like white dust with the body and face of a young person. One inquisitive student started asking her questions that shouldn't be asked. The next day he was gone. To desire the omniscience of this world is dangerous, which made curiosity deadly.

Mr. Barnes was different. His patience for abused, loud-mouthed teenagers was astounding.

"Quantum mechanics states everything in physics can't be pinpointed, it's the science of the very small. There is always randomness," I racked my brain for information. "Things can become distorted when you look at the universe in smaller scales, it's a matter of probability."

"Correct," Mr. Barnes nodded. "The two ideas together," he said to the whole class, but his eyes were only on me, "is the basic idea of the string theory, which is why we exist."

I leaned forward in my desk as he continued.

"We live in a four-dimensional world. North and south, east and west, up and down. Those three dimensions are visible, but time is also a parameter. Space and time are related, any change on one can alter the other. None of you would be in class this very second if you had no idea what time it began. And no one would leave this class if no one knew what time it ended." Mr. Barnes cleared his throat. "If you put quantum mechanics into spacetime, on super small scales they pull and stretch until it all tears apart. All that remains are open and closed-ended cosmic strings. Which form dense networks of giant loops with a strong force of gravity. Each of them has a one-dimensional world, with one reflecting light and another closed loop."

"Isn't this a little over our heads?" A girl asked in a trembling voice. Her protruding bones a good indicator she was just in school to get away from the bigger kids, the weak made easy targets. I attended school because I wanted answers.

Mr. Barnes shrugged. "It is a hard idea to gather for some of you. But for others, this idea is very important." His gaze lingered on me.

"There is more to nature than what is seen..." I trailed off, thinking over my words carefully. "Time itself is a dimension, humans measure everything in time just as they do other coordinates, but that doesn't mean time travel is possible."

His eyes seemed to glow, "But it could be." He sucked in a breath as if to compose himself before he spoke again. "There is only one way this theory can mathematically work, there must be a minimum of ten. There can be more, but I want to focus on the idea of ten." Mr. Barnes began to pace around the room like a caged animal. "Can you imagine other dimensions around us? The world could be so much more than what we see."

But it's what we see that matters if only the unseen could be real, I thought. Eve painted such vivid stories with her words, I could visualize the powerful humans she described. I was only eight when she disappeared, we had one year together and then I was alone. That initial fear morphed to sadness, leading to depression in my teen years. Now I am seventeen and I have moved past the grief. My mentality bloomed into a burning fire of vengeance that is constantly fueled by anger, and a dose of regret.

I will kill them, I thought. *And I will save Eve.* I've had this planned for a while, I was just waiting for the right time. My heart thudded as my chalk snapped in my grip.

I knew it began over the graffiti wall.

The bell interrupted the final sentence of the lecture, "So students, the question remains if we live in the fourth dimension, where are the other six?"

I barely heard him. I was out the door before he finished.

***

I felt at ease outside the suburb. I came to my spot among the dead trees. A few years ago, I followed a white truck to a hazard zone. Items are reused multiple times if possible. I found heavy iron rods as my only prize, because when I went back the next day the dump was gone. I always wondered what happened to the things we couldn't use again, the disgusting stuff like sewage, garbage, and dead bodies. No one else ever wondered these things. Everyone usually stumbled around trying to find a purpose, food, or trouble.

The fourth dimension operates on the test of survival. The young learned to crawl through holes in the shops and scrape for food and the aggressive teenagers would walk through the front door with their fists flying. I'd go for the canned tuna, it was more satisfying than old bread, snatch water, then coffee, and I didn't touch alcohol. There were no shopkeepers, it was a game of steal or die.

They would replenish the storages once a week in two convenience stores in the middle of the night. No one knew or dared to find out who drove the white trucks. All I know is that they were the means of our survival. I decided not to mess with anyone who brought me food.

I hated walking around the suburb, hearing the sevens mumble to themselves. The worst was when pairs cowered by the wall, not even giving themselves a fighting shot. Others found their names and immediately started looking, seeing, touching, and navigating their way around the world. Two by two they grew, or two by two they die.

As always, getting older complicates things. Teenagers manifested into maniacs. Once you figured it out, the driving force for survival was easy; protect your other half. Some would die, of course, that's just the way of this world. Witnessing the process of self-sabotage makes death look merciful. Paranoia starts to rise in their faces and their bodies would tremor. They would start constantly looking over their shoulder, expecting to be attacked at any second. The lack of hunger, or hunger so strong they would murder to gorge themselves on the food everyone else collected. Children would die by their own self-affliction, or seek protection with others, hoping someone would take them in. But it was difficult, no one trusted each other.

UNPARALLELED

And then once you reached seventeen, you're done. Taken out of oblivion, just like Eve, except she was gone before her time. I heard some kids say when you make it to seventeen you get to go to heaven. Others were not that optimistic. No matter the outlook you had, everyone still feared the unknown.

I'm probably the only living seventeen-year-old that was not scared. I have been planning my departure. I went to school to gather all the information I could, I strengthened my body so I would not be weak, and I waited to turn seventeen. I knew I would leave this world either way, no matter if I was a victim or a hero.

I will go over the graffiti wall, tonight. I may die in my attempt to kill the monsters, but that didn't bother me because I will die for a cause. Death likes versatility, but I want full control over the way I'm going to die.

I raised the bar and then threw it down. The physical act of lifting something over my head and feeling the strain in my muscles was empowering. No one likes pain, I grew to love it. I took a deep breath and jumped; my feet left the ground as if wings suddenly attached to my spine. I was airborne for a matter of seconds before my calloused hands embraced the closest branch. I hoisted my weight up easily, swinging my feet along the limbs until I reached the top. Then I let myself fall freely to the ground, landing in a roll. I lifted the nearest bar again, resting it on the tips of my fingers as it settled on the base of my chest. I pressed it over the middle of my head, and then hurled it back down. My hands bled for years but over time they healed with hard skin.

One day, I looked in the mirror and did not recognize myself, except for the pair of dark green eyes staring back. I had a flat stomach with abdominal muscles showing on the surface, capped shoulders, and peaked biceps. My face was slender, outlined by a sharp jaw, and dark brunette curls that cascaded down my back just a shade darker than my shimmering brown skin. My curves were accentuated by dense legs. My body didn't portray how I felt inside. I've never felt whole and I knew there were some parts of myself I couldn't access. There was a shield plastered over my conscience, guarding hidden secrets from a past life.

My breaths were rapid pants as I started to run. Most cars were too damaged, and electricity had major glitches, except for the stores, blinking red lights flashed the time from the dirty windows. Running water worked in the houses though. No one had any kind of weapon except their fists to defend themselves. No guns, no knives, it was all nonexistent.

Unless you knew somebody.

And Eve had known somebody. Just days before she disappeared, she gave me a small knife. It was dirty and the blade was dull, but it was better than nothing. I was afraid of her then. How does a seven-year-old stumble upon a weapon? She assured me it was okay to take. I kept it hidden under my couch. I've never been brave enough to use it.

Until now. I wanted to be brave, at the same time I didn't want the violence in this world to consume me. Everyone was cutthroat enough, killing each other over food, territory, and sometimes pure defense. I was already living among monsters called humans. I would love to tell the people of the past that some things you desperately want to see change, will never change. Humanity still beats to a heart of stone.

I reached my house, shrugged off my damp shirt, and kicked off my shoes. My shorts clung uncomfortably to my legs. I decided to shower and eat and try not to think about how it will probably be the last time. I waited for the fumy sky to turn black. Eve claimed there used to be tiny sparkles in the sky called stars. I wondered what happened to them. She never answered my questions; her answers always came in a poetic blankness. My mind drifted back to the conversation.

"What happened to the stars?" I asked.

"Someone stole them," she answered simply.

"For what?"

"To create a race of monsters."

I wish the night had brightness. What a beautiful world it would be if there was a little light among the darkness.

I watched the sun go down. I put on new clothes and glanced at the mirror. *Take a good, final look,* I thought.

I grabbed the knife under the couch, sticking the hilt in my shorts so my shirt covered the blade. I left, my breath coming and going like a wrecking ball.

As soon as night took over, everyone locked themselves in their houses, except for the artists. I was both jealous and scared of these rebellious children. I wondered if I would have been friends with them if I hadn't been such a recluse, but there was no point in reflecting what I should have done in the past. Loneliness chose me by default.

My hand caressed the little knife against my waist. My checkered shoes dragged along the road making dust swell in the air. The graffiti wall appeared almost too soon. I struggled to inhale like I was trying to swallow a giant rock. A flickering lamp illuminated the artwork. I saw an artist had painted a monster. A pale creature with long pinning fingers outlined by dark eyes, and next to it was an angel with blood running down his shoulders, fearlessly standing behind the monster with his sword raised. Another artist got straight to the point—DAMN THIS SO-CALLED LIFE was scrawled in large maroon letters. I couldn't agree more.

Next to it was the warning, THE MONSTERS LIVE OVER THE WALL.

The words glimmered, I touched the lettering and my fingers came away red. A coppery smell rose from my hand. Blood.

I whipped around and came face to face with a pair of crimson eyes, outlined with protruding veins traveling down its body and a mouth filled with teeth that resembled roots beneath the earth.

I was sent to my knees with an abrupt force. I felt a sting like I had been struck by lightning. My eyes were blotted with black freckles dancing over my vision. A scream came from behind me. I was able to stand, and I ran blindly. My ears were ringing but I could make out the cries echoing from the pink houses in the distance. I put my hand to my side and felt a gaping hole.

CHAPTER TWO

JANCE

We are all subjects of manipulation. I was just as much of a subject as the innocent boy straggling behind me.

No, I corrected myself. *He has the potential to become our greatest enemy. I am doing the right thing. I am protecting my people.*

I was stalling. I looked over my shoulder and saw the boy shiver. He barely reached my torso. His young face observed the glass that encamped this dimension.

He finally met my eyes. "What are you?" he whispered.

I froze. I held my breath as I went for the knife hidden in my jacket. My hand trembled and the boy gasped, I glanced down to see the edge of my sleeve had slid up.

I pulled the rest of my sleeve up slowly. If I had to do this, I would give him an answer. The boy's face turned blank as he gazed at my forearm in awe. If only he knew what these marks on my skin meant and what they were capable of. Forged from the stars and ignited by cuts of sidereal glass, repeatedly and painfully. The webs of silver shined in the moonlight. The boy backed away.

"A Raiden," I answered with the whip of my blade.

It was done. I ignored the ache in my heart that echoed the painful truth in each beat, *murderer, murderer*.

There are two races of superhumans. The Ascendants were the first, they are the original human geniuses. Through maddening physical and mental torture, they mastered the art of manipulation. It began on small scales, first the non-living things and then the living. They can petrify the mind and take someone away from reality. Visions and illusions that could be real, or a lie. The most susceptible minds are humans, easily seduced by the fake portraits of the Ascendants. Their power can make bleeding feel like rain dripping down your skin on a hot summer day. They also unlocked the most coveted ability of all mankind—immortality.

One would think it would be hard to hate the people who created you. I found it quite easy. I wish I could be anything other than what I was.

I flipped my short sword up in the air and caught it. It gleamed in the dark like it was smiling. I traced my thumb gently along the edge as if I were brushing a woman's face. And like a woman, it touched me back with a smile so proud that cut right through me, literally.

"Are you scouting or on a date with your blade?"

UNPARALLELED

I spun to see my best friend smirking at me. "Ronan," I said wiping the blood off my thumb.

"Jance," he returned.

"Quiet night."

Ronan's golden eyes widened. "What is *that*?"

I turned and saw a glimpse of a shadow, and then it was gone.

And so was Ronan, my friend jetted past me at top speed. I ran after him, my feet carried me over the hills as if it were flat land. My heart did not speed up because of the expelled energy, only at the thought of closing on an enemy.

A light blocked my vision. I cringed at the glare that ricocheted off the House of Mirrors. It looked like a greenhouse, anyone would expect to walk in and see the exploding colors of newly bred flowers. But the House of Mirrors was a place that brought your internal hell to life. It works like a mind-reading cage that reflects your darkest fears on mirrors. The Herold sees it all. He knows the fears of his people by watching their performances through the sister mirror located in his room. The Herold, the ruler of the fifth dimension and the Raidens, happens to be my father. I saw firsthand how much of a burden it is to bear. He was confined to that room forever. The Herold could never leave the presence of the mirror, the separation would kill him because his physical mind was permanently bound to it.

I jumped over the last stretch on the final hill, expecting to see Ronan on the other side but there was no sign of him. A sound disrupted the quiet. A scream from a young child. My face twisted in disgust; a demon lurked close by. I drew my short sword, I felt it scrape against my mind, desperately wanting to be heard.

Guard me! My mind warned, but for some stupid reason, I let it in.

"*It's going to kill me!*" the voice shrieked. I tried to run, covering my ears as if it would do any good.

Too late, I thought to myself. My vision blurred into the memory the creature projected.

"*Help me! Help me!*" the voice wailed.

It's not real, I tried to convince myself.

I turned, removing my hands from my ears, but I did not tell them to move. My eyes cleared briefly, and I saw the vacancy behind the crimson bulges in the middle of the creature's face. A naked head showered with red veins like strings. And when he opened his mouth the desperate cry of a child came out.

"*Help! I'm going to die! Please no, I'm going to die.*"

My mind was stolen from me. A young girl, alone and cornered by a man carrying some sort of weapon. A knife maybe? Her image was fuzzy, and all the color had been washed away, she was a shadow of black and white. It wasn't until the scene flashed to the man's face; I saw the color of his rusty eyes.

I tried to withdraw, and my resistance failed. The battle must be won from the inside out.

My body slammed into something sharp and hard. My enemy took advantage of my weakness. I felt my skin being torn from my shoulder and down. My physical pain required my mind to work harder and I forced the memory out of my conscience, identical to needles being yanked from my temple. My sword was still firm in my grasp. I kicked at the creature, he started back, and I immediately sunk my weapon deep into its chest. I could see the sudden pain in his face, and his last cry mimicked the little girl in the vision.

"*Help me!*" And then it was over.

My breath came in ragged gasps, but I was built to endure abnormal amounts of pain. I forced my arms to lift my body, but when my back left the ground a shock jumped up my spine. I laid back down and my head slammed on the hard surface I collided with before I was attacked.

I craned my neck back to see the demon had chased me to the Divide.

The Divide is a dome. A blanket of cut-up glass that enclosed the entire fifth dimension. You could not see over it, around it, or through it, there was a thick looming fog coated behind glass. Except at the very top, it had a skylight. We could see the blue sky and the blinding sun during the day, and the black sky at night accompanied by the moon.

I lifted my hands; the glass was warm, and it vibrated against my fingertips. Children always dared each other to run, touch it, and then run back, and parents would scold them for it. My cousin and I did it when we were young. I never understood this fear of the Divide as a child, but adults feared the unknown, while children embraced the unknown. But as I got older, I learned it was not the Divide itself people feared, it's whatever lies beyond it.

I could feel the bleeding in my back slowly start to recede

and I found the strength to stand. I didn't know the severity of my injury. It didn't matter, the wound would scar and turn into a decoration cascading down my spine, and nothing could ever harm me there again.

I started to walk home. The mansion was nearby, and I spotted a broad redhead making his way toward the forest.

Ronan, I thought, *thank goodness*. Armed with his weapon, he was undoubtedly searching for me.

I should keep moving but I paused to take one last glance at the Divide. I thought about this shattered world, where evil creatures could enter your mind and destroy you with their memories. A place where you could only go so far up and down, left and right because eventually, you will plow into a glass barrier.

The Ascendants wanted to escape far away from their creation. They birthed a race of invincible warriors that did not turn out the way they originally planned. We were not as submissive as they wanted us to be. So, they left this dimension to find subjects that were vulnerable and weak. But if humans were not so blind, they would be able to see the glass that glazed the sky, they would be able to recognize manipulation.

But a few of them do, I thought. *And I kill them.*

They are called Seers, humans gifted with the ability to see the other worlds. Humans who have this sight have the potential to become Ascendants. For that reason, they must die.

My back flamed with sudden pain and I fell to the ground heaving. I clutched the grass and tore it from the roots. It faded to brown and withered in my hand, then I saw green strands sprout up from the dirt, a fresh plump of grass appeared in a matter of seconds. I jerked my head up as the clock rang out, striking eleven. I stood and faltered on.

CHAPTER THREE
EVANNA

I was born with hair like fire and eyes like the deep ocean, uncharacteristic for a Grey. My cousin, Jance, has eyes like pearls, the kind of eyes that were common in our family. I haven't seen my cousin in years. I thought about him and my uncle every day.

I was left to wander the empty halls below the Ascendants hold. The humans didn't know it existed because it was located on the other side of the graffiti wall.

To fulfill the mission my uncle gave me, I needed to blend in with the human subjects of this dimension. I failed. I never found the one who could unite the dimensions, defeat the demons, and give hope to everyone. A hero? A savior? A chosen one? I had no idea what I was looking for.

I maintained my cover as a human for one year. The best year of my life, but I knew it was only a matter of time before

UNPARALLELED

I got caught. I was taken from my home by a Remnant in the middle of the night. The next morning, I woke up in chains with a black set of eyes staring at me. It was Alda. She had been our teacher that year.

I convinced her I had no memory of where I came from. I don't know if she believed me, but she did not torture me any further than a few questions. Either way, she decided she could use me, rather than kill me. The Ascendants knew when someone was out of place in their experiment. I wish I knew why it took Alda a year to figure out, or if she had known all along.

I became a slave to the Ascendants at eight years old. The labors I was burdened with made me wish Alda had killed me. I was forced to live inside this labyrinth as punishment, where I have heard the screams, seen the torture, and watched them perform memory steals. I've wiped down the blood streaks from the walls. Regardless of how hard I scrubbed; the smears still lingered behind. Somethings could never be a clean slate. I became a caretaker to the Remnants. The blood painted on the walls served as the décor and the cries were the music. My nose suffered the reek of burning flesh and the taste of copper was permanently glued to my tongue. I could never go above ground, I could never go over the wall, I could never be around the humans. Therefore, I could never fulfill my mission.

I could never see my best friend again.

It all started when I began telling her stuff I shouldn't have told her. Let alone getting attached to her and letting her think we were friends.

Okay, she was my friend, except I didn't come to the

fourth dimension to makes friends.

I never told her who, or what, I was. I didn't even tell her my real name. Eve is what I called myself. It felt odd, going to a new world with a new identity. I did tell her about the superhumans, but not about the other worlds. Where she is trapped currently is not all that exists. I don't know if I did any good. I think she always thought I had a wild imagination, that I was just telling stories. But those stories were the roots of my upbringing.

I remember being a child, watching Jance rip up the grass, only to see it regrow with scary speed. I thought back to the memory.

"Watch, Evanna!" he said with an excited smile as he unraveled the grass from the earth and then reappear.

"Don't," I said sternly, "destroy our world, Jansen."

He gave me a blank look. "Our world is not destroyable."

He didn't understand. When anything is abused, when anything is taken to its greatest advantage, it will be destroyed. The fifth dimension is called the Lost Paradise. That 'paradise' killed my parents. I was only an infant when it happened. Both lost their minds and their bodies crumbled along with it. My uncle told me they let their heads be invaded by blood memories. That's how Remnants attack, projecting horrid images into the minds of their victims and driving them mad, first destroying them mentally, then physically.

I became Jerik's responsibility. He was a good ruler, not a great one. However, Jerik had proved himself knowledgeable on interdimensional travel. He didn't give me an abundance of advice.

"Getting from the fourth to the fifth is the easy part," Jerik told me. "It is getting from the fifth to the fourth that proves difficult," I remember him looking at me intensely. "Time moves backward, and it moves forward depending on the way you want to go. If you want to go forward, go backward."

Whatever the hell that meant. Anyway, he found a mole that managed to sneak me into the fourth dimension. I still don't know who the mole was, he had kept his hood up the whole time. All I remember was waking up by the trees without any idea of how I got there. Someone had taken the memory from me.

I quickly learned about the manipulation the humans were under. The Ascendants can play their game based on raw emotion, and the removal of memories. Our past gives meaning to our current situations, and our emotional response is based on the experiences we already endured, good and bad. Humans are easy subjects. But when I woke up by the wall, I knew my brain had been tampered with because I am superhuman.

Before I left, my uncle told me I would have to be scarred in a painful way that would make my invincible scars appear not so invincible. I remembered the pain. The mole took away the memory of how I traveled to the fourth dimension, but not the memory of the nearly head-severing scar along the back of my neck. I was only seven years old.

But it worked. Without being cut by sidereal glass, I was not able to heal correctly. Starlight had to kiss our skin for the manipulation to work. There was some beauty in our design, but the creation of the Raidens eliminated all the stars.

I sighed. The demons were spreading death to the humans as I made my way down the white halls. The Cleansing is a sign I can go home. I've never attempted to escape, but I'm assuming the Ascendants are well distracted in their attempt to control the Remnants. Which is impossible, no one truly can. Every new year the seventeens disappeared. Then every seven years everyone disappears, and the event was not exactly subtle either.

Get to Natalya. Perhaps, there could be something in her that my uncle was looking for, I thought. Natalya caught my attention because of the way she handled pain. She had muscularity and grit paired with emerald eyes that echoed her intelligence, and just the right amount of recklessness.

It was a fool's hope, but I was never the wisest of people. For eight years too long I've been subject to this misery. Never in my life was I anything I claimed to be. A child spy looking for someone I didn't know how to find, to a sixteen-year-old who babysat demons and scrubbed dried blood off the walls.

All I ever wanted to be was incredibly, incredibly brave, but I had proved in my recent choices, I was incredibly, incredibly stupid.

Finally, I reached the end of the spiraling halls. I could hear the monsters screaming and I saw them emerging from the pits that looked like a shadowy field. They always sensed when I was close.

Eeeevvveeee!! I heard one cry.

"Shut up," I griped. My hands ran along the wall,

searching for a split.

"Ah-ha!" I yelped. I plowed my weight forward, the door screeching as it broke open. I narrowed my eyes, observing my escape route.

She better be worth it, I thought. I took a sharp inhale of tainted air and plunged into the darkness.

CHAPTER FOUR

NATALYA

I trampled down the path newly outlined with crimson. The only familiar natives around me were the eerie night sky and the flecks of dirt that flew into my mouth as I gasped for breath. But no dust puffed up behind my steps as I dashed toward my house, instead my feet squished in colored puddles. I glanced down at my knife tucked into my shorts, my right hand gripping the hilt. I paused at the sight of red shinning beneath my shirt. I convulsed to the ground and fell on something boney.

It was the body of a girl. Blood streaked along her torso and she looked back at me with empty sockets where her eyes should be. Screams surrounded me in horrid inescapable echoes.

I heard a voice inside my mind, scraping my brain like someone was dragging the edge of a knife lightly against my conscience.

Dear girl. The words dripped with poison. *The girl made of starlight.*

My mind was flooded with a devil's voice and blackness that blinded my sight. "What are you?"

We are all human with our bodies and souls stripped away. We have a common enemy, Natalya Wells, we do the bidding of those who live over the wall, but they do not control us. We are Remnants. And we live beneath the halls of our makers. The humans are now useless to the point of extinction—there are no more who can see.

My eyes swirled back to reality. In my last glance, I saw black shards spraying from an open mouth. I felt a sharpness impale my head and there was nothing.

***

I opened my eyes. For a split second, I thought it all had been a dream. Then my ears started to ring, and someone nearby cried a name I couldn't make out. I sat up quickly and I saw kids sprinting away, determined to outrun their fate. Others stood motionless as if they were welcoming death.

I couldn't detour my eyes from the scene. The pale ugly creatures were slaughtering the entire suburb. This was the first time I could see them in their entirety. They looked particularly human with hunched bodies and elongated limbs. Their skin was torn as if they had contracted leprosy, bordered with veins so swollen they protruded out from the surface, and giant mouths encased with sharp black teeth that could swallow a person whole. Among them, I could see a wisp of red, like waves of hair.

I saw her, but not as the Eve I once knew. I saw her as a warrior. Vicious dark blue eyes and lily-white skin were outlined by flames of hair, and she was walking boldly toward me. She was like a princess, two men with crimson eyes guarded her as if she were the savior of the world. She glided next to the creatures like she was one. The monsters flanked by her side, cowering into a bow. Their hands folded and their heads tilted as Eve convulsed to the ground next to me.

Her eyes locked on mine; they were startlingly familiar. "Natalya," she gushed with affection. She observed me, "You look awful."

I raised my eyebrows, then instinctively threw all my force to stand in half a second, only to fall within the other half.

I yelled, pained invaded in between my ribs and my head. I spat up blood, choking on my words. "What is going on?"

Her face was serious. "A Cleansing."

I glared at her. "Those demons bow to you. What are you? Their queen?"

"They are not called demons or monsters," Eve said. "They're Remnants, and I have lived with them for eight years."

"That's where you've been?" My breath came in labored gasps. I looked around briefly, I could make out figures meeting death as the Remnants moved in a speed unknown to mankind. However, they did not come near us. "I was coming to *save* you—" anger enraged me more than pain. "And you're letting them kill everyone!?"

I turned away from her, and the instant I stared into the blood bath, something changed. My eyes witnessed every millisecond; I could observe the pandemonium in slow motion. A Remnant attacked a girl, she thrashed as the creature buried its teeth in her shoulder blade. Then, suddenly, her body vanished, like it hadn't happened at all. I felt like time was receding, but I knew it was my conscience fading away. I was weak and my injuries were devastating.

"You want to have this conversation in the middle of a battleground?" She asked casually.

I coughed up more blood as I looked up at her, trying to speak through my eyes, making sure she felt the storm raging behind them.

Eve gave me a confused look and opened her mouth, but before she could speak, blackness took over.

CHAPTER FIVE

EVANNA

This is not going to be a fun conversation to have, I thought. I groaned as I picked up Natalya, who was a heavy piece of muscle.

I hauled her body through the chaos. The Remnants parted for me. I shared their thoughts and they shared mine, they respected me as much as they wanted to destroy me. I looked up at the mirrored sky, I saw the reflection of my red hair as I walked. In this dimension, the Divide looked like a mirror. In the fifth, a clear mural coated the sky, and fog surrounded the sides. It was interesting how the same glass could look so different on opposite sides.

My thoughts drifted to the very last conversation I had in the fifth dimension.

"If I find the one," I had asked my uncle as my little hands trembled in my lap. "How—how will I get back?"

Jerik stared at me, his expression was hard as stone. "If you ever reveal this, you will be killed."

"Okay," I answered simply.

"And I will do it myself," he had spoken in a voice that did not belong to my kind uncle.

I said nothing, fear plagued me.

"The trees," he said finally. And he handed it to me, something that was more precious than life itself.

My heart was hurt. The last conversation I had with a family member, they threatened to kill me.

I am more than what I've been set out to do, I thought for a second. My mental empowerment was all I had. Believe yourself to be powerful and that confidence will shine through your darkest moments.

I snapped out of the memory as I gazed down at Natalya in my arms. The flow of blood along her torso didn't ease, and there was some red leaking through her temple as well, but I could see her chest rising and falling. *Good,* I thought, *keep breathing.* "I will *not* let them have you," I whispered to her.

I didn't want to do what I was about to do. I dropped her down next to some random iron bars. She moaned when she hit the ground, swimming in and out of consciousness.

"Shush," I said sternly. Suddenly, a wave of affection hit, a memory replayed in my mind from when we were children. The moment that had given me hope that she was the one I was trying to find.

"Eve," Natalya had said my name like it was the only word that mattered.

I looked at her. We were outside along the dead grasses completing our daily reflections for school. It had been nearly a year since we met. When she spoke, it was like a poem coated with innocence. I thought this innocent girl was special.

But when I looked into those oddly shaded eyes, I knew she was hiding something. "What is it?" I replied.

She sighed. "There is something in the sky."

I brought myself back to reality. To this much older, and not so innocent version of the girl I'd known, who might bleed to death. I remember dodging her curiosity, but that didn't disguise the fact she could see the mirrored dome separating this dimension from the next.

I should have left with her, right then and there, but she was always so excited to go to school. Plus, I wanted to leave under the cover of darkness. I thought with regret.

That was the night the Remnant took me. I woke up the next morning in the Ascendants hold.

The only way she could see the Divide is if her mind can resist the manipulation the fourth dimension was under.

"Natalya!" I shook her, but to no avail. I was impressed that she wasn't dead, and a little worried as to why. No human could live through these injuries. I lifted her shirt, noticing the bleeding was starting to recede.

Oh no, I thought. *How is this possible?* "Natalya," I whispered in her ear. "I will be back."

I rounded the corners of what used to be a quiet little suburb, both just hours ago and thousands of years ago. Now, it had nothing, no inhabitants wandered the dusty roads, it was all marked with red, bones, and torn flesh. But I knew it wouldn't be for long, some of them were already disappearing.

I busted the door off its hinges. My eyes fell on the nightstand. *Top drawer,* I thought, *to the left.*

I yanked it open and buried under old books was a piece of the stars.

I pulled out the shard of sidereal glass. It was still here after eight years of hiding it in the house I once lived because it could only be found, in its true sight, by someone like me. The world always withholds your last hope until the epidemy of your existence. My heart surged with happiness and my smile was reflected in the shinning piece of starlight. This is what I was gifted with before I left home. I felt foolish to not have retrieved it first, but I had to stop the Remnants from attacking Natalya.

I stuck the glass in my cloak. *I'm coming, Natalya,* I thought urgently.

I was stopped suddenly by hands soft as a feather but with a grip like steel.

The beating of my heart froze, and my breath came to a halt.

Alda was unnaturally calm, her long white hair had never been cut. Outlined with pale skin and hollow cheeks. She looked like she had been driven out of the grave and been forced back to life. I shuddered. She was anything but human.

"Eve," her voice rang with an ancient tone. "*Stupid* girl."

This confirmed my choice. I was incredibly, incredibly stupid.

CHAPTER SIX

JANCE

"*What* happened?"

I groaned as Ronan pressed against my injury. I felt weak mentally and physically. We were trained to know if you were physically injured, be mentally sharp. If you were mentally weak, then let your body show its strength. Remnants had the power to attack both.

"I—" I choked. "Did not guard my body or mind correctly."

Ronan snorted. "That much is evident." He quickly turned serious, "What did it show you?"

I lowered my head. "A murder of a child."

I saw Ronan shiver. I remember when he was first rescued, a ten-year-old refuge that no one trusted, and no one still did to this day. He would wake up in the middle of the night screaming about someone's death. Not a murder he witnessed, but one he committed.

"*I killed him! I killed him!*" He would scream in the night. I never asked who, I never asked why. I would wake him and tell him to shut up.

Ronan took a shaky breath. "Don't dwell on it."

"Even though," I started, "it was real."

"Terrible things have happened and always will happen," Ronan said quickly as he threw down the blood-soaked towel. "As long as my family stays protected."

I smiled at him. I knew he meant me. My father was brave enough to take Ronan in as his own. It was like I had a brother. I felt alone after my cousin mysteriously disappeared. He came when I needed someone the most.

Rumors spread about Ronan. It's not every day someone arrives in this dimension. Questions surrounded him like thousands of archers on a single enemy. Ronan had no answers because he had no memory of where he came from.

I remember Jerik in a near panic, pacing around his room. "Someone slipped through the strings, someone slipped through the strings," he had kept repeating.

I was very careful when I asked Ronan what his home was like, he remembered one thing. "Red skies," he said.

I sighed as I brought myself back to the moment. "I'll be fine."

Chills went down my back, it felt good then it made me flinch. Ronan sneered at me like he was enjoying my pain. "This should teach you a lesson. Learn to guard your mind before you die because of your damn curiosity."

"Curiosity," I responded as I rose to my feet. "Is what made the Ascendants so great, who made us," my voice was embedded with sarcasm.

Ronan just stared at me for a second, his amber eyes burning into me. "Exactly," he said glowering.

"I should finish my scouting," I said as I stared back out toward the forest.

Ronan hesitated. "Yes, you should," he said as he stalked past the mansion.

I took off in a run. My feet moved so swiftly they barely made a sound. We were wonderfully and dangerously made. Perhaps, I will always wish we never existed. Even as I began to look at the big picture, beyond the fifth dimension and beyond being superhuman. If I could just focus on the human part.

"There is something is amazing about being human, about being kind," I once told my cousin. I only hoped she listened to me, wherever she might be.

CHAPTER SEVEN
NATALYA

I'm dying, this is the end.

The sharp pain in my head started to feel like the butt of a knife being hammered into my brain in slow swings. My left side of my body felt like it was on fire. I thought pain and I were friends. I felt slightly betrayed. No one knows pain because pain is not controlled *by* you, it is controlled *in* you. I was not deep enough into myself to know how to control this. How to physically manage my breath, how to pretend in my mind that this wasn't happening. Every inhale was a struggle and reality was slipping away.

I couldn't believe Eve. Who she was and what she had become. Where she even went?

She probably decided I wasn't worth the extra weight and left me to die. Fine with me. I'd rather die with my iron bars and my dead trees than to be saved by her.

Murderer, traitor, I thought. I tried to ignore the tears that were desperately trying to drip from my eyes.

On the brink of death, your life is supposed to flash before your eyes, all the good and all the bad. It didn't for me. My life was nothing interesting. I blamed that on living in such an uninteresting place with uninteresting people. And the few things interesting that did happen to me always involved nearly dying.

I sucked in my breath, pain shooting through my lungs and a taste like iron boiled in my mouth. My only regret in this life was that I wished I had spoken when the opportunity was given. Questions that would get me killed and answers that would have been worth dying for. I wanted to know if the dimensions existed. I wanted to go over the graffiti wall and defeat monsters. I wanted to save my best friend. I wanted to be a hero. All I had was desire; I never put it into action.

My vision was sliding as blood seeped into my eyes. I rubbed them with an annoyed moan. I found the strength to rise and I focused on getting my senses back. I breathed through my nose and inhaled the stench of war. I tried to listen, but my ears were still ringing.

I stood and wavered in between the trees as I thought about Eve. Regardless, her one weakness was that we *were* best friends. She may have left me to die, but I know her, people don't change that much. Part of me felt like I failed twice, she vanished when we were kids and now, she is gone again. Maybe Eve originally wanted to save me and that's why she found me, but her ounce of humanity had failed when it came down to it. I want to believe there was a reason for her sudden abandonment, she had rushed away like she'd forgotten something. Eve would turn on a dime if an idea popped in her head. When she needed something, she would try to get it but when she wanted something she wouldn't stop until she got it. Eve had always looked at me like she knew something I didn't, never letting a single secret escape. Deep down, there was a lack of trust between us. If we were truly friends, she would have told me everything.

My hands clung to the trees. They spent their lives letting me climb them and now they are here trying to keep me steady on the ground. I patted the branch I was holding, then reached for the next one. When you can't see far ahead, keep calm and realize that all you need to see is the next step.

I collapsed abruptly, unable to endure anymore. I blinked hard and looked up. I knew I had died because the world was alive.

The trees were covered in lush green leaves bursting from every branch. It was perfect except for one obvious flaw, it was guarded behind a clear, broken shield. The cuts in the glass were prominent, oddly protruding above the surface. As if someone had painted an incredible glass mural over the trees.

Something inside was yearning for me to come closer, like a gravitational pull towards the edge of the world. Suddenly, a crackling sound gave it a voice, like it was splitting open, tearing at its breaking points but unable to pull itself apart. My hands ran over it, it hummed like electricity.

I wanted it, whatever was behind this broken barricade. My hands pushed against it with all my strength. High on adrenaline, the world was spinning while I stood still. My senses were on fire. I traced one of the sharp lines around the glass. My hand quivered as the sharpness penetrated my finger, a bead of red start to ooze on top of my skin. For a reason that I had no control over, I did it again, leaving streaks of blood that stained the crevasses. My finger followed to a single point and the line divided into another, and suddenly the glass spread like rippling water.

The glass continued to segregate. Something deep inside clamored against me. It was stronger than the combination of fear and excitement boiling in my stomach, a chiming in my brain that whispered *destroy it.*

I slammed my palm against the crumbling shards, and it shattered.

Glass rained down as the earth fractured beneath me. A torturing force of nature I've never experienced. I convulsed to the ground and covered my head to defend against the falling shards, although I did not feel them touch my skin, instead, it felt like a gentle mist.

Then there was no sound.

My hands shook violently as I tore them from my face. My eyes opened to see the raining had stopped, and the luminous green trees I saw behind the glass now encompassed me.

I stood slowly and turned all around. It was dark, but moonlight peered through the canopy of leaves that were like leather with sharp points on the margins. I looked closer and saw fruit sprouting, red berries no bigger than the tips of my fingers.

Holly trees, I thought.

I've never seen so much color. A blanket of deep grass descended past my ankles and a creek with crystal water trickled a few feet away, too perfect to be real. I sucked in the air, it had a bittersweet taste as if it were coated with salt and sugar. I could breathe and the pain left my body. I looked down at my side to see the wound was gone.

Getting to heaven was a weird process, I thought.

My fantasy of the afterlife was interrupted, out of the corner of my eye I saw a tall figure standing outside the tree line. It was a boy, my attention settled on him. He was paler than the moonlight and his face was defined with sharp angles, framed by white-blonde hair that fell past his forehead and gleamed like the sun.

An angel? I thought.

He was no angel, and this was not heaven. When I saw the blood running down his back, I screamed.

CHAPTER EIGHT
NATALYA

The boy only stared at me, seemingly unphased by my scream. He was whippet-thin and six feet tall. His lips were pursed together as he gripped something hard under his jacket. I didn't want to wait around to see what it was. I turned and ran as fast as my legs could carry me.

The boy darted in front of me. My breath came in quick rasps while he barely breathed at all. For a moment, we were both completely motionless. His brow came to a point, as if he were confused, he loosened the grip under his jacket.

I grew up with consistent threats all around me; I did not fear him. I checked to see if my knife was still tucked into my shorts, I yanked it out. I caught sight of his cloudy grey eyes and my breath quickened.

"Who are you?" I pleaded.

UNPARALLELED

He didn't answer. A painting of curiosity brushed over his face, I could tell he was still deliberating over something, probably whether to kill me or not. He looked down, his baby blonde hair fell over his eyes, hiding half of his face. His hand flexed under his jacket again. My eyes skimmed over the thick outerwear he wore. A mix of something that looked like leather but resembled armor, slim-flitting and flexible, no less meant to be indestructible.

Suddenly he grabbed my wrist, it happened so quick I barely saw the motion of his hand. I gasped, frightened at the sudden intensity. There was something odd about his hand, his palms were cold like ice. I gritted my teeth.

"Jance Grey," he mumbled as he loosened his grip and gave me a small smile.

Odd, I thought. I jerked my arm away. The instant I was out of his grasp he looked nervous.

"Don't run away," his voice edged with desperation.

Part of me wanted to tell him everything. About Eve and the Remnants attack in the fourth dimension. Part of me wanted to know how my wounds had vanished. And the other part of me wished I was dead; if all those innocent people are dead, then I should be as well. "Why am I not dead?" I said in a whisper.

Jance wavered. "What?" he asked.

I shook my head at him.

"I'm trying to help you."

"Why should I trust you?" I said stepping away from him.

He sighed and pulled out the item hiding inside his jacket, it was a short dagger and it glittered in the moonlight. I felt his cold hand on my arm again, as if he knew my next move.

"Please, do not run away from me, if anyone sees you—" he cut himself off, holding the hilt of the dagger in my direction. I took it, making sure the blade was toward him. I wanted him to know I wasn't afraid to use it. Many are afraid to kill just as much as they fear death themselves. I was not one of the many, I just never had to kill anyone to be feared.

Jance took a deep breath. "Now would I give you something to defend yourself if I was going to hurt you?"

"You were just debating about killing me," I said quickly.

Jance smiled, his teeth were shining white. "There is a reason for that," he said. "But the last time someone entered this dimension with a knife...they were one of us." I saw him glance down at my hip where my dull knife stuck out of my shorts.

I glared at him. "I am not whatever you are."

I didn't care what he was, or who he was, or why his hair had to fall into place so perfectly it made me want to run my fingers through it. It had been easy to mistake him for an angel.

Stop it, I thought. *He's a stranger with a bleeding back.* Although, he did not seem like he was in pain.

"I'm going to help you," he assured.

I sighed and tried to connect with my intuition, which was telling me to go with him. I didn't feel he was lying. Liars have a way of endearing themselves by giving their victims a blanket of good intentions. But Jance wasn't making any promises.

I nodded and he started walking. I followed closely behind him, thinking I could easily kill him. His back was already torn open, all I had to do was drive the knife into the wound. The thought was there for a second, and then my feet stumbled atop some large rocks. He turned; his shockingly bright eyes pierced the dark.

"What attacked you?" I asked.

"A Remnant."

I shivered. "I know what they can do. It's just not just physical, it's mental."

"Pain is mental," he answered briskly. "What's your name?"

"Natalya Wells," I said in a near whisper.

I saw him nod slightly and turn his attention to a hill that could qualify for a mountain. Although it was majestic, nature was out of sorts. Beauty is the most deceiving quality anything, or anyone can possess. Just because something shines in the light, doesn't mean it will brighten the way in dark places.

I let my hand caress the grass as I climbed the hill, it was thick and soft. I was not used to it; grass didn't grow in the fourth dimension. I glanced up at the small flickers of light streaming through the trees, it must be the rising sun.

Jance reached the top of the hill with ease. I struggled to keep from tumbling backward. Jance pivoted to the side only to see me toiling up the hill. He offered his hand and I stilled. I took it slowly, grasping his thin fingers, he felt fragile.

We came out of the trees and I gasped at the sight from the peak of the hill. I could only imagine the magnificent places in the world I learned about in school. I used to envision the relicts by painting the sights in my head. The view from Mount

Everest, the beauty of Niagara Falls, the man-made neon lights of Paris. Places long gone, not even the mark of their existence even exists. If all of them were put together, it would not compare to what I see now.

A wide valley dipped into a kingdom of grey stone. Beyond it was an ocean so blue it resembled the color of Eve's eyes, and merciless waves crashed into nearby mountains. Above the mountaintops, the sky was in pieces. The sun appeared behind a shield of broken glass, shinning down in multiple rays instead of narrow beams. I stretched my arms out, expecting to feel the heat against my skin, but there was nothing. I lowered my shaky arms. Cobblestone streets bordered the grey houses. Smoke rose from the chimneys, configuring a silent and peaceful land. A stone mansion was poised at the end of the valley, illuminating in the broken sunlight.

"The glass...please tell me you see it too," I stuttered.

Jance glanced casually around him, "Yes?" he responded like I was crazy. "No one told you about the other dimensions?"

"Yes," my mind drifted back to the string theory. "Three spatial dimensions and one that measures time. But that's impossible, this can't be *real*. It's just a theory, an idea—"

"The ability to imagine is the greatest power in all existence." Jance raised his eyebrows, "You see this?" he lifted his arms, "It is real. How can it not be real when you see it?"

My eyes met his and I spoke slowly. "Seeing something does not make it real, only visible."

Jance stared for a second and swallowed hard. "Only a select few can see other dimensions, you are one of them. This is the fifth dimension, the Lost Paradise. Created by a superhuman race who superseded human abilities ages ago—"

"Is that what you are?" I whispered fearfully. "An Ascendant?"

"No," he said, his voice defensive. "I am superhuman, but I am not one of them."

"There are good and bad superhumans?"

He grinned. "Is anyone, deeply and truly, good?"

He stomped on the ground as if he were afraid something was going to jump out from under him. "We need to go," he said and started down the hill.

"Where are you taking me?"

"To my best friend."

I grimaced. "My best friend betrayed me."

"Well, mine won't," Jance said with confidence.

Everyone thinks that. I thought but I didn't dare speak. *You don't expect it from the ones you love, that's why betrayal's piercing is so deep.*

I narrowed my eyes on Jance's back, the bleeding stopped but the wound was still ghastly. "I don't think it's my safety you should be worried about. You're going to bleed to death."

I could see a smile spread across his face as his neck craned toward me. "Impossible," he spoke with unmatched confidence.

I rolled my eyes. "You're just a boy."

Jance stopped suddenly, causing his feet to slip out from underneath him, the first ungraceful thing I'd seen him do. He recovered on his elbow. I also slipped down the hill at lightning speed, the grass was silkier than what I thought. I felt an arm stop me from my catapult, I grabbed it.

Jance's face was inches from mine. I blushed in the proximity; his breath against my face felt strange. I've never had anyone so close to me before.

"We've only been aquatinted for about five minutes; you don't know *what* I am." He let me go and stood.

I used my hands to steady myself up. "That's true," I said at Jance's comment. "I don't know what or who you are, but I chose to follow you," I said while gripping the dagger in my hand. *It doesn't mean I trust you,* I thought.

Jance reached the bottom of the hill in a matter of seconds. "And why did you make that decision?" he hollered in my direction.

I groaned. I was tired of this hill. "Because you decided not to kill me, that's how I base all my decisions," I said with a heavy load of sarcasm.

Jance gave me a small grin.

The sound of our footsteps changed as we went from the grass to the cobblestone streets. I looked at Jance. My mind was racing as I tried to put the pieces together. His stature, smooth movements, the fact that he carried a weapon, and his supernatural ability to heal fast. I flashed back to Eve, she talked about people with unique powers and beautiful patterns on their skin. Was he one of them? What was he hiding under the armor?

Stories, I thought. *Am I foolish enough to disbelieve them?* I realized not believing in something, could be more dangerous than believing it.

My eyes wandered, the echo of my footsteps along the stone path was so loud. My senses felt heightened, the blood on Jance's back suddenly leaked a deeper crimson. I felt my brain fogging up.

We approached the grey mansion. It wasn't exactly beautiful, but it was quadruple the size of the other houses. Beyond it was a soaring tower and a huge clock was perched at the top.

I gestured toward the mansion, "Who lives there?"

Jance didn't cast a glance toward the mansion. "That's called the Herold's House. It's where our leader lives. We're going right behind it." Jance stuck his arm out, stopping me in my tracks.

I frowned. "Don't put your arm in front of me like that. I'm not a child."

"Quiet," Jance glared. "Sometimes there's no time to talk—"

"We've been talking this whole time," I said with irritation.

"Listen," Jance said ignoring my comment. "Stay right by my side, I don't know who could be watching." He took off his thick jacket, he wore a long sleeve shirt underneath that covered the knuckles on his thin hands. "Put this on with the hood up."

Looking at it closely, I could make out the black and silver colors with bloodstains on the back. I took it and stuck my arms through quickly. Jance tossed hood over my head and my thick hair fell through the front. Jance tried to stuff my curls back in the hood, while I twisted my face in disgust, it smelled like boy and blood. He gave up and we stalked around the Herold's House, his body shielding mine.

I breathed deeply as a small stone house came into view, Jance pushed me forward and then pounded on the door with urgency.

Who appeared in the doorway was probably the most attractive redhead I had ever seen, he had porcelain skin and amber eyes speckled with gold. He stood even with Jance but doubled him in mass. His expression was unreadable as his eyes went from me to Jance. The muscles in his arms were thick, flexing as his hand gripped the door frame.

"Jance..." he groaned with disparagement in his deep voice.

Jance ignored him and turned his attention toward me. "This is Ronan," Jance smiled, then looked at the boy, "and this is Natalya."

"Is she a—"

"I don't know," Jance cut him off.

Ronan opened the door wide. "Let's talk."

Jance and I stepped through the door frame. There was an entryway with a couch sitting along the stone wall and a narrow hallway leading to a kitchen and two rooms. Ronan closed the door quickly behind us.

Jance pivoted. "You two can talk, I'm leaving."

I rolled my eyes. I was not going to be left alone with a strange boy for the second time in a day.

"Where are you going?" Ronan asked.

"I have to go back. I'm scouting for another hour. She

appeared through the Divide."

Ronan was speechless, he gave Jance a bleak look.

"I don't know what to do..." Jance said hopelessly.

Both Ronan and Jance were looking at me like I was some sort of alien. I gave them the same expression.

"She can sleep here," Ronan said with compassion. Jance's face lit up at his response and he gripped Ronan's shoulder.

Jance paused in the doorframe. "I'll be back soon," he said, taking one last gaze at me before he dashed outside.

I didn't need his comfort. But for some reason, when Jance was out of sight, I felt my heart lurch.

Ronan turned toward me awkwardly. My breath came in and out at a rapid pace. He wore the same clothes Jance did, covered head to toe in tight material.

"Um," Ronan struggled for words. "You can have the spare bedroom."

I nodded shyly. Ronan walked down the hall and opened a door. I peered in, there was a dark wooden bed with pillows and thick blankets. It amazed me how simplistic and orderly the house was. Ronan didn't appear to have any personal items lingering around, only the essentials.

"Can I get you anything?" Ronan asked.

"No, thank you," I answered.

He closed the door with a bang.

I kicked off my shoes, laid on the bed, and shut my eyes. My mind was weary, but as my brain tried to shut down to sleep, I forced it awake.

Start with the facts, I thought. *I am in the fifth*

dimension, it is real. I don't know how I got here exactly. There was an attack. Eve came back, she helped me then betrayed me and left me to die. Everyone is dead.

The rest of the night was filled with my screams and cries. I kicked at the bedsheets as if they were choking me, I threw the pillow against the stone wall. I made a mess of things. I was always so in control, but I had finally lost it.

I heard Jance come back into the house. My crying never ceased.

Ronan never came. Jance never came. Should I expect them to come? I had only barely met them, and now I felt like I needed them. They were either hard sleepers or they didn't care. I felt especially betrayed by Jance.

I was embarrassed and I felt selfish. I loved being alone. But the result of these past events made me realize I *couldn't* be alone. The fourth dimension was all I knew. There were always bodies trapped in the suburb; I hadn't given myself the chance to know the souls. Except for Eve and she had turned on me. And now Jance, I had no choice but to trust him and understand him. It scared me to the core.

I couldn't handle it. The attack, Eve's betrayal, the deaths, the reality of another world. I couldn't sleep among strangers. I trust no one.

I dug my nails into the upper part of my hands, the hard, calloused part. The part that made me feel even a little strong. Deep down, I wasn't strong at all.

Tears still slid down my face as I left the room. I felt drunk. I've never been drunk to the point of no return, but this must be how it feels. No control, feeling everything, and then nothing at all. I concluded I was drunk on emotion and trauma. I wandered along the little hallway, there were two other rooms. One was a bathroom with a sink stained with pink grit. I twisted the knob of the next door, nothing happened.

I staggered to the front of the house, throwing open the door and slamming it shut behind me. My sobs still came in pathetic bursts as I escaped into the early morning.

CHAPTER NINE

EVANNA

On this note, the humor of the situation had dissipated.

First, I had to sit in front of a committee of Ascendants, which always creeped me out. I've made plenty of mistakes under their service that always ended in public harassment. I told the Ascendants they should not mistake immortality for perfection, everybody screws up, they looked at me like I had two heads. Saying that again was not an option. If I couldn't say anything smart, I wasn't going to say anything at all. Which was difficult; words tended to come crashing down like a waterfall right out of my mouth.

Second, I was interrogated by the snake herself. Alda could bury someone six feet under with her tinted midnight eyes. Except for this time, they were filled with something I never saw in an Ascendant before, fear.

"Where is the girl?" she asked.

"There's a girl?" I snarked.

What happened next, I do not want to revisit. Pain, just pain.

It wasn't a petty tap on my mind, it was a crushing weight against my brain as she tried to intrude my thoughts.

I won. I saw a flicker of rage in her eyes. It almost mimicked the way a mother would look at her child if the child had been a murderer. In a sense, we are their children.

"*Scarred One*," she whispered lowly.

I stared back at Alda without fear, but I was no longer concerned about myself. I am over. I was worried about Natalya, did they want her because of her association with me? I worried about Jerik. Would they know that he had sent me on purpose? Would they act and try to invade the fifth dimension? Could they?

Shocking that they incarcerated me, which was only the next worse thing than the job I already had. The difference was, instead of sleeping outside the walls from the Remnants, I would be imprisoned in the pits with them.

I sat in a dark room with demons. They attempted to feed my mind with their horrid life stories. Some just wanted attention, I heard them whisper my name.

Eve. Eve. Eeeevvvveeee.

One of them gave me another name.

Ocean Eyes. It seethed through teeth like black nails.

My breath caught in my throat. In the process of being bound to the Remnants, I had shared some of my past.

Memories from when I was just born, the ones I could not remember but were still in my mind regardless.

My father had always called my mother ocean eyes, and I inherited them. The fact that parents had died when I was an infant, and having that part of my forgotten subconscious resurface, was a different kind of pain.

The Remnant calling me crawled along the floor. I kicked at it and it retreated with a hiss. I watched the red eyes surround me. Some liked to talk, some liked to sing, and others quoted lines of poetry. Poetry that had been dead for a long, long time. A few I could make out their remains to be male or female. And others were so far gone that any aspect of being human had vanished.

I knew the Ascendants did this to drive people mad. Even their own people. I don't know what qualifies as a good enough reason to destroy your own kind. I knew some that had been sent to sleep with the Remnants. On average, most killed themselves if the Remnants didn't kill them first. I wondered what they had done to deserve death. What are these elite superhumans trying to accomplish? I wanted to find their reasons, but I couldn't even find my reason for being here.

My uncle sent me to find a special human. He didn't give me many details, other than 'the one who can *see*.' I had no idea what he meant. *See* what? But I knew it had to be a Seer. Now I know I was wrong about Natalya.

Natalya, I thought deep in my mind. *I'm so sorry.*

I remember when I told her, that a long time ago the sky was blue. She loved stories, and she soaked up whatever I spilled out. She burned with curiosity. The type of curiosity of wanting to know everything, even if the knowledge destroyed her.

I drew my knees close to my face and put my head down. Right now, I felt like a failure.

I reached under my cloak, taking out the bit of sidereal glass and it ignited within the black pit. The Remnants cried.

"Shut up!" I squealed at them.

I concealed it in my lap and traced the edges. I earned a few scars over the years. Not nearly as many as I would've if I lived and trained as a real Raiden. But the few scars I do have were red and inflamed. I always tended to my injuries alone. The Ascendants didn't care as long as I could do my job; heaven forbid I die in the process.

I fumbled the glass in my hands and felt its sharpness dive into my skin.

I watched my wounds turn white. I felt the blood pulse through my body. I heard the disturbing moans of the Remnants, I inhaled the reek of this slaughterhouse, tasted the blood that whelped on the insides of my cheeks, and saw the sea of red eyes staring back at me. I was both fire and ice. I froze and burned all at once.

I gasped and stared. New scar tissue has a different texture quality compared to the skin surrounding it. A Raiden's scar is the same process sevenfold. Starlight flows through our veins and a single cut from sidereal glass ignites the manipulation. I was a Raiden regardless if I had touched the glass or not, but now the process is complete, and I am unconquerable. My fingers grazed my new invincible scars, like crystals that formed on the epidermis. Beautiful torture.

"I am a subject of manipulation," I said out loud.

Yoouuu think you are the only one? one Remnant answered.

I glared at it. I could tell it was female, she even had the voice of a woman. A newly bred demon that will only deteriorate with time.

What did you do? I thought. *To earn a life so demented. Lingering between creature and human.* A wave of sympathy washed over me. "No," I answered her. "I do not."

The creature moved on, with a look of remorse in my direction.

Another Remnant approached, a full-blown one, skeletal and pale with red veins showering its skin and eyes that mimicked a battleground.

Eeeevvveee, escape? It asked curiously, speaking to me like I was an old friend.

"Or you can kill me. I'm dead either way," I said nonchalantly.

You become one of us? It whispered.

I laughed. "I have screwed up. But never in my life have I done something bad enough to deserve your curse."

Its body coiled, crawling on all fours, I could barely tell that it had hands and feet. *Your girl could not be manipulated, and we know the reason.*

My heart pumped faster. "What do you know?"

Oh yes, Evanna Grey, we've known all along. Do you think we return from over the wall without knowing the truth?

UNPARALLELED

The moans grew louder in the pit and my eyes wandered, they were slowly coming forward, like drops of blood falling from a black sky.

We hate all the superhumans, it said with vengeance. *You have torture and fallen starlight in your blood, and it shines on your skin. But your mind is never as strong as your body.*

I felt a rush of anger, the sidereal glass still in my grip. I turned it toward them.

Light spread throughout the room as if the sun exploded. The Remnants scattered and screamed. I held my ground as the Remnants moved like ghosts. Their echoes were unleashed along with the memories they carried. Real nightmares that would never cease to destroy them.

I felt one grab my ankle. I kicked at it viciously, but the Remnant's grip was tighter than a leech. It was so dark I couldn't make out the spidery body of my captor. I made my fingers into a claw and whipped my hands about and I pulverized something squishy. Skin that felt like scales and veins like worms. I yanked back, disgusted.

Out of nowhere, there was heat and pain. I screamed.

There's too many of them and they can defeat me physically, I thought. *But they will never take my mind.*

I built an iron wall over my consciousness. The scars on my body may be few, but my mind was made of them.

Another lash of pain came, a few seconds passed in agony before I fell into darkness.

CHAPTER TEN

NATALYA

The air was crisp and firm. My eyes narrowed at the sunlight glistening over the hilltops beyond the clock tower. I startled as it chimed. Any clock that went off at six in the morning was terrifying enough, but this one echoed against the glass dome surrounding this world, making the noise unbearably loud. My eyes followed the broken sky, trying to see if it had a beginning or end. It did not. The sun was not a circle of fire; its rays cascaded in distorted patterns, making the blue sky look like a puzzle. I hated puzzles; my mind always saw the pieces never the picture. Nothing but a fractured image of peculiar lines. There was no need to try to put something together that was made to be broken.

The puzzled sky faded as my gaze traveled downward. When it kissed the treetops, the glass lost its transparency, it became a giant grey cloud that I couldn't see through at all. I turned around in circles, it was everywhere like I had fallen beneath the world.

Eve said there was a difference between being brave and being stupid, but that difference was a very fine, but obvious, line. Such as deciding to hold a knife by its hilt or by its blade.

Be brave or be stupid, I thought. I didn't know the right answer and I ran off the path toward the forest.

It was stupid to go back. If I were brave, I would have stayed where I was. But I was human, I wanted to go home, I wanted the familiar, even if the familiar was bad for my well-being. Humans always did that. It's easy to get lost in comforting tendencies as life passes by. It takes a lifetime to realize all the lives one soul could have lived if they stepped into the unknown.

But I didn't want this.

My shins swept along the grass as branches entangled my arms, the leaves of the holly trees left small scratches along my skin. All I could see was green until I came face to face with the one person I did not expect, myself.

I stared at my reflection and raised my hand to touch my face in the frame. The gigantic mirror I realized was an entire house made of mirrors. There was something eerie about it that made me want to turn and run, but at the same time, I wanted nothing more than to keep my fingers on its unusual warmth.

The ground shook and merged into a new formation. Crackling noises leaped through my eardrums. I couldn't fight this contraption.

A terrifying instinct, the same one that brought me to

this place, spoke to me in a familiar ring from the bottom of my soul. *Destroy it,* my inner siren whispered.

It was like being hurled through space. I do not remember moving my feet before I plummeted into the shift. My body was yanked from reality into a blur of black and white, lasting all of five seconds.

I sat up and gasped for air. I was on a cliff. There were dark blue skies filled with birds flying east. I stood quickly and followed the birds, leading me to the edge. I was welcomed by the view of a crystal sea that bled into the sky like a perfect painting. I glanced downward; it was a long fall to the ocean waters.

I tried to gather my thoughts, but mentally I wasn't operating at all. Only my body drove me as if I were sleepwalking. My mind officially unattached itself from me.

"Natalya!" I heard in a recognizable tone. Then I realized, the voice was my own, I was hearing myself talk...to myself.

My tongue was mute, words couldn't come from my mouth, but my name continued to rebound in consistently increasing volume. I put my hands over my ears reflexively, not consciously, my body still trying to protect me. It was no use, my mind felt like it was going to erupt. I had no control over my thoughts or movements. I was under manipulation.

Then like a fleeting emotion, it disappeared. The need to think, the need to analyze, the need to connect the dots, was gone. And it was the feeling of ultimate freedom.

I took a deep breath of the fresh sea air and sprinted with full force off the ledge.

UNPARALLELED

I wanted to laugh and scream at the same time. My arms were stretched out like the wings of a bird as I flew over the waves; they roared as they crashed into each other.

I landed on a large rock below the cliff gracefully, as if I had been given the agility of a wildcat. My body felt free, but my mind was still frozen. I saw something waver in the ocean. It was a man, struggling against the waves.

"Help me!" the man cried. "*Please!*"

I did not need my mind to make this choice, my body moved on pure adrenaline. I threw myself down on the edge of the rock and extended my arm out. The man's hand reached for mine and he caught it instantly. I met his face and opened my mouth, but my terror couldn't come out in a scream. It was not a man. A Remnant glistened back at me, smiling.

"Got you," it said with a familiar voice.

It was my own. The Remnant had stolen my voice.

The creature snatched me down into the sea. I had never been in an ocean before and now I was hurled in its beating waves and bottomless depth. The seawater stung my eyes and throat, I tried to keep them shut. I had no time to take a breath before I was covered by the water. Kicking my arms and legs, I managed to reach the surface. I breathed in cold air.

The Remnant was looking right at me, the waves seemed to flow around it instead of taking it down, the demon moved like a snake in the water. The sea was not on my side.

The red-eyed man came next to me and my voice whispered in my ear, "*Getaway, swim away.*"

I was confused if I was my own enemy or my own friend.

I tried once more to let out a shrill of terror, there was nothing. This mimicked my fear of my need for control. I never trusted myself enough to simply let go, to release these strings that tied me. Mr. Barnes mentioned how the world was encompassed by cosmic strings. No one took the time to see the world on its smallest scale, just as no one took the time to know me on my smallest scale, because I kept it behind too many barriers. I was just as infinite as the strings, but along the way, I was bound to unravel. There comes a time when the strings wear thin and before you know it, you break.

And then it changed, barely a second passed and The Remnant's eyes turned in to a desperate blue. The creature morphed into something more feminine. The veins turned soft, red strands fell past her chest, and I knew exactly who it was.

"Eve," I said, my voice finally returning to my throat.

Eve's body became victim to the waves, submitting herself to be taken by the sea.

I had all the parts of me again. Suddenly, I realized I had free will, a choice. Eve had abandoned me, betrayed me, but would I let her drown?

The answer was simple. *No,* I thought, *never*.

My heart fluttered with the things I would say to her. For all that it is worth, we may never see each other again. We saw the world so differently because our stories are different. Know this, I am far more powerful than you gave me credit for, but I am gone forever, in a new world I will not return from. I have shattered the glass barrier. However, you may still find me in the strings of words I bound together; if you take the time to read them. I will dive into the depths for you.

I did not hesitate as I plunged underwater until I found Eve's thin shape and pushed her to the surface. Then the scene was consumed by a black swirl and I went with it. A crushing pressure forced the last breath from my lungs.

***

I gulped in air, which was without the taste of the sea, and my eyes opened to a new horror.

I was in a white space with no walls. I looked to the right and saw Jance. His head bowed, his eyes closed, and his hands folded in front of him. Black whip-like strings were attached to his wrists, his ankles, around his neck, and midsection. The places where the strings gripped his skin were stained red.

"Jance," I said with concern. Every time I see this boy, he's bleeding.

There was no response. I extended my arm to touch him. Suddenly, a tightness flicked along my wrists. I looked down to see strings digging into my skin, tied to my body like a snake to its prey. My right wrist was bleeding from trying to reach Jance. My eyes shifted and I saw my reflection in a mirror, but it couldn't be a real representation. No strings bound me in the mirror, instead, I was held up in the air like a puppet.

The strings, I thought. *They hurt if I move, why am I not allowed to move?*

Turning my head, I saw that Jance had a mirrored version of his tied self. I knew it would hurt, but I craned my neck over Jance. The string around my throat tightened, restricting my breath. Next to Jance was Ronan and next to him was Eve. Faces that I had known made a long line down the white abyss, random kids that lived in the fourth dimension. And they all were hanging from whips with their heads bowed, eyes closed, and hands folded in front of them.

My reflection smiled. My breath got caught in my throat, I was not smiling.

Footsteps began to echo in the blankness, growing louder and louder. I should keep still, but my curiosity overruled the pain. I turned my head again and the strings pulled harder, making me choke.

I gave in and straightened my back. A strange shiver went down my spine as random lines appeared on the mirror forming words. The strings clenched as my mind opened. I could see the words in their inverted state. I always had a talent for reading backward. It created a poetic verse that read,

"Bend your neck

Close your eyes

A manipulated subject

To be criticized

Invincible to the knife

Scarred in the way deserved now

Take a bow

And give away your life"

I felt the string around my torso constrict, I jerked my head down. The strings forced my hands to fold in front of my body, then they released their grip. For once I felt like I could breathe. But if I moved an inch, the strings would tighten as a result of my disobedience. I gasped when I saw my new reflection. The image of myself was bowing. The poem filled me with rage. My eyes stung with tears as my emotions heightened. I glanced at the blonde boy next to me.

Invincible to the knife, I thought. The wounds on Jance's wrists were healing, being replaced by scars. *Scarred in the way deserved now*. It was the last line of the poem that released all my inner turmoil. *Take a bow. And give away your life.*

I raised my neck, the strings cut me. I saw myself, bowed and subjected to these strings, and I decided in that moment I'd rather die than be directed by the snakes over my head.

No, I thought. *I am not a subject of manipulation.*

My body moved with a sensation of anger I didn't know was contained in me. The strings pulled at me with the weight of a freight train and tore at my skin like thousands of sharp knives. I refused to believe the pain was real.

I felt the strings uncoil from my body. I eyed myself in the mirror, my reflection held a brave face. An instinct flickered, identical to a flame that could ignite a wildfire. Any spark, given the opportunity, can burn down the world. The inner voice compelled me, *destroy it.*

I held my hand over my face as I broke through the mirror, my reflection smiling at me. The glass shattered, and I demolished into shards as I became glass.

***

I felt the soft grass catch me and I gasped at the scene of a broad man holding a knife to Jance's throat.

Everything happened in slow motion. Jance whipped out his blade as if it were an extension of his arm, deflecting the other man's knife, and kicked out his feet. Jance was fast but the man was strong, he grabbed Jance by the neck and raised his weapon.

I screamed as I ran toward Jance. I proved useless as I stumbled and fell back on my knees just the knife dove into Jance's back.

And it fell right out.

Jance stood, unharmed but breathless. The knife rebounded off his body like the sun rays off a mirror. Immediately, the burly man approached me, his expression enraged. His sleeves were cut, and I could see long white marks like diamonds crystalizing over his arms. They didn't follow any pattern like a tattoo. They just looked like long, white—

Scars.

I knew who these people were, and I sucked in my breath. Jance acted quickly, coming up behind the man and twisting his arm. Then man knocked Jance down in a violent motion that would have killed a normal human. He continued toward me, knife at the ready.

I tried to scramble to my feet, but the man seized me by the hood of the jacket Jance had given me. I gagged and I was thrown to the ground. I looked into the eyes of my unknown murderer.

Is this how I'm supposed to die? I thought.

He brought down the knife.

Yes, it is.

UNPARALLELED

I did not close my eyes or hide my face. Instead, I looked up at the broken glass shielding the sky.

Suddenly, the man stopped. His face twisted into disbelief and the knife fell from his hand.

CHAPTER ELEVEN

JANCE

The second I laid my eyes on her I knew she was different. But I couldn't help but question that again, as her weakness showed when she ran away. And yet here she was, inches from death, and her eyes showed no fear.

She was one of us.

What was even more satisfying, was seeing my father's Right Hand drop his weapon in complete shock. The fact that he had almost killed me was irrelevant.

"What?" Natalya said through ragged breaths.

Ace said nothing but motioned for Natalya to give him her exposed arm.

Natalya turned over her right hand, there was a wound on the outside of her forearm. Blood smeared up and down her skin, she wiped it away casually. Her eyes widened when she saw it was no longer bleeding, but already in the process of healing.

I smiled, but I could tell she was holding her breath.

"Impossible, she's a Raiden," Ace said folding his arms over his chest. He turned on me, "I almost killed her."

Before I could respond Natalya cut in, "You almost killed *him!*"

"Natalya," I said quickly. The last thing I needed was her rising to my defense, it will hurt us both. "Don't."

Of course, she didn't listen. "No!" she yelled and took a charge at Ace.

Ace looked bemused as she slammed her weight against him. He smirked and shoved Natalya to the grass with an easy push. "You've got a lot to learn little girl," his devilled eyes shot to me before he stalked away.

I walked to her side. "Natalya Wells," I said. "I'm rather interested in your story."

Natalya's eyes were glued to Ace as he started down the hill. "Who is that? And why was he trying to kill you?"

I shrugged off her questions. I knew why. It was because I showed the boy my scars last night.

Natalya's eyes wandered over me like I had a script all over my face. I wondered if she would know if I lied, but I don't think she would believe the truth either. "We have rules," I stated simply, "and I broke one of them." My hair hung down into my eyes and my clothes covered my skin from the middle of the neck down. I rested my back against one of the trees.

Natalya frowned. "I thought you were going to bleed to death last night, no human could bleed that much and live. Now, you're leaning on your injury as if it didn't exist anymore. And what just happened, the knife couldn't stab you..." she trailed off, looking mystified and afraid. "What are you?" she breathed out her question. "What am *I*?" her voice barely a whisper.

My head jerked at her question. How was I supposed to answer? A superhuman? A protector? An invincible warrior?

A murderer, my conscience echoed.

I was something other than human. No, I am human. At least I told myself I was. I wanted her to know that too. She grew up human, but I knew the bitter truth. They would strip away every iota of humanity she had.

I said nothing as I held out my covered arm.

Natalya's eyes cascaded over it, unsure.

"Touch my arm," I said.

She reached out hesitantly. I tensed my muscles and felt the power beneath my skin rise, the intense flow of something foreign in my veins. When her hand landed on my wrist, I knew she felt the hard coldness beneath my sleeve. That whatever laid over my skin wasn't human flesh.

She jerked away, snatching her hand back as if she had touched fire. "What *are* you?" she asked again, her voice ringing with fear.

"You mean what are *we*," I corrected. "We're Raidens." I looked at her curiously. "Now, you want to tell me how you're one of us?"

Natalya seemed to drift away as if she had fallen back in time. She locked eyes with me, her irises were rich green, a color that only stood out if you looked close enough. "I don't know," she babbled with disbelief.

"You were either born a Raiden, which means you came from Raiden parents, or you were made into one."

"I don't remember a life before seven," she spoke quickly. "I was put in the fourth dimension like everyone else. I had to find my name on the graffiti wall—"

I shook my head. "Everyone comes from somewhere. The fourth dimension is the Dead Land, no life sustains there. You were part of an experiment. As far as your memory, there are such things as being manipulated to the point where your mind thinks it didn't happen."

"How?" she questioned.

"The Ascendants manipulated their subjects by emotion. By taking a fundamental feeling and driving it to the greatest extreme. To make someone forget past thoughts, they make the subject think it didn't happen at all. Long ago, humans called this denial, which stemmed from different emotions, like sadness—"

"I know what emotions are," she snapped, cutting off my words. I watched her eyes slowly close as she took a deep breath.

I sighed. "Come on," I offered my hand to help her up.

She took it, but her fingers curled around my hand uncomfortably. "Where are you taking me now?" she asked.

"The Herold," I answered. "He's already seen you." I motioned to the House of Mirrors behind her.

"In there? Like hell I'm going back in—"

"No," I smirked. "The House of Mirrors has a little sister that plays the scenes you experienced. There is only one appointed viewer and that's the Herold himself. It's just a mirror in his room, you'll see."

Her face fell. "Your leader just saw everything that happened to me inside there?"

I nodded. "Don't worry, he sees everybody's and he's the only one that will ever see it. Don't tell. Whatever you do, don't discuss what you saw with anyone, other than the Herold." I hesitated at my next question. "I take it you figured out what it does?"

Natalya hesitated. "I'm not sure. But does it separate your mind from your body?"

"That is always the first trial," I said lowly.

She looked somewhat relieved as she glided her feet along the tall grass. "It's your biggest fears, with situations and people—"

"Stop," I said quickly. I swallowed the lump in my throat, no matter how much Natalya's fears would tell me about her, I, out of all the Raidens, should be the last to know. In this world, secrets were never secrets to begin with, the Herold sees all. "Do not tell me the rest," I said softly.

We walked on. Exposing the bright day as we escaped the trees, the sun splintering in all directions.

"What covers the sky?" she questioned.

"The Divide, it is made from trillions of broken cosmic strings. It's been in existence for thousands of years, as well as the dimensions."

"The Ascendants made it?"

"Yes."

"They are the enemy?" she asked with a bitter tone.

I shrugged. "If you want my opinion, they should all be strung up and stripped of their brainpower. That would be worse than death for them." I bit my lip. I tried my best to be kind but sometimes my sense of justice and entitled anger overruled it.

"Jance," she said. I stopped as my eyes went to her, the way she said my name was almost a plea. "Tell me everything."

I smiled. "I will."

She looked at me suspiciously, then her face twisted to hurt, and it was gone within an instant. "Just answer my questions if I ask. I get curious."

"Okay," I nodded. I couldn't shake her saddened look from my mind. "The person you need to see first is the Herold."

Her dark green eyes had a hint of blue, like the tips of violent waves. "Take me to him," she said with bravery.

I guided her toward the mansion. Its magnificence had worn off for me, but Natalya marveled at the house like it wasn't real at all. The black fence creaked as I pushed it open. The cobblestone walkway lead to a large wooden front door, I opened it effortlessly.

We stepped through the doorframe. The inside was coated with shades of gray and two extravagant staircases embraced each wing of the house, light poured in through large windows. The strong illumination made it feel like the sun itself was in the room.

"The windows have sidereal glass in them—" I cut off suddenly as she tripped up the stairs. I grabbed her arm, trying to be gentle as I pulled her up. I felt my heart dive toward my stomach, and I let go.

Natalya cleared her throat. "What is sidereal glass?"

I pulled out my sword and held the blade in the light, the rays spread like a shower of lightning bolts. She gasped and turned her head away from the brightness.

"It is glass made from the stars," I explained. "There is nothing like it. It's the most coveted weapon to ever exist and only Raidens can handle its power. Not even the immortals have the ability to wield it." I put my sword back in its sheath and tapped on a nearby window. "It eats light, in a sense. When the sun goes down, light still shines from within the glass. We were designed to be the bearers of light. Raiden, meaning God Spirit. It is also related to the word radiant."

A beautiful smile spread across her face. "That's incredible. My best friend," she said, her voice had a hint of sadness, "told me about people with patterns on their skin."

"Who was she?" I asked.

A wave of depression washed over her, but she masked it well with anger. "Her name was Eve. She left me to die in the end."

I nodded. "Betrayal hurts...but don't worry, everything exposes itself in the end. Just never in the way you imagine."

She shrugged. "I am not driven by revenge."

I said nothing, but the way her eyes narrowed said something entirely different. Eyes that mimicked a bottomless green sea were full of vengeance.

"The Herold is down this hall," I uttered, making the long trek toward the double-doored room.

UNPARALLELED

I threw them open briskly. Ace stood next to a tall thin man. He was well poised, with locks of pale blonde hair that were tucked neatly behind his ears. Despite his gentle features, his face was cryptically framed by a tight jaw. The man's stormy grey eyes burned into me with disappointment. I felt the familiar chill run down my spine. It happened every time I met the eyes of my father.

"Jansen," he said with a mix of gentleness and pain.

"Father," I responded. "Herold," I added out of respect.

I felt Natalya's eyes leer at me. I could feel her anger. She cast a look of disgust toward Ace.

My father sighed. "Leave Jansen. I want to have a conversation with our new subject."

I looked at Natalya apologetically, her glare at me deepened.

I bowed my head, closed my eyes, and folded my hands, the way of greeting and departing yourself in the presence of ones higher than you, and I scurried out. I made my way down the hall, putting as much distance between myself and my father. However, I didn't let him linger on my mind too long. It was Natalya who encompassed my thoughts.

I should have gone to her last night, I thought. Guilt washed over me, as it always does, and I knew I would never be free of its company.

CHAPTER TWELVE

NATALYA

I took a deep breath as I stood in front of the Herold. Jance was the spitting image of his father. I don't know if I was enraged Jance for leaving me, again, or because he didn't tell me he was the Herold's son. At this point, I was just looking for reasons to condone my anger toward him.

A deep wooden desk sat in the middle of the room and two sets of flowers were perched on both sides. To the left was a bouquet of large white roses, and to the right was a smaller bundle of black.

"Do not be afraid," the Herold spoke to me gently. "My name is Jerik Grey, I am the leader of the Raidens."

"I'm not afraid," I half-lied. I was curious about the memorizing flowers, the whitest of white, and blackest of black I had ever seen. "Interesting flowers."

Jerik smiled, the same smile Jance had. "Thank you, I give the prettiest ones to my wife."

I frowned. "There are better gifts, flowers die."

He chuckled. "What do you think is a better gift?"

I narrowed my gaze. "Knowledge, Herold. I value knowledge, it's eternal."

"Wise. She is right, knowledge is not a subject to death," Ace said.

"This is my Right Hand, Ace Huntington. He will be your commander in training," Jerik said. "But we will discuss that later."

My breath stopped, which at least kept me from saying something I would regret. I figured Ace was being kind because we were in Jerik's presence.

"What is your name?" Jerik asked.

"Natalya Wells."

He cleared his throat. "Well, Natalya if you value knowledge your best gift rests in the libraries. I'll tell you as much as I can though. Beginning with your name, Raiden girls have a first name ending in 'a,' while it's traditional for boys to have names ending in 'n' not all of them do. Names are like eyes," Jerik's grey pearls twinkled. "They are windows to who you are."

"Grey, like your eyes?" I questioned, feeling a little more at ease.

"Yes," Jerik assured. "The Grey family embodies all the leaders in Raiden history. We are the descendants of Raiden himself."

I startled. "Raiden was a person?"

Jerik laughed. "Coming from the fourth dimension you haven't even heard about us, let alone know our history."

"I heard stories," I noted, thinking of Eve.

"Raidens do not inhabit the fourth dimension. It is called the Dead Land and it contains all the destruction of past humanity. It is the Ascendants playground."

I nodded. "Nothing lives or grows. We were confined in little houses; the roads were coated with sand and dirt, we were constantly fighting for food—" I paused, realizing I was rambling. But Jerik was listening, his hands were folded on top of his desk with a tense grip. "There were these artists who painted on the wall that separated the monsters from us," I continued. "Then we were attacked. All the children that lived there are dead. I don't know how I got here—I saw a glass mural, and a living tree was shielded behind it. It *called* to me. Before I knew it, the glass shattered."

"The Ascendants killed everyone?" Jerik inquired.

I swallowed hard. "Those red-eyes demons did."

"Did they say anything?"

"What?" I frowned.

"The Remnants—did they say anything?"

I nodded. "One said I was made of starlight. A-and," I stuttered, "it said, 'there are no more who can see.' Then they killed everybody."

Something passed over Jerik's face. At first, it looked like worry, then it twisted into an emotion that mimicked anger and despair. He cleared his throat. "The Ascendants are experimentalists and the children were their subjects," Jerik confirmed. "The Ascendants kill according to their mission—"

"Explain how that is justifiable?" I interrupted, my volume rising.

"Not everything that is seen is real," he said.

I frowned at him. His words echoed what I had said to Jance earlier. "I don't understand."

Jerik smiled slightly. "There is hope beyond apparent death."

"You're talking about life after death?"

"No," he murmured. "I am talking about life unbound from death."

"I refuse to become desensitized to death and dying," I said with frustration. "You cannot bring people back from the dead. You may be superhuman, but human is still a part of that word. It is impossible to *not* be bound to death. You've been living under this glass sky for too long, Herold."

I thought Jerik would react by slapping me across the face or worse. But Jerik's eyes grew sad and the mirror behind him rippled like water. A feminine figure slowly appeared in the mirror.

Jerik seemed frozen in time. I looked at Ace.

"His mind is connected to the mirror, when evoked with great emotion it produces images," Ace said nonchalantly. "And he can never leave its presence."

I swallowed hard, so Jerik was permanently stuck in this room. I turned my attention toward the mirror.

The waves turned red around a small body with a thin face and eyes like the ocean. My eyes widened and my heart took a nosedive.

The girl in the mirror was Eve.

CHAPTER THIRTEEN

EVANNA

When I died, I thought it would be more eventful, gory, and heroic.

But no, I was left dangling with a rope around my neck.

I don't even know if I saved Natalya. The sidereal glass had to touch her skin for her to pass through the Divide. Now, I may have doomed her. What if she was lying there dead? What if the Ascendants took her? It's all my fault.

My heart told me something different than my head, that she wasn't dead. I started to believe it. Why not be optimistic in the last moments of my life? At this point, it doesn't help or harm me. I thought of the way the sky would have parted for her, glass that kissed like rain as it gently fell. The secret of entering the fifth dimension is the starlight in our blood once it is ignited by sidereal glass. We were made from the universe; therefore, it falls apart for us.

The more I believed she was alive, the more faith I had we would eventually escape to the fifth dimension together, and she would survive its challenges. She was harder, guarded, and seemed highly angered. I only hoped she could channel that inner storm to save herself. The Raidens would break her then remake her into a subject. By blood, she is a Raiden, but she was not as raised one. Her mind was never trained to shield away the monsters, who will penetrate her exposed consciousness with ease.

I struggled to keep my grip on the rope, my hands clenched above the noose, lifting my weight so I could breathe. I had a few scars on my hands. They were the only reason I was able to hold myself up for so long. About two hours now, I figured.

They left me alone at least. No one was watching me desperately try to cling to life. I was thinking of ways out of this, I can usually map out an escape plan. Right now, I only had one thought occurring, and it was a bad thought.

I closed my eyes and envisioned. I thought of how I walked among them. My footsteps in the blood of the humans and I parted their pathway. As I called out in my mind, I felt my heartbeat slow.

And then I heard the sound. *Eeeevvveeee,* one whispered.

I willed it to find a way.

I felt the presence of one through the walls. It was weak, but it was coming.

My eyes were starting to blur, but I saw the door jolt and

my hero came through, bleeding from the sides. Its skin was shredded with dark red sockets. I shuddered as the creature approached me. It tapped on my mind.

There was a price to pay for my release.

The Remnant knocked again. Like a parasite, they thrive on their victim in order to live. Their subject frees them. Just like anyone who places their burdens on the shoulders of others when they cannot carry their own, not recognizing they will destroy their host. The Remnants suffer from constant stabbing headaches, but when they inflict their memories on someone else, the pain goes away.

This one wanted to die. I had seen a suicidal Remnant before, and I knew what it was going to show me. Dying seemed like a better option.

I braced myself as I clung to the strings, desperately trying to hold myself up. I let down my guard.

"You are beautiful," a voice whispered.

Then there was a series of faces of beautiful girls that passed over my vision. I could make out their emotions. Some were smiling, others were crying, and a handful was running away. The last girl lingered with a robotic gaze, except her eyes were alive with love.

My body fell to the floor and my mind swarmed with confusion. The demon lingered in front of my face for a moment and then began to choke and scream. It withered as its skin became a cloud of ashy dust, and then disappeared. No blood or other evidence of death remained. To die from the inside out is a death only one so lost could want.

I sprinted down the labyrinth. First, I had to get to the sidereal glass, surely it was still in the pit with the Remnants, the Ascendants wouldn't be able to recognize it. I turned the corner and the pit was empty. I scanned the depths, and my eyes fell on a piece of reflecting light in the darkness. I ran over and picked it up with delicacy. I began to tear at my sleeves as I darted out the door.

The bodies of the human children had vanished. During the Cleansing, the Remnants tore the subjects open, covering the ground like a red blanket. And now it was gone like it hadn't happened at all. The Ascendants would start over. Wipe the memories and begin again with whatever new idea they had. What an amazing power; to utilize time to counter death and death to renew.

I couldn't help but wonder where the Remnants had gone? Not even the Ascendants could control the Remnants, only barricade them.

I ran down the dirt path, then something wrapped around my ankles, and I fell.

The dead roots of this world were alive again, crawling out from the earth like living snakes. I turned my body over to see their masters walking toward me. Cloaked Ascendants, they always wore cloaks with hoods to shadow their faces. They moved like swirling dust. I saw their arms dance as they directed the constricting roots to entangle me.

I took a hard hit to the head and fell into unconsciousness.

UNPARALLELED

***

"What is your name?"

"Evanna."

"Your full name?"

"Evanna Grey."

My interrogator brought the hatchet closer to my neck. "Evanna Grey, are you ready to die?"

"I do not fear pain. I do not fear death," I said the last words of Raiden firmly. The first thing they teach Raiden children in school is the last words they're supposed to say before they die.

It was stupid of me to think that I could get out alive. Stupid but not impossible. Even now, with a hatchet inches from my neck, I still searched for a way out. Only my hands were bound, the rest of my body was free.

I had gone through various forms of torture before I came here. Insurance that would save my life if it came down to it. The Ascendants had a cruel obsession with severing the neck. They are mind dominate people; being hanged or beheaded was worse than having a sword through your heart. Because the mind rules, the heart is not important.

I sucked in my breath as I felt the whip of air from the hatchet rising.

And then brought down on me like thunder.

I heard a snap, a yell, and then I ran.

Luckily, they wanted to behead me outside. It was a straight shot back the dirt path to the trees. I heard footsteps behind me, I glanced back, my killer struggling to keep up.

The trees! I thought seeing them in the distance.

My breath didn't waver, and my feet didn't fail me. I was not their slave. I was not their subject of manipulation. I am a Raiden, and I didn't have my head nearly severed off as a child for nothing. I will not die in the Dead Land.

When I reached the trees, I felt for the piece of sidereal glass inside my cloak. As I looked down there was the fifth dimension, all spread out in shattered glass on the ground.

Impossible, I thought.

I looked up and in between the dead trees of the fourth and the beautiful green lush of the fifth, there was a dark hole, an empty void of nothingness. The missing pieces were scattered throughout the dirt.

Natalya, I thought. *How?*

I had to act quickly, I assumed she made it through.

I whipped out the piece of sidereal glass and cut my skin.

As I placed my bleeding hand over the glass, I watched it open, the Divide parted into a paradise of tall feathered trees and rich grasses.

I thought of the Remnant who set me free. His deeds did not involve the bloodthirst that I had expected to see. There was deep emotion locked in a spiraling betrayal. I felt my heart breaking from the memory that wasn't mine but was now mine to bear. The faces of the girls permanently locked in my consciousness forever, and I couldn't save them.

I did my best to leave the memory in the Dead Land where it belonged.

CHAPTER FOURTEEN

NATALYA

"*Eve*," I muttered in shock.

Jerik snapped out it. "I saw her in your fears."

I opened my mouth, but no words came out, I was trying hard not to scream or cry.

Jerik sucked in his breath. "Evanna Grey is her name. She was my sister's daughter."

"She betrayed me," I said bitterly. "Left me to die in the fourth dimension. I thought she was saving me at first when she dragged me away from the Remnants. But she took off and left me by the trees—"

"No," Jerik shook his head. "Natalya, you are misunderstanding. She didn't abandon you, she saved you. You mentioned trees, that is where the Divide parts." Jerik spat out his words in a jumbled mess. "She was trying to bring you here and she succeeded. She must have known you were a Raiden."

"The Divide shattered when I touched it," I reflected.

"No, that is impossible. She must have cut you with the sidereal glass. The Divide doesn't shatter by a naked touch, but it does open like a portal if it is exposed to Raiden blood."

I frowned, trying to remember. I was in and out of consciousness from the Remnant attack. When I touched the Divide there was blood on my finger.

But my finger wasn't bleeding before I touched the glass, only after I touched it, I thought, *it probably doesn't matter.*

"Sounds like Evanna failed her mission," Ace said in a low tone.

"But she brought us Natalya," Jerik said with a hint of sympathy, and a blaring smile plastered across his face.

I didn't say anything. I didn't know what to believe. I only stared at Jerik's eyes, they reminded me of Jance, for some reason it comforted me. Jerik dropped his gaze, I watched the image of Eve fade as the mirror returned to reflecting my image.

"To speak of your fears, observing you was quite amazing," Jerik started.

"Is that a good thing?" I asked.

"We shall see," he stalked around the room as he spoke. "Height, depth, betrayal, and manipulation. Most humans age without maturity, never coming to know their true selves, one of the many reasons they failed themselves. You have an advantage. The House of Mirrors has shown that you are not only a Raiden but one with phenomenal capabilities."

I thought back to my experience, the water, the cliff, the

drowning man, the choking strings. I didn't see anything about my fears that seemed phenomenal.

Jerik pointed to the mirror. "I see what happens when a Raiden enters the House of Mirrors. Only I can witness the scenes, then I relay to Ace what your fears are. It is my main responsibility as the Herold."

I looked suspiciously at the large piece of glass; a portal that dives into the subconscious. "That is a frightening power."

He nodded. "It is a burden I bear." Jerik turned to the mirror, and written lightly on it was the poem displayed I saw in the House of Mirrors. I gasped.

"The House of Mirrors manipulates fears through images and situations that are fantastical. Never reveals words. Writings appearing is something I have never seen in all my years as Herold. Have you seen it before?"

"No," I said simply. I began to feel weary, my stomach surged with hunger. I took a shaky breath.

"The poem has been around since our creation, it's one of the things we kept from our makers." Jerik eyed me curiously and then turned to Ace. "Leave, Right Hand."

Ace looked surprised at first, but then quickly regained composure. He bowed and exited the room.

Jerik came close, his voice low, "There is something else I saw in the mirror that I feel is too dangerous for anyone else to know."

I swallowed hard. "And what's that?"

"Two of your fears, betrayal, and manipulation are controlled by other forces, not by you. Your anger is a mask for fear. You cannot control if someone is going to betray you, and your fear of manipulation is a fear of being controlled, which induces a rebellious attitude. You cannot fear those things here. We are all subjects of manipulation."

My heart dropped out of my body and my fury was burning hotter than a thousand suns. My fists clenched in my hand. Jerik was watching my body language, his top lip curled into a vicious grin. "I will not live my life on strings," my voice was a mere whisper in the storm raging within.

He held my gaze, there was a threat behind his translucent eyes. "You may go, Natalya," he said as he retreated behind his desk. "I expect you to be training with Raidens in your age group. I must warn you; it will be painful."

I looked at him dead in the eye as I stood. "You should know that pain is not one of my fears."

"Control your anger—"

I couldn't handle it anymore. I stalked out of the room and slammed the door.

I was panting as I trekked down the hall. Jance stood at the very end by the bright windows. His attention immediately went to me and his face twisted with concern. "Are you okay?"

"No," I confessed.

Jance moved closer, "Come with me, let's walk."

"I don't think going for a walk will help me right now."

"Walk and talk," Jance insisted.

"I'm already on information overload right now," I said as my mind whirled.

"I don't think that's possible for you," Jance boomed with

confidence. "You have a strong mind. I know my father thinks so."

"What's the deal with Ace?" I asked quickly, trying to change the subject.

"Do *not* worry about it," Jance snapped, with a venom in his voice I hadn't heard before.

I held my hands in the air, "Alright then."

We walked outside, the sun raining down behind the glass kept the heat at bay. The land was a perfect temperature.

"Did you ever feel like you were destined for more? More than a human pawn trapped in the fourth dimension?" Jance asked as he led me back down the cobblestone path, which was now bustling with Raidens.

I observed them, they walked calmly but moved with haste. They wore clothes that traveled to their wrists and ankles. I frowned. Their scars were so beautiful, why didn't they let them show? Will I hide my scars? I reached for my wrist and remembered the torture in the House of Mirrors. I shuddered, it made me pull my sleeve down. *Ah,* I thought, *now I understand.*

Gazes were drifting toward me and one Raiden caught my attention. He smiled at me. I had to look up to meet his eyes, pools of blue stood out from his black complexion. I returned his smile.

"Quit flirting, I'm trying to be serious," Jance said with a hint annoyance.

I shifted my focus away with sadness. I never thought anyone in the fourth dimension was attractive. I guess superhumans were more my type. When I came here, I had mistaken Jance as an angel. "Sorry," I said. "He was nice to look at."

Jance rolled his eyes. I took a deep breath. "Honestly," I paused in thought. "I've never known who I was, no one knew who they were. I didn't think I was 'destined' as you say. I had planned to die...but on my own accord to save my best friend."

"Oh, how egotistically heroic," he bellowed.

"Hey," I lashed back. "I wanted to do the right thing."

"Just because you want to do the right thing, doesn't always mean it's for the right reasons," Jance spat out his words.

I paused, my defenses within were rising, but I bit my tongue and stayed silent. Part of me understood what he was saying.

Jance sighed. "Ronan appeared in this dimension just like you," he said. "Except his memories were completely gone."

"He doesn't remember anything?" I said urgently.

Jance shook his head. "He knew his name," he said casually, then offered his hand.

I stared; he was all bone and limb. I could see the fibers flex under the surface. I took his hand, feeling the hard scars in my palm and it chilled me to the bone.

We walked off the path and into the tall grasses. Jance's grip was my comfort, but its coldness did not fade in my warm palm like I was holding hands with stone.

CHAPTER FIFTEEN

EVANNA

There was a rush enfolding me in wind and my heart felt trapped in my throat. I was hurled through falling stars until the glass-covered sky lingered above me. It was like I never left. The trees soared high, the grass nearly descended past my knees and the temperature was dormant. Home was the same, but I was different. I was a slave who I babysat demons and I'm haunted by memories that are not my own, especially the last one. The faces of girls tapped against the back of my mind, reminding me of a story from when I was little.

Mendax, Mendax

Liar, Liar

Or so the story goes. An innocent child who heard and innocent story that secretly snuck in heartbreak, betrayal, and something worse than death. It amazes me how things you were told as a child you remember when you are older, except now it had a new demented meaning.

When my uncle told me that I was going to the fourth dimension, I never thought I would end up like this. Of course, I pictured the possibility of dying, painfully dying. I never imagined meeting someone like Natalya.

Natalya wasn't afraid of living a life full of danger, but she was afraid of existing in the Dead Land. Her soul was stir-crazy. A human with a mind, a heart, a brain, and a damn strong will. She was different from everyone else. But was she part of the Ascendants game?

How could they know? I thought. *She was never scarred.*

Alda instantly demanded to know where Natalya was, and even tried to invade my mind to get the answer. But my best friend had slipped through their strings.

The way I saw her fight for breath from the Remnant attack. Breathing painlessly because she would not bow to death so easily. Not only did she cope with pain, but she was also addicted to pain. That was inhuman quality, except she was superhuman.

We were a failure to the Ascendants. Even though nothing could touch us, our invincibility was incomparable, they still made us a little too *human*.

I felt a tear slide down my face. I wiped it away quickly. *I don't cry*, I thought, *I'm Evanna Grey, I don't cry*. But there was the proof, even with the slight scars on my hands where I could never be scarred again, I was wiping away tears.

Before I left to go to the fourth dimension, I discovered a

note from my mother. I had snuck into Jerik's room looking for something to take with me. In the top drawer of his desk, I found a destroyed piece of paper with three words written in red ink, at least I hoped it was ink, it was my mother's signature. I shivered as my small hands ran over the scripted letters,

Love conquers all—Amelia Grey.

I did not take it with me. Jerik must have kept it for a reason. I knew he missed my mother more than I did. She was his sister, and I never knew my mother and I never will know her.

But I did know one thing, I was nothing like my mother. She must have been so full of hope, I had none of that even as a child.

Eight years later, I must accept what I've done, more like what I haven't done. The only hope I clung to, was the slight chance that I hadn't killed my best friend.

I was home, and my consequences were waiting for me.

CHAPTER SIXTEEN
NATALYA

Ronan's lion eyes roared with anger when Jance explained what had happened. Ronan didn't seem to pity me, he looked at me like I was totally stupid. I didn't blame him, but as Jance continued Ronan grew somber, I saw him flinch at the mention that my memories had been manipulated.

"You guys use the term manipulation a lot. What exactly does that mean?" I asked randomly. I sat on a large leather-like couch that smelled like blood and roses, it creeped me out.

"Manipulation," Ronan started as if he was spitting out words from a dictionary. "The skill to deceive through abusive tactics. The ability to control. The Ascendants can make you see things that are not there, visions and illusions beyond anything you can imagine."

"Sounds like they can rule the whole world with their

mind," I said with wonderment.

"They can, and they do," Jance sneered. "They could not stop the evil that threatened them. They are scientists, visionaries, geniuses, immortals—but they are not warriors."

Who would want to live forever? I thought. "So, they made the Raidens be their protectors?"

He nodded. "We were created to be invincible," Jance continued. "The idea of a person who could be injured over and over and come back even stronger."

"Those strange patterns I saw on Ace's arms—" I started. I remember seeing the white crystallization over his skin. And what happened when Ace went to stab Jance's back, how the knife rebounded off his body. "Invincibility—"

"Scars," Ronan cut in. "Once we are scarred on our body, we will never be harmed in that specific place again, and that scar becomes invincible. In humans, scars are always lighter than the skin. It is the same idea, except ours shine like stars and harden over flesh." His eyes went to my injured wrist. "May I see?" he asked politely.

I hesitated, but I slowly rolled up my sleeve and showed Ronan. He observed it closely, turning my arm over. It had healed in a long, jagged scar, and it was inflamed.

Ronan sighed, "It will heal better in time. Most Raidens get their first scars when they are very young, in the beginning, they look just like that. The genetics just kicked in from the House of Mirrors I assume?"

"Yes. I honestly never knew..." I trailed off, feeling overwhelmed. I pulled my sleeve down quickly, I didn't want to look at it. "How do the Raidens manipulate?" I asked hesitantly.

Jance smiled. "We don't, you can trust the Raidens."

"But still you must become familiar with manipulation. There are four kinds," Ronan said staring into the fire as if he was entranced by the flames. "Manipulation of the body and manipulation of the mind were the foundations of our creation. Then there is the manipulation of time, and the rarest— manipulation of words."

"The body and mind are most important, those you will master once you start training. You won't have to worry about the last two so much," Jance said. "The Ascendants don't exist in this dimension anymore."

"Why?" I asked, my voice growing a little louder.

"It goes back to the War of Mind and Invincibility," Ronan added. "Raidens were sent into the House of Mirrors to come out with a blank mind, emotionless and submissive. However, we came out with our humanity intact, but fear was our primary driver. The Ascendants didn't think we were a complete failure, so they enslaved us utilizing the fears the House of Mirrors exposed. It worked for the first few hundred years of our existence. Before we were called Raidens, the Ascendants referred to us as Scarred Ones. We undertook strict rules, small living spaces, and cruelty. But there were always some who fought the ternary of the Ascendants."

I leaned closer, engrossed in the story.

"As time went on," Ronan continued, "a man by the name of Raiden assembled the Scarred Ones to rebel against the Ascendants. The rebellion was started by a single murder.

UNPARALLELED

Ascendants are immortal, no one had ever seen one bleed or die. We were trained to think it was impossible. Raiden had a magnificent talent for concealing his mind. No one knew what he was planning," Ronan took a deep breath. "The story goes that Raiden snuck out of his quarters one night and stabbed an Ascendant. The Ascendant died; bled like an ordinary human. The action ignited a war unlike any other. The Ascendants fought with their minds and manipulation, the Raidens fought with our weapons and invincibility. The death toll was nearly equal on both sides."

"Who won?" I asked anxiously.

"No one, but kind of us," Ronan concluded. "In the end, the Ascendants abandoned the fight and ran off into another dimension. I call that winning."

"The fourth?" I pressed.

Ronan nodded. "Since then, we focused on rebuilding the fifth dimension in our image, the Lost Paradise it is commonly called, and we renamed ourselves Raidens, in honor of the man who freed us. Reorganized the structure of our militia and here we are."

"If the Ascendants control by emotion, what was the purpose of taking them away?" I asked.

"The Ascendants wanted to create a race of superhumans that could fight off the evil that exists, but not excel their power," Jance stated. "We had the minds to survive the game of fear. Your personal hell strips away everything you are if you choose to let it in." His tone turned serious. "It's easy to control a mindless machine, and you don't have to be an Ascendant to do that. Even the humans of the past accomplished this."

"Stealing the soul," Ronan commented.

"A subject of manipulation," Jance mumbled.

The whole thing was so twisted. I swore to myself I would kill an Ascendant if I ever saw one like I needed more motivation. But I am superhuman, a Raiden. I am not something to be manipulated. *No matter what Jerik says,* I thought.

Suddenly, there was a loud knock on the door. Ronan rolled his eyes and lazily pulled it open.

Standing in the doorway was a girl with scarlet hair. Somehow when I saw her, everything melted away. "Eve," I uttered in complete shock.

I stood motionless and she bolted, throwing her arms around me. "Natalya," she said my name with passion.

After a moment, I gave in and hugged her back. Feeling like at least the love of my childhood was mine again. The only person I had left who loved me and I had loved in return.

The world we had lived in was soulless and dead. But I had Eve through it all, who could fill a thousand souls.

CHAPTER SEVENTEEN

EVANNA

"I knew you were different," I said to Natalya as we walked along the halls of the Herold's House. My room was at the end of the hall on the right. Jance said it hadn't changed.

The lush trees in the forest welcomed me home. I went to the house behind the Herold's, the one that was meant for the Herold's heir. I knocked on the door expecting my cousin, but instead, a large boy with red hair stood in the doorframe, with golden eyes that looked me up and down before his gaze rested on my face. Behind him, I saw Natalya and I broke. I didn't know how that was possible, I was already shattered into a million pieces. She had made it. And she was alive. I could tell she had been angry with me. But when I hugged her, I felt her forgive me right then and there.

My cousin, despite the painted look of disbelief on his

face, was the spitting image of Jerik. I told him that I used to be the tall one, and he laughed as he encamped me in an embrace I didn't know if I would escape from. His friend, Ronan, didn't say anything as his eyes lingered on me. I decided I wasn't going to trust him, I glared back with a warning in my eyes. I made a mental note to keep an eye on that one. I love my cousin, but Jance always loved too deeply too quickly.

I avoided my uncle. It was easy considering he was trapped in that room. Regardless, the fifth dimension was bursting with the news of my return, and I didn't want to hear any of it. I do not care what they think, because anything they were told about my departure was a lie. My focus was only on one person.

"And now, here we are," Natalya said pulling her long curls out of her face.

"Yes," I said. "In an entirely different world."

"It's beautiful."

"That it is." I swallowed hard. She didn't know the horrors of this place yet.

"I'm sorry. I thought you betrayed me," she murmured slowly.

"I would've thought the same thing."

Natalya shook her head. "You would've never thought that about me, Eve."

I frowned. "Why do you say that?"

"Because," Natalya's mouth crossed in between a smile and a wince. "You trusted me in the fourth dimension. You told me about the Raidens, the superhumans with scars."

"You needed to know," I said.

"There is more I need to know. The Cleansing—what happened?" Natalya asked with an edge in her voice that was sharp like a knife. "The Herold didn't make sense when I asked him, he said life unbound from death—"

My breath caught for a moment. I witnessed many trials and errors the Ascendants would inflict on the children. They would feed them fear, joy, pain, doubt, excitement. It's like the mind being tailored; cutting and threading until it would fit just right. However, the Ascendants could never manipulate to perfection. So, they began to manipulate something beyond the living, something dangerous to mess with. I sighed, knowing that I won't tell her the whole truth. "The Ascendants will not give up hope in trying to find the perfect subjects."

"Where do the original subjects come from? These children don't just come out of nowhere, do they? We all arrived at the age of seven with no idea who we were or where we came from."

I looked at her face. I had suspicions, although I never dug too deeply. I knew there was the possibility the Ascendants were manipulating outside the fourth dimension. Somewhere no one dared to go, no one touched outer realities. I took a shaky breath and half lied, "I don't know."

She turned away from me and was silent for a moment. I couldn't tell if she believed me. "Eve, a Remnant told me that there are no more who can see. See what?"

The question trickled out of her like sand in an hourglass. I closed my eyes. My mission had been to find the one who can *see*. A special Seer, someone my uncle desperately wanted. I am beginning to put the pieces together that my uncle may not be the only one seeking them.

"The Ascendants only have one mission, to find those who have the characteristics of an Ascendant and dispose of the ones that don't. They are extremely rare, they're called Seers. If none could see that's why the entire dimension was cleansed."

Her eyes sparkled like emerald flickering flames. "The artists..."

I grinned. "Yes, they were Seers."

Her face twisted into a panic. "Do the Ascendants capture and kill them? Is that why most never returned from the wall?"

"No, it's the opposite. They take the Seers and train them to use all the power encased within their mind, then they morph into Ascendants. They have to keep replenishing; Ascendants can't have children."

"So, the fourth dimension is an experiment to uncover Seers?" She questioned. "And they just killed the others? For no reason at all?"

"Precisely," I said. "Humanity is disposable according to the Ascendant elitists."

Natalya looked like she was going to be sick. "I can't believe it, why couldn't I have done something. Why couldn't you have done something?"

I looked into her eyes. "Because there was nothing I could do." It was true. I had no power to stop them. I witnessed so much within the Ascendant's hold...it made the Remnant attack look merciful. "These are the same Ascendant's that created the Raidens," I admitted. "They're immortal, and they will continue experimenting on vulnerable subjects."

"They want to create more superhumans?" she asked.

"I don't know exactly," I took a breath and I changed the subject. "Regardless of the experiments, we cannot go back we can only go forward. Natalya, you broke their system. I never suspected you were a Raiden until you were nearly dead in my arms."

"Neither did I," Natalya said. "What did you think I was?"

I tried to choose my words carefully. "A Seer," I answered, it wasn't technically a lie. "It doesn't matter now. Don't think you'll be jumping through glass to get to different worlds, it doesn't work like that." *Although it does for some,* I thought.

We walked slowly to my room. "It does matter Eve. Why were you sent to the fourth dimension?"

This will never end, I thought. *Endless questions, I am going to hear them in my sleep.*

Honesty is the best policy. However, I wasn't even honest with myself. I just became what was expected of me. I've been lying to myself my whole life. A lifetime of self-discovery only to uncover more lies than truths about who I am. So be it. There's no better liar than an honest liar.

"I was sent on a mission by the Herold and I can't tell you what it is. Like I said, it doesn't matter, I failed. I was a slave to the Ascendants, buried underground to care for the Remnants." I inhaled sharply. "Eight years I endured, and the things I have seen will stay with me forever. I do not want to talk about it."

Natalya bowed her head and closed her eyes as if she were in pain. I didn't want her to feel sorry for me, there was no time for her to feel pity toward me. I know she can do this, she had so many qualities I feel foolish for overlooking. She would do anything for the ones she loved, yet her personality was hard. It reflected in her muscles that flexed when she was angry. Violent green eyes that echoed an overwhelming fierceness. She never demanded attention with loud charades, she commanded it with her silence. She was coated in humility that undermined her abilities. She knew she was strong, what she didn't know was how brave she was. That was all about to change.

We turned to the right. Sure enough, my room was how I left it. I saw my sketches still lying on my bed. I picked up the pad with care.

Natalya followed. "I never knew you could draw."

I shrugged. "It's a side of me I want to get in touch with again." I stroked the portrait of a woman with hair and eyes like mine.

"Who is she?" Natalya asked.

"My mother," I choked. "How I thought she might have looked."

Natalya put a hand on my shoulder. I smiled to assure her, then someone tapped on the door.

We both turned to see Jance in the doorway. "Let's go."

Natalya looked confused. I put down the portrait of my mother and grabbed her hand. I touched my side with my other hand, the piece of sidereal glass still resting in my pocket. I vowed to keep it hidden. I don't know why I felt the need for it to be a secret. I just learned the best way to survive was to follow my gut.

CHAPTER EIGHTEEN
NATALYA

I felt numb as I walked mechanically down the halls of the Herold's House. My eyes focused on Ronan and Eve ahead, they looked like two-toned red roses. Eve, the color of blood, Ronan the color of a sunset. I snapped out of the daydream as Jance walked beside me.

"The Black and White Parade is the young adult army," Jance said informatively. "Ages fourteen to nineteen, when you turn twenty you can be a part of the adult army, called the Flood."

"Okay." I nodded, seemed simple enough.

"And," Ronan cut in, "the best soldiers are called the Elites."

Jance cast an annoyed look. "Ronan is up for Elite, even though he's still eighteen. Raidens sometimes bend the rules for ones that excel in combat."

I raised my eyebrows. I saw Ronan start to walk with some pride in his step, I rolled my eyes.

"Ace manages both armies," Jance added.

"Great," I said.

"Yes," Jance answered quickly. Ronan and Eve were chatting casually. I wondered if I should tell them about Ace nearly killing Jance or if they would believe me. "Don't bring it up," Jance said lowly as if he could my thoughts.

I sighed. There was too much on my mind. I felt like Eve was lying about the kids in the fourth dimension, or not telling me the whole truth. The guilt was like the sky and all its storms resting on my shoulders, seeing the people I walked the same dirt path with slaughtered before my eyes. I shivered. Now, I have a new responsibility to myself, and the people around me. I spent most of my life chasing Eve with a burning vengeance. Now we are finally together and I refuse to lose her again. If I am going to protect her and myself, I have no choice but to train, fight, and endure the process to become a Raiden. If I succeed, maybe then I can uncover the mystery in the Dead Land and destroy the Ascendants. I could do it with the help of the Raidens. To get where I need to go, I must focus on the present. I cannot dwell on the past and continue to carry the weight of the dead, or I'll be dead too.

The grey clock tower came into sight; it was tall enough to touch the glass sky above. I heard new footsteps joining the stones, I kept my head down but my eyes wandered.

Young people were piling in. Everyone wore the same

tight clothing that covered them head to toe. My eyebrows raised when I met the eyes of the boy I had seen earlier. I caught a glimpse of a sleeve that was cut short, exposing bright crystal scars contrasting against his skin.

When I walked among the fourth dimension, I hardly paid attention to people because they all looked and acted the same. But here, no Raiden was like the other. Jance stood out with his striking white-blonde hair, and so did the girl up ahead, her hair was blacker than the night sky and it gleamed against her snowy complexion. She walked close to a boy with narrow olive eyes and sandalwood skin. The appearances were striking, but what was even more impressive were the personalities. I could see it in the way some stalked the ground while others seemed to glide over it. They all had their own confidence, yet each one looked like they could hold the glass sky up if it were to fall.

The tower seemed to grow taller and taller the closer we got to it. "Wow," I exasperated as I craned my neck to the sky.

"This is the fortress of Camden," Jance said. "It's the place where all subjects come to be educated. From weapons to libraries, you name it, it's in there." Jance grinned a little. "My grandmother used to say that Camden goes further down than it goes up, as if some other world exists underneath."

My eyes grew wide, "That would be quite a basement." I smiled back at him, "Is it true?"

Jance laughed, loudly. A mix of annoyed faces turned toward us, Jance didn't seem to care. "Of course not, it's just a story."

UNPARALLELED

We gravitated around the fortress. I felt my heart skip. The mass of bodies suddenly enclosed around me, and it made me feel claustrophobic. As if he had sensed it, Jance grabbed my arm and diverted away from the crowd. "You need proper training clothes. Come with me, we still have time."

Camden had an extensive number of stairs. I groaned as Jance once again hopped up the flights as if it cost him no effort. My legs were burning by the time I reached the top. Jance yanked the doors open, the sound reverberating throughout the endless halls of the fortress.

The floor at the bottom of the entrance sparkled with colors, and a huge fountain in the center was filled with obnoxiously blue water. The strangely patterned entryway continued down a short hall, with multiple doors on each side. Two large staircases parried the stone walls, leading up to a second level. I walked down slowly, trying to take it all in. I surveyed the frightening heights of the floors above. It never ended, like it would eventually lead to heaven.

"Who built this?" I asked.

"The Ascendants. This fortress has been here longer than the Raidens," Jance said in a matter of fact tone. "This is the only place that wasn't harmed in the war." He looked briefly around the entrance and then focused down one hallway to the left. "This way."

I followed him. While the entryway was colorful, the halls were dark and gloomy like a cave, my shoes sliding against the stained tile to scraping against the stone floor.

Jance went to the last room on the right. "There's

usually extra clothes in here," he said as he opened the door in a quick motion. I peered in and it was nothing extraordinary, just a walk-in closet lined with multiple colors of the thickly clothes Raidens wore. There were extravagant and deep shades of greens, purples, reds, and blues. Towards the end was full of black, white, and various shades of gray. I observed them all as I lifted the outfits off the rack. I felt something hard in a pair of pants, I found a long sword attached. I swiped my hand back immediately.

My eyes landed on a black and white outfit. The pants were black in the front and back with white stripes along the sides. The shirt was more white than black. My hand grazed over it, the sleeves felt stretchy and vulnerable. There was a black vest that fastened below the chest. I picked it up and instantly felt the weight fall in my arms. I turned it over, the back of the vest was thick and broad with four separate slits that rose above the fabric, places for holding knives.

I turned to Jance. "I like this."

Jance sucked in his breath slightly. "Black and white are the colors of the Raidens. When the Parade marched into war against the Ascendants, they were all clothed in black and white. Hence the Black and White Parade." Jance touched the clothing with a sad look in his eyes. "This was my mother's. She was the top subject when she graduated from the Parade."

I hesitated. He's never talked about his mother. "Is your mother...dead?"

Jance shook his head. "No. You just haven't met her yet. She'd like you. You can change in here, I'll wait outside," he pushed the door behind him.

My body was tremoring slightly as I kicked off my checkered shoes and removed my clothes.

I slid into the elastic armor. I was fighting to pull the clothes up as they squeezed over my body. They were snug and foolproof. I wiggled and jumped, eventually fitting into the material, it felt like I had put on a second skin.

"Are you done?" Jance asked briskly through the door.

"Almost," I said breathlessly.

I stalked out of the room and slammed right into him. Jance looked annoyed, I ignored it and smiled excitingly. "I'm ready."

"Okay," Jance answered and wasted no time as he dashed down the hall. I was tired of trying to keep up with him. I hung back, glancing around the fortress as we left.

Jance lessened his pace, guiding me past Camden. Up ahead I could see figures of people lined up along the crevasse of that blasted hill that lead up to the forest. "The Parade meets at the bottom of the hill," Jance said. "We're supposed to do basic partner combat drills today—nothing too crazy. You'll start gradually."

I nodded. However, my heart still thudded with uncertainty in my chest. My stomach flooded with nerves as Ace's bulky figure appeared in front of the crowd.

"Subjects!" His voice echoed.

Instantly, the figures formed a line facing Ace. They moved like a colony of ants, scattering until they found their place. Before I could blink, each subject was perfectly aligned with their heads bowed, eyes closed and hands folded low in front of them. Everything was quiet.

"What are we doing?" I asked Jance, my voice trumpeting the silence.

Jance gave me a short glare as Ace approached. I could tell Ace was the type of man that could strike fear into anyone. When he spoke you listened, I felt myself shrink back as he gave me a bold stare.

I met his eyes, dark and deep, figuring I wasn't supposed to do that. I did it anyway. The others may bow their heads, but Ace didn't deserve my respect.

"Subject," he said almost gently, making me release the hold on my breath. "You have quite the story that I don't think is true."

"Believe what you want," I said quickly. "And my name is Natalya."

"You are a subject to me. And it's not about believing," Ace responded wisely. "Believing is thinking something is true when you've never seen it."

I couldn't find a response. Ace twisted his gaze into a threatening look. "Subject of manipulation," he said harshly, "take a bow and give away your life."

I remembered the trial in the House of Mirrors, the strings tightening around my throat, then loosening when I obeyed. With regret, I matched my body to Jance's, bowing my head, folding my hands, and closing my eyes. I did not see Ace walk away I only heard his footsteps grow quieter.

I felt frozen in this stance, and like time slowed down.

UNPARALLELED

Ace must be walking down the line, looking at every single Raiden.

"Today!" he yelled. "We will run."

All the young Raidens broke their stature, I did the same. My heart leaped at the idea of running, but the faces all around proved they felt differently.

"I can run," I whispered confidently to Jance.

"Not this kind of run," he spoke low and soft, but his face was twisted with anxiety.

"Why?"

Ace was suddenly by us, he looked directly at Jance, "Oh she will run."

Jance's eyes grew wide and he opened his mouth—

"Ace!" Ronan yelled before Jance could speak. "She's not running."

Ace jerked his attention toward Ronan, his deviled face tightly scrunched. "Do you lead the parade, Surestrike?"

Surestrike? I thought.

Ronan did not falter, "Maybe I should."

Ace just grinned and said nothing.

Jance lowered his mouth to my ear and spoke with gentleness, "You have to swear to stay by me, no matter what. If you lose me, Ronan will be close."

"Two groups like always," Ace continued stalking back and forth along the line.

Ace started at the right end of the line. I saw three Raidens descend back, Ace skipped three and then counted three off, repeating the process down the line. When he came by us, I knew what three he would count off.

"One," he said toward Jance and he launched immediately backward.

"Two," he mandated Eve. She hesitated, but Ace gave her a punishing look and she stepped back. She glanced at me, not with pity but confidence.

I watched her lips as she mouthed the words 'be brave.'

I gave her a short nod.

Ace approached Ronan, "Three." But Ronan stood steadfast in his original place.

"Surestrike," Ace said his name like it contained poison. "Step *back*."

Ronan remained like a statue. Without warning, Ace threw a hand across the side of Ronan's face, leaving a bright red mark against his porcelain skin. He still did not move.

"Ronan," I said. He barely glanced at me.

I was touched that he was standing up to Ace on my behalf. But it made me feel like I had slapped him across the face myself. "Just step back," My voice came out in a desperate whisper.

Ronan looked at me with narrow amber eyes.

"I would do what your girlfriend says, Surestrike." Ace said impatiently. The comment made me blush.

Ronan just rolled his eyes and breathed out, finally backing out of line. Ace counted off the rest.

I peered behind my shoulder. Eve grinned at me. I tried to whisper Ronan to show him my appreciation, but he wouldn't look at me. Jance had his head bowed, I briefly gazed at him before I turned my attention forward. I tried to shake off the hurt I felt when Jance had stepped back so easily. Then again, he was the Herold's son, he was held to a high expectation. Jance shouldn't give Ace any trouble, since it was already evident that Ace was out to kill him and Jance denied it to his own father. What kind of blackmail did Ace have on Jance?

Ace trailed back down the line shouting, "Subjects, you know what to do!"

At that moment, a loud *bang* echoed throughout the entire dimension, I startled and turned toward the clock atop Camden, chiming like thunder. The young subjects lowered their stance, preparing to run.

My hands shook as I kneeled. On the second chime, my body jumped forward, but no one else moved.

When do we go? I thought. I had no plan other than to follow behind the crowd if I can keep up.

The third chime rang out and once again everyone remained still. My breathing turned shallow and I wasn't even running yet.

"You run when silence rings." A soft voice spoke behind me.

I turned to see the boy, his dark curls framed above his forehead, and his bright blue eyes were startling up close.

The clock echoed for the fourth time, but it stopped in mid-chime. I frowned, mystified at the three and a half rings.

In the seconds of silence, they ran.

I was taken by surprise as the Raidens shouted out battle cries and sprinted forward like a stampede of crazed animals. I was several strides behind as they ascended the hill. Gathering all the momentum I had, I shot upward. All my muscles burned, and my face scrunched under the explosion of energy.

I reached the top of the hill breathless. The Raidens continued to run straight into the forest. There was no time to rest, my legs barely carrying me into the thick trees. The air in the forest was different, I was breathing in more dust than oxygen. Thin lines of the sun snuck through the branches of the trees, offering enough guidance to see ahead.

My gasping stopped when I heard screams.

The trees grew thicker and the branches took an odd shape. I felt a sting as a thorn made a long cut up my shoulder.

I yelled. And then another sharp edge grazed along my forearm.

I need to stop, I thought. But the others were not stopping. They continued to run into the depths of the thorny trees. The pain spread as I felt cuts and tears up and down my back and legs. I put my arms over my chest, a poor attempt to protect myself. I felt a pierce against the side of my head. It was finally enough to make me stop.

I bent over as waves of nausea washed over me. I shut my eyes, I didn't want to see my injuries, all I could feel was stinging pain and blood trickling down my skin like I had been whipped with shards of glass.

I jolted as a pair of arms encased me and forced me up. "Keep going!" the voice encouraged.

I did. I ran once again feeling a cut here and there, but not nearly as bad as before. The Raiden behind me was shielding me from the thorns.

The forest seemed to break apart, light shined from above and I let out a breath in relief. The Raidens were cut up but not as bad as I was. The arms around me retreated.

I felt a burst of strength. Something sparked within my fibers and my mind let go of the pain. My eyes glanced down around myself, torn and bloody from head to toe, sweat stinging the open gashes.

And I smiled.

A smile of pain. The smile of love for the pain. For a reason I couldn't comprehend, I felt invincible. I moved faster, catching up with the rest of the crowd. They ran through the forest, up hills, over rocks and fallen tree trunks. I jumped and cleared anything that crossed my path. When I came neck and neck with the front runners all eyes were on me. I turned to see a girl, she had a few scrapes, but the biggest red stain was very small compared to my shredded skin. I could not figure the girl's expression, but I could read the word on her lips.

"*Wow*," the girl exhaled.

The edge of the forest was near, and my adrenaline surged. No one is going to get past me. I gritted my teeth and pushed forward. Finally coming to the Raiden in first place, a lean boy with narrow eyes. There was a long cut down his face, but other than that he didn't appear hurt. I traced my eyes over his torn clothes, I could see the white marks along his skin. He had lots of scars to protect him from the thorns. My competitor and I were tied as we descended the massive hill. I could see the rest of the Raidens at the bottom watching with anticipation.

I controlled my movements down the hill. Just yesterday I was slipping and sliding, barely able to keep up with Jance. Now, I was broken, bloody, and in perfect control. I left the previous frontrunner in the dust.

The Raidens cheered. The faces coming clear as I ran right into the crowd and they caught me in a heap. Hands pulled me to my feet, I was gasping and laughing. I heard the rest of my competitors congratulating me from behind. I was surrounded by superhumans. I finally felt like I belonged.

My eyes fell on the boy who helped me through the thorns. I walked shakily toward him. "I—couldn't have," I gasped, "done it without you."

He smiled, "The glory goes to you." His voice was like liquid, it flowed over his lips like a fountain.

My breath finally caught up. "Thank you," I smiled.

The boy gave me butterflies, he lowered his head closed his eyes. "My name Shai Cassteel."

I didn't want him to do the whole bowing thing. When I meet someone, I would rather look at them in the eye. "Natalya Wells," I said looking into his blue pools.

"We've all heard about you. News travels fast around here," Shai said.

I nodded shyly as Ace's large figure appeared behind Shai. I stepped aside. Ace was expressionless; he didn't seem impressed or displeased. He stood with his arms folded over his chest.

"Do you have something to say to me?" I asked sarcastically, I was over the unreadable attitude of his.

UNPARALLELED

At my comment, I felt a sting on the side of my cheek. My neck whipped to the side and a crack traveled down my spine at the sudden shock. I kept my head turned. I didn't want to look at him. My bloody marks began to pulse.

"Do *not* speak to me that way, I've had it with your mouth." Ace said firmly.

Jance was suddenly there. My eyes went to him and then back to Ace. "You tried to kill Jance," I tried to speak as softly as I could. "And you're trying to humiliate me."

Jance stood without a hint of truth on his face. I narrowed my eyes at him. Jance did not cross me as a good liar, but he had perfected a poker face. I saw him sink back into the crowd. I couldn't see Eve or Ronan.

Ace slapped me across the face again, sending me to the ground.

"Subjects!" His voice was louder than the chimes on the clock. "Round two," he said to the other group Raidens.

Everyone returned to their bowed position. I thought it was freakishly robotic how they were able to switch to the subjected stance.

I couldn't stand, my body was done. I was shaking and fighting back tears. Perhaps it was true, pain was all mental. Physically the body can take what the mind could manage. The slap Ace had planted across my face was more painful to my pride because it was not deserved. The slap or the cruel words and lies Ace had said so far. Everything I felt easily morphed into anger.

"You're a *liar*," I said through my teeth.

Ace laughed, he knelt in front of me and met my eyes. He came close, I shuddered as he whispered in my ear, "*Mendax, Mendax.*"

I frowned at the foreign language. Ace quickly retreated before I could ask what the words meant. He spoke loudly as he addressed the Raidens but still looked down on me. "Congratulations subject, you've won the race."

The Raidens let down their bows and cheered once more. I shifted through the crowd of praising Raidens. Some clapped, some said congratulations, but they *all* bowed. It made me feel awkward. My smile vanished among the low figures.

I felt a thin hand on my shoulder. I turned, Jance's grey eyes were clouded and dark.

"Jance," I breathed.

"Natalya!" a voice echoed behind him. Eve pushed past her cousin, and I was almost knocked over by the force of her embrace, she didn't seem to care that I was wearing a coat of blood. Her body was shaking, but her grip was strong.

"You were phenomenal!" Eve exclaimed. "I don't know anyone else who could have done that."

"Don't Raidens train like this all the time?"

"You don't understand," Ronan's voice rose behind Eve. "We've been training and preparing for this our whole lives. You are unscared. That run could have easily killed you."

I wasn't surprised at his, "I think that's Ace's mission. To kill me." I paused, and my gaze faltered on Jance. "And Jance, he tried to kill Jance."

Ronan looked away and Eve looked confused. Jance

looked outraged, but his expression quickly turned to worry as I felt my body weaken suddenly. My breath sped up and I was on the ground.

"Natalya," was all I heard. And then everything went black.

***

My eyes opened to a grey surrounding. I felt a mix of sudden pain and victory. The pain came first, my head throbbed like a giant stone had been repeatedly thrown at my skull.

I ran the race. And I not only managed to not die but win the damn thing.

I blinked my eyes and the walls of stone came clearer. I was in a large bed and layered with plush blankets. I turned my head to see Jance, wide-eyed and smiling. It had to be a trick of the eye because the room suddenly seemed brighter. His delicate features with hair only a shade of away from white it could pass for grey. Jance was pure light.

"You and I have a habit of meeting under strange circumstances," Jance said with attitude.

I gave him a small grin and sat up slowly.

Jance's smile faded as his eyes fell on my arms.

My heart stopped when I looked down. First, there was fear and then a sense of amazement. Where just hours ago was torn flesh, raw scars now layered over the surface. They were not pretty, and the sight sent shivers down my back. Pink and puffy crooked lines bulged down my arms as if I had been infested with large worms growing under my skin. I turned my forearm over, exposing the wrist where I got my first scar from the House of Mirrors. It was a shiny mark that had risen slightly above the epidermis, like a vein that carried a beautiful shade of gold blood. I gasped and quickly covered it. Jance jumped at my sudden movement.

"What's wrong?" he asked.

"Uh," I gaped for a moment. "I—I'm cold, do you have a jacket?" That was probably a stupid thing to ask since I had plenty of blankets.

Jance fell for it and removed the navy jacket he wore. I reached out to grab it, but he came graciously toward me and helped my arms through. I put it on quickly and jerked it shut. It's not like I didn't appreciate his kindness, but I could not take another second looking at myself.

"When will the scars look like normal?" I stuttered.

"Everyone's body is different, for some it takes time and for others they change immediately, just be patient. I think the most powerful scars are the ones that heal with time and grace." I saw Jance shudder a little.

"Raidens get scars when they're kids right?" I asked, still trying to shake off the mix of drowsiness and shock.

Jance breathed out a sigh. "When you turn ten and enter the House of Mirrors. Then if you pass, meaning if you live and come out with your sanity, you get sent on your first scouting."

"What's a scouting?"

"That's what I was doing when you appeared out of oblivion the other night. It's like a perimeter check. Just walk around your route and kill any threat in your path," Jance said as he folded and unfolded his hands repeatedly.

"They send ten-year-old's?" I said defensively. I did not care if this was a different dimension, a child is still a child.

Jance shook his head. "Not regularly, and some places are safer than others. But our numbers are low. They send ten-year-old's who are ready, and they scout in places where their strength lies. I was placed along the outskirts of the forest. Some are sent south near the ocean, underground, or by the cliffs. It's the Herold's job to mandate scoutings."

I nodded. "Because he sees everything that happens in the House of Mirrors."

"My father knows everyone's strengths, weaknesses, hopes, and fears."

I shifted a little under the blankets, pulling the jacket tighter. "That's terrifying"

Jance nodded and continued, "I met my first Remnant along the tree line. I thought—" Jance choked on his words. "I thought that it was my father. But it wasn't of course, it was only a manipulation in my mind. I was almost killed. Cut and bloodied just as you were, except I was only a child." He stopped again, looking like he was going to say something else, rather than his words that followed. "But I lived through it," he smiled. "Everyone goes through horrible things, the ones who succeed utilize them to become stronger. Defying the natural human instinct to run from fear. Instead, we run to it."

I smiled slightly. I saw his face become distant. His long sleeves covered his arms and peaked collar surrounded his neck. I tried to picture him in less clothing...well not in *that* way. But I tried to envision the bright lines all over his body. How it would make him look. In my mind, he already looked like the sun. I imagined the white scars over him, bringing out more of the paleness to his skin, his light blonde hair shining where his nearly colorless grey eyes vanished. I shook the mental image away, feeling my face get hot.

"How do you keep the Remnants from invading your mind?" I asked, knowing this might be the most important skill I need to survive.

Jance flashed up. "The same way you strengthen your body. You've proven yourself strong physically and your mind is just as strong, maybe even more powerful. To strengthen it, you will go back to the House of Mirrors. It builds a shield around your mind over time, the more you practice, the harder your mind will be to invade. You won't be scouting by yourself for a long time, so don't worry."

My face fell. I didn't know exactly where the scouting premises were but the entire fifth dimension was a vast place in an encamped space. I survived the Remnants once, I could do it again. And I wanted to do it on my own, without Jance or Eve. I didn't want an escort every time I stepped outside. I've learned to be alone for too long, to not be alone anymore. "I can defeat them."

Jance raised his eyebrows. "I know you can," he said confidently. He stood from my bedside and walked toward the door. "If you're feeling better you should eat. There's food in the kitchen and clothes in the wardrobe. This is your new room."

I swallowed hard, there was something peculiar about the Herold's House. It was a mansion with very few people, it felt empty, but I'm thankful to have a place to stay. "Okay," I answered. "Food would be great."

"My room is just down the hall to the left," Jance said as he swung open the door and held it.

I was able to stand up but my legs still shook. "I get to live with you and your family?"

"The Herold's House is home to Raidens who don't have one."

"Ah," I said shifting my weight tenderly from foot to foot, walking felt foreign.

The truth was I never had a home. Being alone was not scary for a person like me, I loved solitude. The company of others had never been necessary for me to be happy. But the ones I did need, I loved fiercely. Since I recently discovered this new world, I was more eager than ever to spend time with people. These superhumans stole my heart and made me want to be like them.

Jance and I walked down the staircase; the stone was cold against my bare feet. "Where's your mother?" I asked randomly.

Jance just frowned at me. "You ask too many questions."

"Because I'm relentless," I stated bluntly. "You said she would like me when I picked out her—oh no. I'm so sorry about your mother's clothes." I bit my lip, they were probably ruined now, shredded to bloody strips.

"They will be perfectly fine. Our clothing is unique. It fabricates back together after some time passes." Jance danced down the stairs and this time my pace matched his evenly.

I nodded, not surprised. "So, where is she?"

Jance shrugged. "In her room."

I gave him a dissatisfied glare but let it go. I followed him to the lower level. Everywhere I turned there was grey, some random pieces of furniture were different shades of charcoal and black. Jance went toward the back of the house and through a set of double doors. There was a large table that looked like a fancy version of a picnic bench. Jance motioned for me to sit down as disappeared into the kitchen. I slid in and leaned against the short backrest, wincing a little as my tender scars pressed up against it. Jance returned with a bowl of something that smelled like seasoned beef and vegetables. I barely gave him the chance to set it down before I grabbed the spoon and started eating like a wild dog. It was delicious, a beef stew with carrots, simple yet wonderful.

After gulping down nearly half the bowl, I could speak again. "Who's the cook around here?" I asked.

Jance laughed, "We cook for ourselves mostly. Evanna made this a few hours ago for all of us. There's plenty, eat as much as you want."

"You don't have to tell me twice," I finished the last bit before a minute was up. I swallowed hard and realized there was something off about the ingredients. The carrots were too sweet, and the meat was too tender, almost melting in my mouth.

Jance went back into the kitchen at least three more times to retrieve more stew. We chatted casually about the fifth dimension. Jance told me there was a farm to the west, with animals and crops. Retired Raidens catered to the management and distribution of food. There was a beach toward the south.

UNPARALLELED

I've always wanted to see the ocean, the freedom of the sea always intrigued me. I couldn't quite figure the exact distances. The fortress of Camden was as far east as you could go without running into the mysterious Divide. It encircled the entire fifth dimension like a giant fishbowl.

"Have you ever been to the far west?" I asked working on my final bowl of stew, my stomach continued to expand several inches.

Jance nodded. "I remember going until I could see the other side of the Divide. That got me in trouble."

"Have you seen all sides of the Divide?"

Jance shook his head. "No, the forest is too thick to see through, the trees never stop growing. When I went sailing, I saw it from a distance, the water exposes the clouded glass from miles away. The Divide is always staring in your face. No matter where you are it lurks all around..." Jance trailed off for a moment. "All you have to do is look up at the sky and see the sun in pieces; or pull a piece of grass and watch it shoot up again. We are constantly reminded of the manipulated world we live in, the Lost Paradise."

"Why 'lost?'"

Jance grinned. "Because this place is *not* paradise, but damn, it used to be—the Ascendants wanted to create a perfect world. A world so 'perfect' that it uprooted any form of the natural world. Everything here has been pulled apart to its smallest unit and then multiplied sevenfold. Spend some time out of these four walls and you'll understand what I mean."

I nodded. I made a mental note to go for a walk

tomorrow and try to wrap my head around what Jance was saying. "So, why'd you get in trouble when you went to the west side of the Divide?"

"There's a dark story behind it," Jance answered simply.

"Isn't there always? Tell me," I pushed.

Jance took a shaky breath. "When the fifth dimension was created, it was an open meadow with the most beautiful flowers of many colors and surrounded by green grass that grew past your knees. Where children danced, the old rested and everyone was happy. It was a paradise."

I smiled. "Sounds magical."

Jance played with his hands, intertwining his fingers, and avoided my eyes as he spoke. He could never keep his body still. "There were no Raidens. There wasn't a raging sea or a violent forest. The Remnants didn't exist and there was no need for a fortress like Camden. But it became that. The meadow is still there, and it stretches from the outskirts of the farmland. It's a burial ground and below it there is a place called the Undercity. That is where the Ascendants experimented and failed repeatedly. Until they finally had one succession, us."

"It sounds like a place filled with answers."

"Answers?"

"Yeah," I said, glancing toward the window. The sun had set long ago, and the sidereal glass window had lit up the room as we talked. "Why wouldn't it? If that's where it all began. I just found out I was a Raiden yesterday, and I want to know how we were created, or manipulated, to become the superhumans we are. The answer would be where it all began."

Jance rubbed his hands over his face. "Possibly," he said lowly.

I went and sat right beside him. His grey eyes larger up close, hiding under his hair. His breath was slow and even. I could see the pulse vividly in his neck. "Is it true we are made from stars?"

"Yes," he said nonchalantly.

"I do not understand," I responded, shaking my head.

"Some form of magic," Jance answered in a dismissive tone. "Which is a form of manipulation, another word for magic. It can be used for good just as it can be used for evil." Jance's voice was nearly a whisper. "The Death Meadow, the thicket right above the Undercity remains the most beautiful place known in this land and it's filled with evil. You can hear your ancestors screaming. If you pick the flowers, blood will drip from their stems. Some of the flowers even hold memories like the Remnants."

"What a dreadful thing to do to a pretty flower—is this only story?" I smiled.

"I wish it was," Jance said seriously. "We are here because of scientific purposes, bonded with forms of magic. Everyone knows the stories of the Death Meadow, going there is basically a death wish, but some must cross it, like the Elites. And even for them it's scary." Jance said shifting his weight closer to me.

"Because living in this world isn't scary enough," I commented.

"Scary isn't the problem, pain is." Jance retreated his gaze from me and looked toward the sidereal glass illuminating from the window. "But we are made to endure the greatest pain."

CHAPTER NINETEEN

NATALYA

I walked Natalya back to her room. She thanked me and gave me a small smile, but that was it. I shook the feeling; I shouldn't expect anything else. When I closed the door, I let out a big breath of frustration. I hurried to my room. Luckily, it was exactly how I left it. Sometimes my mother would come in and organize it. My room was not messy, it was chaos in perfect order. I had books splayed all over the bed, ones about history, science, and even the supernatural. I've read most of these books through multiple times hoping I would find something new.

I learned the history of the world before the fourth dimension by searching through hundreds of books in Camden's library. I read about guns, bombs, and machines, all telling stories of how destructive the world was. People blowing each other sky-high, the ability to shoot bullets faster than light using an automatic weapon. The horrors of homicide and vicious discrimination of individuals. I studied the reasons for the wars in the world, and I only found my jaw clenched and my hands tight enough to break the binding. I would end up slamming the book shut and tossing it across the room.

Some Ascendants who originated in the world foreseen such wars. They were not prophets, that was only a superstition. However, they were insanely smart. They predicated the rises and falls of humanity by watching past patterns. I had tried to pinpoint the exact time in history when the first Ascendants created the dimensions. I tried to find the first inkling of the strings unraveling. I could never find a specific timeline.

Time was a strange thing, especially here. The clock that rings three and a half times—a fluke in the system. The sun goes down, at least I always thought, a few minutes earlier and earlier every day. I observed this since I was old enough to understand the idea of time. The days seemed to last longer if you enjoyed them and took them moment by moment. It's only after years passed that you see how fast time can go.

After the war, the Ascendants left behind the information they did not think to take with them, and that was books. The Raidens had pieced together the information of why we were made, but not *how*. Or how the Ascendants seemingly disappeared into another dimension. Once the Raidens had regained themselves, we were bloodthirsty. After a few decades, the thirst for revenge eventually dried up. My father told me that some groups of Raidens would still ally with the Ascendants. My father was not a cruel man; he could have easily made a law that forbade anyone to even discuss the topic of the Ascendants. Jerik said to let them waste their time, it's pointless, just like researching the supernatural and the manipulation of words.

I agreed with him to an extent. Why go searching for your enemy when you live comfortably? But I understood revenge. An Ascendant had never hurt me personally, then again, I did get an occasional compulsive feeling to slit their throats. I would remind myself to be kind, be forgiving. It was in the past and eventually mortality takes care of vengeance. The vengeful Raidens died and new generations came forward. Revenge does not run in the blood; it only runs in the mind. And the mind changes over time. Then again, it was hard to sleep when you know your enemy still exists.

In school, I learned how the Ascendants created dimensions from nature, by pulling apart the smallest building block and repeating it over and over. Like the way we were scarred over and over, until the moments before death. But there were no details. How did the Ascendants rally the stars? Why did some experiments die? How did the ones who lived survive the process? But no matter how many books I read, no matter how many teachers I asked, how many times I approached my parents, my questions always remained unanswered. I don't think anyone is hiding the truth, I'm seriously convinced no one knows.

I looked out the sidereal glass window in my bedroom. I got a direct view of the Divide. I have spent countless nights staring at the clouded glass, following it upward until the shattered sky became visible. *Why* could we not see anything else but the sky? Asking those types of questions was the same as asking why is the sky even blue? And why is it red in Ronan's only memory? No one knew the answer. Eventually, I stopped searching and studying, I stopped asking stupid questions.

The first three things they teach you in school are the manipulation of the mind and body, and your last words. They briefly discuss the manipulation of time and words. There was a story that goes along with the manipulation of words and a family that is tied to it, the Merciless family, my mother's family. A line of Raidens that have the same curse as me.

I had no peace out in the open. I was consistently pulling my sleeves down. I did it in private just out of habit. I felt exposed when Ace nearly killed me for the thousandth time. I do not think Natalya noticed the difference in me, not yet at least. She was too wrapped up in everything that happened to her. I know Ace wants to kill me; he wants to find the right time to do it without anyone important witnessing. He knew I had told the boy what I was before I killed him. It wasn't the first time Ace had caught me disobeying the law. All Seers must be killed, and they cannot know what we are. If not followed, it was a crime punishable by death. Ace technically didn't do anything wrong.

My mind whirled with thoughts of Natalya. She made me want to ask stupid questions again, mostly because she was filled with them. The second I saw her in the forest I thought she was a Seer. But she struck me before I could strike her. Seers look distant and untouchable. Her composure was strong, like she had seen the world crumble, and only she had risen from the remains.

UNPARALLELED

Today, Natalya proved that she was not only a Raiden but one hell of a fighter. I could barely look at her before she took off in the run, and the waiting minutes passed in torture. When I saw her sprinting down the hill, she was a bloody shell of the human she once was. Yet she was smiling, handling pain in expertise that requires a form of insanity.

I leaned back on my bed, my head spinning from everything that's happened. I thought deeply about the secrets I had to hide from Natalya, and bitterly from Evanna as well. When I saw my cousin, I could barely breathe. I felt numb for an instant and then felt everything all at once. Relief, happiness, and an abundance of love. Finding out Evanna and Natalya were best friends in the fourth dimension made them liabilities to the secrets I kept.

I remember how my heart dropped out of my chest when I saw my scars as a child, and it still does to this day. I was flooded with a mix of shame and mystery. When I look at myself in the mirror, I see something that is not normal. I am on the borderline of possible exclusion and death if I'm not careful. I have no choice but to hide. I let myself fall into the sync of everyone else, but I was only pretending.

A knock at the door interrupted my thoughts, "Yes?" I invited.

The door swung open. A young woman with long dark hair stood in my doorway. I startled; she was beautiful. She had been here before, four days ago I remembered.

"Jance, your father requests you immediately," she said with a cooling voice.

I nodded, and she hurried back down the corridor.

My father would review Raidens consistently, keeping up with how their training is going and how well they are managing scoutings. It was normal for Raidens to come and go. Still, I couldn't shake the wave of uncertainty that came over me.

I waited until her footsteps grew to a faint patter, and I headed toward the Herold's room.

CHAPTER TWENTY

NATALYA

I opened my eyes to the break of daylight coming through the sidereal glass window. I was so tired. I barely remember Jance closing my door before sleep took me last night.

I stretched my arms and my eyes caught sight of my scars. They were less swollen and more vivid in color. They were not white yet, but the redness had lessened enough for me to look at them without having to turn away. I stopped and stared at the single hint of gold traveling down my wrist. I ran my fingers over the scar, it was like diamond dust, dense at the base with a powdered texture on the surface.

Throwing myself out of bed, I grabbed Jance's jacket to cover the sight of the new skin. I rushed to the bathroom. The stone floor was cold against my feet. The sink was filled with clear water but there was no faucet, I dipped my hands in and it was surprisingly warm. I washed my face, dirt trickled off my skin as I scrubbed. When I was done, the old water began to disappear, and new water rose to the surface like it was a living thing. I looked in the mirror and sighed.

I came out of the bathroom and glanced at the wardrobe. It was made of darkly colored wood. A smell of fresh pine burst through the door when I opened it. *The trees*, I thought. The blackened wood resembled the tree trunks in the forest perfectly. Looking inside, I picked a random pair of black training pants and a royal purple long sleeve shirt. I was prepared for the struggle this time as I jerked the tight clothes over my body. I slipped on a pair of lightweight shoes that hugged my ankles. Satisfied, I left the room to see if anyone else was awake, but the halls were quiet.

I decided to venture outside. It was a bright morning, as every morning was here. I sat on the stone path to watch pieces of the sunrise behind the glass sky. I traced my hands over the grass like I was touching a newborn. I dug my hands into the spongy grass and pulled it up from the roots. Suddenly the grass turned stiff and the green faded into a dingy yellow. I frowned, letting it fall out my hands. Then I saw the grass sprout up, growing from the spot where I had pulled. Tall and bright green, no evidence remained of the damage I had done.

This isn't real, I thought. There's a possibility that this world may be unreal just as the other was dead.

CHAPTER TWENTY-ONE

EVANNA

I woke to a loud thump and I scrambled out of bed in a panic. Any sound could make me paranoid, the trauma from the fourth dimension still had me by the throat. Just because I was gone from that place did not mean I could escape it. I breathed in slowly, trying to calm myself. The air had a taste in the fifth dimension, like sweet wine, in the fourth it was pure dust.

I yawned and heard another thump. It was coming from upstairs. I groaned and pushed my long hair out of my face. I turned to grab the piece of sidereal glass out from under my bed and tucked it into one of my deep pockets. I gallivanted up the stairs even though my legs felt like bricks from the run. I was going to kill the idiot that decided that seven in the morning was a perfect time to train.

Listening again, the thumps were coming from the

right wing of the house. I glanced back down the left hall, there was nothing. Everyone was still asleep except for whoever was making the uproar. I stalked toward the noise and the thumps grew louder. I knew this house like the back of my hand. The clamor was coming from the very end of the hall in the training room.

Another thump exploded from behind the doors. It didn't sound like someone throwing knives, it was like the crack of a whip with more fire behind each blow. I swung the doors open.

Ronan was standing with his bow and arrow strung. The room was quiet and I could see the immense concentration on his face. I heard him take in a deep breath as he drew the arrow back against his cheek, I saw his chest relax as he released the arrow and it ran itself deep through the heart of the target. Perhaps I had imagined it, but I thought I saw a flicker of light at the tip of the arrow like it had ignited a flame.

Ronan spun in my direction. His face gaped with astonishment, like I had just walked in on him naked or something. His hair stood out like a red rose in a dark storm. His clothes were deep shades of grey and black, clinging tightly to his body that I could see the outlines of muscles in his arms, back, and chest.

The shock on his face faded. Ronan smirked, his gold eyes shining in the light. "Don't," he started, "tell Jerik I just did that in the house."

I returned his smile, "I won't," I said as I walked toward him, I kept my gaze fixated on the floor. "That was very brave of you, standing for up Natalya before the run."

Ronan shrugged. "No big deal. I think you're brave, I've always been curious about the fourth dimension."

"There's not much to be curious about," I finally glanced up at him suspiciously. "Where did you come from?"

Ronan's eyes grew dark. "All I remember is arriving here without any idea of who I was aside from my name and one memory—I murdered someone in a place with red skies."

His hands went to his belt, and he pulled out a small knife. I observed it closely, it was simple, with a black hilt and a shiny red blade. What made it unique was the initials inscribed at the base, a large 'S' interlocking with a smaller 'S' in red, and the name SURESTRIKE stood out down the middle on the blade itself.

"It was covered in blood," Ronan said as he returned the blade to its sheath.

"From another dimension?" I questioned. "You killed someone? There lies our job description."

"Remnants—"

"Remnants were once people, Surestrike," I cut him off. "Regardless of what they have become. But I will agree with you, they did do horrible things." I bit my lip. No one knows what torture they endured to make up for the deeds they had committed. But I'm not the person who is fit to judge moral punishments. All I know is that I carried some of their memories in my mind. I shuddered at the thought of the girls, the last faces in the memory I saw in the Dead Land.

Ronan swallowed. "I've never thought of it that way."

I grinned and shook my head. "We all do bad things, I guess some are more cursed than others." I sighed, "So you don't remember anything?"

Ronan shook his head, then paused as his eyes diverted from me. "No specifics, just red skies."

"The fourth dimension had a red sky...kind of. It was hazy and orange. I wouldn't be surprised if you came from there, Natalya did—"

"No," Ronan turned his back to me. "The sky was like pure blood."

I wasn't going to let him get away that easy. "Then you know more than you're admitting."

"You mean one of the other dimensions?"

I nodded. This was based on an old scientific theory. For everything to operate correctly there must be a minimum of ten dimensions to make all the worlds go around. The only dimensions known that are in use are the fourth, the fifth, and the sixth. Seven through ten are known as voids where no life exists.

At least, that's what they tell us, I thought. After living in the fourth and fifth, I did not want to believe that was all. The Dead Land was filled with experiments, dangling on the strings of Ascendants. And the Lost Paradise encased the Raidens in a glass dome with a world that was too far manipulated. The rumors are that the sixth dimension is unreachable, so no one bothered. The Lost Paradise is the only world Raidens should care about and what exists outside is not our problem. That's what we are made to believe, that's what our leaders tell us, and that's what parents relay to their children. There's a matrix, however, the possibilities beyond our existence. Very few consider this idea or try to expand their awareness of other dimensions. I am the exception. Even as a child I was always curious about other worlds and I never stopped bothering Jerik about it. I think that's why he picked me to go to the fourth dimension. He could have sent any seven-year-old. But I had my own ideas about life. If there are other worlds out there, wouldn't you want to know? Why would our leaders want to keep it a secret?

Power, I thought, *control. The best way to control an audience is to assure them they are not being controlled.*

There lies the art of manipulation. I'll be damned if they try to control me, not again. I swallowed hard as I met Ronan's eyes. "I want to believe there is more out there."

Ronan chuckled, "I don't doubt your intuition." He shifted toward me with a dreamy expression. "I believe, the Ascendants didn't escape the fifth dimension alone; they took some Raidens with them. Raidens that didn't join the rebellion or ones they captured. I think some were my ancestors. There's no one here that carries the name Surestrike. Of course, I see why they took us." Ronan raised his bow and fired once again in a motion so fast it startled me.

He smiled, "I never miss," Ronan said confidently, running his fingers along the string of his bow. He looked at me with interest. "Are you always up this early?"

"No," I responded with irritation. "Your shooting woke me up."

"I could train you if you would like."

"Training?" I said, raising my eyebrows at him.

Ronan nodded enthusiastically. "You've been gone for a long time, Jance said you left when you were seven."

I said nothing and glared down at the floor. I didn't want to entertain the subject.

Ronan cleared his throat, "Let's see if you have the capability of a sniper." He offered his bow to me.

I embraced it with both hands, it was weightless and cool to the touch. The bow gleamed with a red tint reflecting off the weapon. Ronan had arrows pinned to his belt and his pants had little slits where arrows ran down the sides of his thighs. Even toward his shins, I saw little arrowheads peeking out.

I faced the target, "I thought you carried arrows in a quiver."

"Not if you're in a hurry to save your life. I carry them in my hand usually. The belt and pants are an easy grab, and extra storage," he said with a grin.

That's not funny, I thought, but the instantaneous smirk on my face betrayed me.

I straightened up my posture and loaded the arrow. It has been a long time since I touched a bow. I suddenly felt awkward and that was a feeling I rarely got. I wasn't sure if it was because of archery or the other redhead in the room. "How—"

Ronan yanked the bow from my grasp. Before I had time to blink, he had fired the arrow. Not caring about the details of where the arrow was placed on the string or what hand he used to launch it. I could tell archery was like breathing to him. His bow an extension of his body, showing how deadly he could be. I was shocked to see the arrow had landed in the bullseye. Same as it did when he took his time to release the arrow.

"That," he said brightly, "is how you shoot. Don't waste your time on nitty-gritty stuff, just learn to shoot straight."

Suddenly he ran to the other side of the training room and hopped on a wall that mimicked the side of a cliff. The idea was the same, with cracks and crevasses that were tricky to see immediately. With one hand and foot he clung to the wall like a spider and with the other hand, he whipped out an arrow from his belt and strung it to the bow. He used his foot to pull the string back and shoot. The arrow landed in one of the targets carved with the dimensions of humans, right in the heart of one.

I jogged over to him with amazement. "How did you—"

"Practice, practice," Ronan said confidently. "And it's in my blood."

"You think so? How can you be sure if you don't know your family?" I asked before he could interrupt.

Ronan's breathing slowed, he only hesitated for a second before he answered. "They're dead, more in likely, but I don't know because I can't *remember*," he implied as he extended the bow toward me. "You try."

I took it. "Where do you want me to start? On the wall or the floor?"

He smiled a little. "Stand where I was shooting before." He showed me to the right side of the training room in front of a few simple targets.

I strung the arrow and pulled the string back until it laid

against my jaw.

Ronan stood beside me. "Hold it a little higher so you touch the top of your cheekbone next to your eye, don't be afraid of it."

I did as he said and pinned my eyes directly on the target, concentrating. I jumped slightly as Ronan wrapped his hand over mine on the bow. His touch was warm.

He closed in on me as he spoke gently, "Your bow is like your lover, you want to hold it close to your body." He adjusted the bow slightly. I felt my cheeks grow redder than my hair. "Now the key is to breathe and relax."

I inhaled and cleared my mind, as much as I could with Ronan breathing down my neck, my heart began to beat harder. *I endured tremendous torture, held myself up while being hung, kept sane while living with the minds of the damned, and yet I find myself trembling at his touch.* I thought to myself, I didn't like it.

I shook away the endless thoughts. No, it had nothing to do with Ronan. I'm just not used to people being in my space. He probably helped dozens of girls with 'archery.'

"Let it fly," Ronan whispered, and I released the arrow. It landed toward the left, but at least it hit the target.

I beamed.

Ronan smiled, "Not bad. Do that again and aim slightly more to the right." Ronan grabbed another arrow and handed it to me.

I arranged the arrow as Ronan showed me. Tugging it to the top of my cheekbone and holding the bow close. I breathed in, aimed more to the right, and released the arrow, it sank in the heart of the target. A wide smile appeared across my face as I peered toward Ronan, he was not smiling.

"Impressive," Ronan said with folded arms.

My grin faded, I guess that was the closest thing to a compliment that Ronan was going to give me. I handed the bow back to Ronan. "Can we try something else?"

Ronan was already heading toward a wall lined with different weapons. Long swords, short swords, different bows, arrows, daggers, and knives. I glanced at the wall where the human figures were imprinted. Those poor drawings had earned their time on that wall, they used to be pretty outlines now they were bombarded with stabbings. Some of the figures were tall and straight, others bent and sagging. But they all meant the same thing, Remnants. "Those practice targets," I said motioning to Ronan, "are in the shape of people."

Ronan grabbed two medium-sized swords off the wall. "That's what Remnants look like. I would think of all people, you would know that." He said a little too sarcastically.

I opened my mouth and then closed it. His words hurt and it must have spread all over my face like a disease of emotion.

"I'm sorry," he said with regret. "I—I shouldn't have said that."

"You're right, you shouldn't have," I snapped.

Ronan didn't answer. He walked over and held the hilt of the sword in my direction.

I took it. It felt familiar and dangerous. Like all Raiden weapons, it looked a lot heavier than it was. It was tipped with sidereal glass and the rest of the blade gleamed in silver. It looked like someone tried to mix water and oil, they contrasted from one another making the blade appear more lethal, a double-edged sword. The sidereal glass that traced along the sword and the scars on my body was created out of the same thing, the stars. It was strange knowing that such a power existed in the sky, far beyond the Divide of this world and however many other worlds out there. The first earth, were the air was clear and everything lived and died in the proper time, were humans struggled against the simple concept of life.

I shook my head. "It's been so long. So how by a simple touch, does it feel like it never left me?"

Ronan took a step closer, he lifted his hand and caressed my face, forcing me to look up at him. "Because it never did leave you. Like us it is invincible, and therefore it is eternal," he paused for a moment and removed his hand, although I could still feel his impression on my face. "Can I tell you a secret?"

"Okay," I said casually, trying to sound uninterested.

"I heard," Ronan's voice flowed like water, "that the sixth dimension is made of it. Skyscrapers and streets of sidereal glass that sparkle in the sunshine and illuminate at night. A city that is never dark. And that," he lowered his tone, "is where the *others* are."

I twirled the sword in my hands and smirked. "Oh," I spoke carelessly. "And who are these 'others?'"

He glared at me. "They have a name and they are," he paused and rubbed his arm, "a lot closer than you think."

I raised my eyebrows. "For a boy without a memory you

sure do have a lot of stories."

"It's the truth Evanna." He looked at me with those cat-like eyes, amber and bright.

"I believe you," I said, only because there was a small percentage of me that did. Ronan, I realized, thought like me. Reality is more than what our eyes can see.

Ronan withdrew from me and tossed his sword up in the air, catching it right before it hit the ground. "There are still Raidens looking for the Ascendants."

"Yeah well," I said casually. "They're worse than the stories. I say let them be in the fourth dimension."

"It is because," Ronan said forcefully. "These Raidens would rather fight back against them, over admitting defeat and locking themselves away in this broken glass world. I have a feeling this isn't over—"

"I don't want to be trapped in this glass world either Ronan but going to the fourth dimension for revenge isn't the answer. I have seen enough of violence, death, and damnation," I said angrily.

At that, Ronan said nothing. He sighed and swung his sword at an invisible enemy. "Sparring with me and others will ignite that fire in you that you've always had, you're a Grey, you're destined to be a brilliant warrior."

I shrugged, "I don't think too much about being a Grey, I don't feel like one. I'm just Evanna."

"Alright, I'm just Ronan."

I smiled at him and he returned it.

"The winner in any fight is determined by your intuition,

your ability to predict what your enemy is going to do next," Ronan imposed. "However, no amount of knowledge or skill will guarantee your life, fighting is a game of chance. Come at it with the attitude that you are ten times better than your opponent, but don't get cocky to the point you become lazy." Ronan crouched down slightly holding up his weapon, "Hold up your sword."

I looked at him with a guarded expression.

Ronan straightened up, "You don't trust me."

I examined his golden eyes, "I don't trust anyone Ronan."

"You are smart not to." Ronan's lip curled as he raised his sword toward me with a quick motion.

I blocked him, our swords clanging against each other. Ronan disengaged and moved down toward my feet. I dodged his attack with ease.

"I was going slow and eyeing where I was going strike to you. No good fighter will ever do that. Someone with skill will try their best to stare at your face and try to read you. Now, what I want you to do is try to kill me."

I raised my eyebrows. "Oh, don't tempt me."

"I am tempting you. I won't fight back, only block. I want to see what you got. Unleash the magic that runs through your veins." Ronan said holding up his sword again, not taking his eyes off me.

I moved to the side of him never breaking eye contact. Gripping the hilt tight, I swung fast and hard towards Ronan's neck. His eyes widened as he blocked, not expecting the attack. I quickly aimed toward his ankles as if to chop off his legs. He jumped, avoiding my blow and he danced away. I swung and jabbed at Ronan until we were both gasping for breath. I felt something wake up inside me, like a sudden need to try to take Ronan's head off, only for fun of course.

He held up his hand to stop the fight. "You are good at keeping eye contact; I wasn't sure what body part you were going to try to take off next."

I was sweating, wiping my forehead. "Thank you," I breathed.

"Now, let's fight for real." Ronan surmounted.

"What!" I shouted.

"Think fast!" Ronan's sword came by my side, I yelped, swerving away from him, forgetting that I could move that fast.

I parried most of Ronan's swings, but it was challenging to get a move in. Ronan was stronger than me. He was muscular; with big arms and abdominals, their outlines making a feature through his sweaty shirt. The kind of body that was bred for strength and invincibility. Poor Jance had always been scrawny, but that was characteristic of most Greys. I was quite petite myself, but I am not to be underestimated. I was getting sick of moving away from him. A scowl formed on my face as I half-closed my eyes and a yell came from my throat. I whipped toward him, aiming to the side, I felt my sword sink into something. My eyes widened as blood appeared on his hip, I gasped. Ronan shook his head and nodded toward me, encouraging me to continue. I did but Ronan upped his game. I felt his sword cut the top of my shoulder and I inhaled sharply, it was hot like fire.

Ronan lowered his sword immediately. "Stop!"

I froze and backed away from him; drenched in sweat that made my shoulder sting. I looked at it and noticed a little blood on the surface, it wasn't a deep cut.

"Is your shoulder okay?" Ronan asked with concern.

"Yeah, what about your side?"

Ronan breathed hard. "Just a minor cut. I'm sorry we had to stop."

I pushed the hair out of my face. "Why did we? Afraid I'm going to hurt you?" I inquired, giving him a sarcastic smirk.

"Ha-Ha," Ronan said mockingly. "No actually, I would have killed you."

I laid the sword on the ground, "I wouldn't be so quick to assume you'd have the upper hand."

"Wouldn't dream of it," Ronan said, picking up the swords and hanging them on the back wall. "Some things about me are hard to understand."

"Well, if you can't understand things about yourself, maybe I can help you figure them out," I admitted openly. The words felt foreign on my mouth, I rarely talked about myself. Let alone have a curiosity about others. Natalya had been the one to trigger my compassionate side. The story of oneself is long and complicated and the worst part is it never stops. Even after you die people keep talking about you.

Ronan breathed deeply, avoiding my gaze. It wasn't the first time I felt like something important was being hidden from me. Natalya gave me similar feelings. I look her in the eyes and think there is another world behind them. The hands of the ticking clock will eventually return to the same place, and so time reveals all secrets, no matter how hard you try to keep them.

"Thank you," I said. "For training me."

Ronan looked relieved at the change of subject. "We can do it every day if you want. I'm here every morning before breakfast."

I half smiled, I hated getting up early, but the idea of spending more time with Ronan motivated me. "Better get ready, I'm a hard worker."

"And an amazing fighter," Ronan said as we walked toward the door. He put his hand on my back, I shivered. "Tomorrow then?"

"Tomorrow," I said and immediately left the room.

CHAPTER TWENTY-TWO

NATALYA

Breakfast felt awkward. Ronan and Eve were stalking each other with their eyes. I stared at her, she shrugged. I stifled a chuckle. She had come down ahead of Ronan from the fourth floor. I wondered what they were doing up there so early in the morning.

Jance came down groggily, he looked like hadn't slept all night, he wore long loose clothes.

Ronan talked while making pancakes. "What I recommend you do Natalya, is go to the weaponry. You'll meet Shai's father, Donavan. All Raidens usually have a favorite weapon, mine's the bow. Both Jance and Evanna have short swords, I think it's a Grey thing."

Jance and Eve winked at each other.

"Okay, I'll check it out."

"If you have questions," Jance said as he handed out plates. "Now would be a good time to ask."

"Names," I stated simply, and confused looks spread around me. "They have meaning?"

"Yes, and legend," Ronan said stirring the batter. The motion made my heart feel at ease, something so human.

"Tell me about your name."

I saw Eve's face twist in curiosity.

"Surestrike," Ronan flashed a smile toward me when the batter hit the griddle. "I'm probably a descendant from a long line of snipers." Ronan gawked down at his pancakes like they were a masterpiece. "Names are also just trademarks of appearances like the Grey family are known for their eyes."

"That seems kind of strange," I commented. I inhaled through my nose, it smelled like brown sugar and cinnamon.

Ronan grabbed himself a plate as he spoke and gave the first pancake to Eve. "We trained hard this morning," he said with a wink.

I couldn't hide my smile as I saw Eve's cheeks grow red, and Jance's sudden protectiveness was written all over his face. Ronan's smirk faded as he met Jance's eyes. Ronan cleared his throat and continued, "It's not strange. Grey is the color of the Raidens. The Ascendants embraced black and white, symbolizing law. For there to be law and order everything must be black and white. The Raidens embrace various shades of grey, showing that we believe in bending the law in certain situations."

"Really?" I said surprised. He stacked a few pancakes on my plate. Jance looked at Ronan impatiently. "From what I've gathered, this doesn't seem like a place that bends on anything."

Ronan was stuffing his face and finally tossed a pancake at Jance, which landed in his lap. "Times have changed. I wish I lived in the good old days."

"What? The days when the Ascendants enslaved us?" Eve asked sharply.

Ronan sighed, "No, the days that came right after that."

"Well at the end of *this* day, it doesn't matter," I said. "The past is over, and the future is nonexistent. There is only the present, and we all have to accept that and make the most of it."

"Wise words," Jance said, collecting pieces of pancake.

"What was the past like?" I asked Ronan.

He sat down at the table beside me. "Freedom," Ronan said swallowing another large bite. "Freedom to run, freedom to do whatever the hell we wanted, and Remnants didn't run wild. It was nothing like now. We are all subjects of manipulation like the Ascendants wanted us to be."

"What changed?"

Ronan shrugged. "The rules. Raiden was the leader for a while, he helped redirect the chaos after the war. After Raiden and all the other veterans of the war passed on, we were free from the Ascendant's reign, but we needed someone to guide us and the line of Herolds began. The concept of this new leader was not to overpower but be humbled by enduring the fears of the people. The use of the House of Mirrors was reintroduced to manipulate our minds and shield them from the Remnants, who started to enter this dimension at alarming rates. The Raidens figured that the Ascendants were experimenting and failing again. After years of peace, the Raidens had grown soft. So, we had to start acting quickly, toughen up, and protect each other and defend the fifth dimension. It was one of the hardest times in history. The Herold had to bring the hammer down and create new ways to make us stronger, like running through sharp trees. Then militia was reinstated."

"Why enforce the idea of being subjects of manipulation? It all seems so demeaning," I asked.

"The Herold is the ultimate example," Jance spoke slowly like he was in pain. "My father can never leave that mirror."

I looked at him sympathetically.

"And," Eve cut in. "Because that is what we are. You cannot undo what you were made to be."

I shook my head. "You don't always have to be what you were made to be. Or become what the world has done to you. If bad things happen to you, do you become a bad person? I would hope not. Who you are depends on your choices."

Jance smiled. "Sounds so human."

Ronan groaned. "That's why it sounds so naïve."

Eve kept her face down. "Maybe in some other world, those words would be beneficial, but you're taking it out of context. We were designed to be something specific. I don't think you're understanding that."

"What do you mean?"

Ronan's voice grew angry. "You're not human Natalya!" He paused and took a shaky breath. "Being superhuman doesn't make you fully human. We were created underground by people with minds so insane, that they would do torturous things to another human. To scar them again and again until the brink of death but they wouldn't let them die. Teaching the body and mind to defeat the need to die. The least you can do is respect who you are. We are subjects of manipulation because that's how we were created, thousands of years ago after the old earth was destroyed and the dimensions were brought to reality."

I was silent. I did not know about the creation of the Raidens. But the fact that I am only what I was made to be, and be told I have any control over it? No choice in the matter? Words can play tricks. Words that praised how we were created to be invincible sounded so good. Heroes make the world a better place. Replace those words with manipulated, scarred, tortured, it instantly makes us sound vulnerable, even evil. *Thousands of years ago,* I thought.

I dropped my fork as the clock on top of Camden rang out. I had a sudden flashback to what Mr. Barnes had taught in class. Four dimensions, the fourth being time.

My mind finally connected the dots. "We are not the only subjects of manipulation here."

Ronan raised his eyebrows.

"Time," I whispered. "This, the fifth dimension. It's time moving faster than time."

The clock stopped on its last half-chime.

I thought of the grass, how it had shriveled in my hand, and then regrew. I swallowed hard. "It is possible. Time isn't constant, it's an illusion, or relative, depending on where you are. Time is just above the dimension we are spatially in." I tasted blood on my lip as my teeth gritted into the skin. The pain felt good. "This is what the world is destined to be?" I burned my gaze deep into the three faces around me. I turned to Eve, "The fourth dimension—you said some of those kids were made into Ascendants. I know you, Eve, you wouldn't let anyone be mercilessly killed. Time moves backward there, and here it moves forward. The Ascendants are manipulating time."

Eve's eyes shot to me. "They would pull the skeletons from the ground, and I saw the flesh layer over the bones as they rose," her voice broke. "You have to learn to differentiate what is real and what is not real—"

Something inside me unhinged. "You are going to tell me *now* what is real and not real? All those years and you never told me anything! You didn't speak about who, or what you are Eve. You won't even tell me what you were searching for in the fourth dimension!"

Eve struggled for words, "I *couldn't*—"

I was tired of questioning everything. "For once in my damn life all I want is something real, and for someone to be real..." I trailed off. My heart hammered.

Eve stood, but she did it with a frightening calmness. "I told you what you needed to know," she said slowly. "I thought you were the one I was looking for!" Her voice rose as her blue eyes blazed with fury. "But you weren't the one...and I *failed* because of it." She whipped out of the room, the kitchen door waving behind her.

The boys were quiet. I looked back and forth at Jance and Ronan, my eyes settled on Jance. "What *was* she looking for?"

Jance responded simply. "I don't know—"

I threw my hands in the air. "Fine, then just please explain to me the time manipulation."

"You are existing in a different space. Like time zones except instead of zones they are dimensions." Ronan said.

I snorted. "Why didn't someone tell me this before? My whole life I fought, I starved, and I've mourned for those children—" I cut off my words, my anger thrummed inside me like it had a heartbeat of its own. "Look, I want to save them if I can. The Ascendants are probably manipulating more kids in the Dead Land as we speak, they're playing their death's on repeat, you heard what Eve said. Please, we are superhuman, help me—"

"The fourth dimension doesn't concern us," Jance cut me off casually.

"*What!* Do their lives not matter to you?"

They just stared at me blankly. I was so angry. I was tired of my own questions that will never be answered. I was tired of being around people who seemed to only care about themselves, and not for the ones who have no voice. I stormed towards the door.

Jance stopped me, grabbing my shoulders in a fluid motion. "Look at me," he said gently. His voice was like a quiet river against my raging sea. "Natalya, there is something about the Seers you do not understand."

He rubbed my shoulders, but even with every gentle swipe of his hand, there was no comfort. I squirmed away from his touch.

He let me go. "Listen," he breathed. "Look at me. Am I real? I am right in front of you. It's true, not everything that is seen is real. Not all that is visible, is reality. The key is to see behind the masks and know their games. This world, and every world out there, will play tricks on you. We do not have access to the Dead Land, we cannot be responsible for the Ascendants undoing of humanity. There may come a day where we can figure out a plan, but we must focus on one moment, one *world*, at a time." He paused, "Natalya," his hands went to my wrists, "you have us, you have me."

He still wasn't understanding. Why is it the first instance I begin to put my trust in someone, they fail immediately? My body wanted to run, but I was mysteriously frozen in place. I wanted to push Jance's hands away, but I did not have the strength.

"Look at your own body—" he said as he went to roll up my sleeve; the place where the gold scar was hiding. Suddenly, I was back in control and instantaneously grabbed at Jance's wrist, catching him off guard. I dug my fingers into the loose undershirt trying to stop him, but it tore with ease.

Jance was frozen and Ronan's mouth gaped.

I took in Jance's whippet-thin frame, his ribs and collarbone outlined by an abundant amount of lean muscle and I could make out delicate lacey patterns, more detailed and organized than the typical jagged marks. His scars formed different star-shaped illusions. The crystallization over his skin was not white, but a silvery grey, like iron sparkling in the light. No formation was like the other, my eyes followed to the point where it ended at the base of his palm; the same place where my discolored scar was. I realized my hand was locked on his arm, it felt glued there. What I felt on my hand wasn't human flesh, it was an iciness that leaked beneath my skin.

He drew back his arm. I met his grey eyes, which were swirling like storm clouds. "Get. *Out!*"

And I did.

I ran out the door. Tears blurred my vision. My body plowed into the large door of the house, throwing it open with vigor, it made a large thud that echoed throughout the mansion. I didn't care. I felt a surge of adrenaline as I charged down the path, instead of opening the gate to the fence, I cleared it with a solid jump.

I am superhuman, I am strong I thought. I felt tears begin to creep down my face. *But I am not invincible.*

I collapsed against the fence. I slid down the rods that enclosed the mansion and looked above. I was greeted by the broken sky and the sun peeking through the pieces. I wanted to feel the sun soak into my skin but there was no warmth, I wanted to feel the wind whip through my hair, but the air was lifeless. There was no sun or sky in the Lost Paradise. They were hardly in the Dead Land either. I may never witness nature in its true form. I dug my hands into the plush grass and tore it from the ground repeatedly as if the cure to all my worries laid beneath it. Once again, the grass replenished itself within a matter of seconds. But I kept tearing into it, trying to destroy the indestructible world.

CHAPTER TWENTY-THREE

JANCE

"Jansen," Ronan said my full name like poison on the tip of his tongue.

My mind whirled, I was speechless. My breath came in angry little bursts.

"She's going to run to Evanna—" Ronan cut himself off for a second. I turned to look at him. "Does your cousin know?"

I shook my head. "No."

"We can play it off, I'll go find Natalya, make up something. I'll say it's normal for some Raidens, but it shouldn't be discussed to others—"

I snorted loudly, trying to pull my torn shirt back over my head. "Very discrete."

He sighed. "I wasn't going to put it exactly like that."

"She won't go to Evanna, she's mad at all of us right now.

I don't think she's the type to go running to people. I think she just closes herself off." I said flustered.

Ronan came closer. "You like her?"

I turned to him. "She intrigues me. She ripped my clothes off."

"Under different circumstances," Ronan interrupted, "that would be a turn-on—"

I pushed him, and he smirked. "Will you *stop*. Something isn't right, she got really angry within seconds."

Ronan's brow furrowed. "It's not easy coming into a new world and having no idea who or what you are. She probably just cracked and lost it for a second as we all do sometimes. So, she saw your scars, maybe she didn't notice the difference."

I shook my head, doubting the possibility. "No. Something isn't right. And come on Ronan, she saw them in their entirety."

"Despite the scars, I think you did the right thing," Ronan's voice lowered. "She shouldn't be told about the Seers yet. Once she understands who they could become, the threats against Raidens, then she'll understand. She is one of *us*, not one of *them*."

I turned my back to him.

I understand your fury, Natalya. I thought to myself how I would explain this. *I am responsible for the murder of the Seers, these children, who have gifts beyond my own imagination. It's not right. But I can't do anything about it. I am the monster.* I looked down at my forearm through my torn sleeve, the silver marks shining with brilliance. *I am cursed,* I thought.

"Why did you ask if I had feelings for her?" I stammered. "When you were gawking at my cousin, who has been through so much pain already, and the last thing she needs is someone like you *touching* her."

I didn't turn to see his face, the momentary silence said it all. "You're right," he said, exhaling the painful realization.

I heard his footsteps fade behind me and the backdoor slam. When I turned, he was gone.

I felt shaky. I wanted to believe I was kind. But somethings could put a major dent in my ability to maintain a kind nature. My disease sabotaged it. I can be empathic, or I can be awful. It all depends on what side I choose. When I was far away and reading, I felt like I was kind. Although I was in solitude, so there was no way I could mess up. I do not know what set Natalya off, perhaps it was the way I touched her shoulders. She reacted like she hasn't been touched before.

She should be touched with gentleness, I thought. I shivered, and instantly cleared my head, putting the thought out.

The side I had little control of, the hysterical side, was not characteristic of a Grey. I yelled at her to get out; when she was already confused and angered. Regret ran over me like a wave and it threatened to drown me. I need to take accountability for my own actions before I put full blame on her reaction.

I turned and looked at the sidereal glass window, it was as merciless as ever, mixing my reflection with the morning sky. My eyes were nearly colorless. They changed sometimes according to my emotions, dark grey to clear. I blinked hard, but it was useless. I knew what I had to do next.

CHAPTER TWENTY-FOUR
EVANNA

I heard a knock on my door.

I surged at the thought that it might be Ronan. I glanced in the mirror to make sure my crimson hair fell into the right places. It was my mother's hair. There was a sporadic string of blood-red hair throughout the Grey line that is typically flooded with baby blondes with pearl eyes. Occasionally, deep blue eyes or red hair would pop up. Somehow, I ended up with both. Together I do not even look like a Grey.

I opened the door to see my cousin, who looked just as distraught as I felt. I threw my arms around him. He felt familiar...and cold.

"We haven't had a chance to talk," Jance said in a low voice.

I retreated from the hug and looked up at him. He was

so tall, I used to be taller than him. Everyone thought I was the oldest. I smiled. "It's okay Jansen. It's all over now. What happened to me doesn't matter."

His eyes were full of concern. "I understand. But I wish you would tell me, why did my father send you away?"

I sighed. I knew this conversation was bound to come up. I hesitated, and when I hesitate, I always lie. "Just Seers."

A series of unreadable emotions passed over Jance's face before he finally spoke. "Seers?"

I nodded. "This is why I couldn't tell Natalya about the fifth dimension. I thought she was a Seer. I failed miserably on my mission because of it. Of course, I managed to find another damn Raiden."

Jance shook his head. "Seers are such a commodity lately..."

I looked at him intensely. I lowered my voice and stepped closer to him, "Are more Seers passing through the fifth dimension?"

Jance's expression was bleak, I could read the sorrow passing through his crystal eyes. This burden kills him. Jance received the job best suited to harden his child-like heart. The Herold's heir is responsible for the seeking and killing of Seers. It is a law that is hardly talked about, but everyone knew. Any Raiden who stumbles upon a Seer must kill them. But they rarely appear right in front of us. Seers have a unique ability to shift from dimension to dimension, and the worst part is, they do so unknowingly. The Ascendants have more knowledge of these humans with superhuman qualities. All the Raidens know, is that they must be hunted down and killed, otherwise, they could grow to be an Ascendant, our enemy. That's why Jance scouts the tree line. The trees are always the way in.

Jance took a shaky breath. "Yes, way more than when we were kids. Killing them on sight, it just doesn't—"

"Feel right?" I finished. My heart felt like it was breaking. Is it justifiable to kill those who may become a threat? But how would you know if they are not given a chance? "You must have known Natalya was not a Seer then."

Jance turned away. "She's livid. We had a big fight after you left. She wants to save the children trapped in the Dead Land."

I closed my eyes slowly. "Did you tell her?"

"No Evanna, I did not," he said bitterly. "I think that will be the hardest reality Natalya will have to accept, we have to kill them. They must die for us to keep our superhuman race safe."

I shifted. There was an echo of disbelief in his voice. "Jance, you are not the only one to question that idea. I feel your empathy in my heart. I've seen what's been happening to these children. It is the single most unspoken evil done in all the worlds. The Ascendants bring humans in, and they determine the ones who are worth it and the ones who are not. I do not know Jance, but I don't think the humans are truly *killed*." I had a deep theory, Jance's eyes were locked on me. "Time manipulation, the Ascendants have humans on their strings. They are the ones that created us ages ago. They're the elitists, and the leader is named Alda. I think they are trying to manipulate time. Control time, you control death. I saw it happen Jance, bodies rising from the ground..." I shuddered. I didn't want to relive it.

He sucked in his breath. "Natalya assumed correctly then? You think the Ascendants care more about time rather than hunting Seers?"

I nodded. "It's a theory, but I've been watching them. Why else would they target average humans? Ones that have no sight. We both know where they come from..."

"The earth, the real one," he answered.

I nodded. It still existed. There is a past, present, and future and they all can coexist in different realms. The dimensions keep them all in order. If the dimensions were destroyed, all the superhumans would have nowhere to go. If we lived in the past earth it would drive humans to insanity. If the Ascendants are playing with time, that could only mean they are trying to figure out ways to manipulate the outer reality. Perhaps, some of the Ascendants have already walked the earth.

"How do we fight against this Evanna?" Jance's words dripped like beads of water. "Who is going to take our side? We will be shunned by the majority, our leaders, and my father—"

"Any voice being drowned by the masses is the one that deserves to be heard," I said with confidence. "But the world won't break by words alone."

My cousin looked at me in awe. "Evanna, you are incredibly brave."

Or incredibly stupid, I thought to myself. "So are you," I confirmed. "We will find a way to fight this," I touched his shoulder. "I'm thankful you didn't tell Natalya. She needs to focus on training her mind and body and become a Raiden. She will try to save the world with nothing but a dull knife, a stubborn heart, and a fragile mind. Trust me."

"Ronan said I did the right thing as well; it just doesn't feel like it."

I sighed. "It's hard to keep secrets from the ones we love." I glanced at him; my hand still lingered on his shoulder. An interesting coolness flooded over me.

"Do you want to talk about what happened? In the fourth dimension?" He asked with an ache in his voice.

"The Dead Land was a *horrible* place. The Ascendants separated the children by a wall, and they lived in an encampment on the other side. A long, flat building that extended for half a mile. Vast halls that never ended, one always leading deeper into their hold. Below it, they kept the Remnants in pits. I catered to them..." I trailed off.

Communicating my past was almost like reliving it. Jance didn't understand, Natalya didn't either. I didn't expect them too and I didn't want their help. Not the way they are approaching me about it. Silence is power, and I must deal with my demons by fighting them with the weapon in my mind. How brave am I truly? Brave enough to push it all away and try to pretend it didn't happen. Move past my past once and for all.

"Evanna, I'm so sorry—"

"Don't be," I cut him off. A smile spread across my face. "Do you remember when we were kids? And you would rip the grass and watch it regrow within seconds? How fascinated you were? I asked you to not destroy things even if they couldn't be destroyed. Think about me then. I need you to understand how I want to be remembered. I want to be here without the annoying judgment of others and their fear of what my past has done to me. I want to hold on to that little bit of myself I left behind."

Jance reached down and took my hand. "I think of those times too. But nothing stays the same forever. Time is a cruel punishment and a great blessing."

"You remind me of someone."

"Who?"

"Natalya." I breathed. "I grew up with her. Like you did with Ronan."

"Fascinating, now we're all *friends*."

I pushed him. "Come on, Ronan is kind and very attractive."

Jance paused like he wanted to say something, but then managed a grin. "I guess whatever makes you happy."

I reached up and hugged him. "I do deserve it."

"Everyone does," he said with a hint of sadness. "Love."

I pulled away and rubbed his arm, which felt icy again. I frowned a little, the fifth dimension was consistently warm, stiff but comfortable. He backed away from me like he was afraid of my touch.

"I've got to go see the Herold."

I nodded. "We'll come up with a plan Jance."

He gave me a reassuring smile as he slowly closed the door to my room.

He was right, time does change things. But there was something different about Jance. All those chills that crept up my body when I touched him. He was hiding something, and I am determined to find out what.

CHAPTER TWENTY-FIVE
NATALYA

I wiped the tears from my face and stood. I decided to walk around and pretend I knew where I was going. I needed a distraction. The cobblestone paths lead to small houses. I could see letters of last names engraved on their gates that read WAYWARD, ARLING, STEEP, GUARDER, CASSTEEL, FREE, and MERCILESS. It reminded me of the names written on the graffiti wall a whole world ago.

The streets were not busy but running into Raidens was inevitable. I recognized some of them from the Black and White Parade. Some smiled kindly toward me, others kept looking onward. One elderly lady hobbled down the path walking arm in arm with a young boy around the age of eleven. Both were dressed in poor, loose clothes. Her sleeves were cut short and her arms were scarred to the point that I barely saw any skin in between the crystal marks. The boy had scars as well, they were slightly red and swollen. I glanced away when they passed me, but I couldn't help looking over my shoulder, curious to see what house they belonged to. The boy opened the gate labeled MERCILESS.

I headed toward Camden and saw a crowd of Raidens dressed in royal blue. It must be the Flood, the adult army I remember Jance telling me about. A few of them wore navy blue, those must be the Elites. The adults still looked young. Even though they are not immortal, the Raidens sustained their youth longer than humans did in the past.

I peered down a hill to see a clear building. The foundation of it was layered with stone, but most of it was held up by windows of sidereal glass. Across the top of the building it read Weapons of Cassteel. I could see all kinds of sharp objects hanging on the walls through the glass. I jogged down the hill. I remembered Ronan advised me to go there. I could think of no better distraction than playing with swords.

Upon entering, I saw a man standing behind a counter. I breathed through my nose, it smelled like steel on stone.

The man smiled at me. "I've heard lots about you, Natalya Wells. I was wondering when you would find your way here."

"Does Shai live here?" I blurted.

The man was short with umber skin, black and blonde hair, and blue eyes that resembled the same ones that saved me during the race. The man seemed to glow with pride at the mention of Shai. "He is my son," he paused and turned to a back room. "Shai!"

Shai appeared in the doorway, shirtless. I could feel my cheeks flood to a rosy tint. His black skin glittered with sweat and his white scars beamed with light. His features were different from his father, except for the eyes.

"Natalya," Shai said in a silky voice.

I said nothing but nodded toward him.

Shai's father bowed down at me. "I'm Donavan Cassteel. And my son told me about your amazing performance in the race. I've always questioned the notions of Ace Huntington, and how he was leading our young Raidens. Looks like my reason for suspicion has been justified. How are you healing my dear?" Donavan's words were fluid and he spoke like he was very old.

I shrugged, "Well if it wasn't for Ace, I would have probably never known what I was capable of. I couldn't say I would run through giant thorns and tear myself up all on my own."

"Yes, perhaps we all need people to test our limits," Donavan said patting his son on the shoulder. Shai smiled softly.

"What can I do for you, Natalya?" Donavan asked kindly. "I'm sure you didn't come here to just talk, although you're welcome anytime."

"Um, yeah. I was told that Raidens could have a sort of calling to a weapon?" I said, shyly glancing around the glass walls. I felt overwhelmed being surrounded by dangerous items of all different shapes, sizes, and colors. However, every single one of them was tipped with an edge of sidereal glass.

"You've heard correctly!" Donavan walked up to me.

"Everyone is destined for a certain weapon. For some, it takes longer, while others just pick up a weapon and they know. Like the feeling I had when I first laid eyes on my wife. Love at first sight."

"Destined?" I asked confused. "Raidens believe in destiny?"

Donavan got a faraway look in his eyes. "The Raidens believe in very few things, I, however, believe in destiny. And I've raised my son to believe in faith, hope, and love. If there's nothing to believe in, and if there's no one to love, then what's the point of existing?"

I nodded slowly, unsure of his words. I glanced back at Shai who seemed to have lost interest in what his father was saying and had retracted into his own mind. Of course, when my eyes lingered on him a little too long, he looked up. "I'm going back to work father," Shai said with a low bow.

"Yes, yes of course. Thank you, son." Donavan said as Shai returned to the back room.

I almost felt sad to see him leave. Shai had an aura about him that gave me instant satisfaction.

"So, Miss Wells, any weapon you'd like to try out?" Donavan asked enthusiastically.

I didn't wait for the man to hand anything to me. I began picking up weapons like a child with new toys. I grabbed a short sword, the same kind Eve and Jance carried. It was lined in a simple dark grey that contrasted against the sparkling sidereal glass along the blade. I examined it for a moment, then I started swinging it around. Nothing. It was pretty, but there had to be more than just beauty.

I continued Looking around the walls. "Why are there no weapons made strictly out of sidereal glass? If it's so invincible why combine it with other materials?"

"Good question," Donavan commented. "Sidereal glass is very precious. Long ago we created weapons to be forged with all the naturals in the earth. Each weapon is never short of sidereal protection, a little goes a long way. I assure you, Miss Wells, you'll be safe with a weapon just tipped with the star glass."

"I better be," I said scanning the rest of the wall. A scary-looking longsword hanging high on the wall caught my eye. It was all white and clear. I stood on my toes to pull it down. It was about the length of both my arms combined. I raised my eyebrows at Donavan.

"Longswords, beautiful weapons. The Cassteels are well known for our skill with them. Although, they're a bit heavy to lug around." Donavan said rocking back and forth on his heels.

"This is incredible." I admired it as I began to swipe at an invisible target. Then, it suddenly hit the wall with a loud crash. I swung it again, this time it's weight almost made me fall over. I felt like I was trying to control something that did not want me to control it.

"They're tricky to handle sometimes. That one has a mind of its own," Donavan said, struggling not to chuckle at my clumsiness.

I sighed. Maybe I could learn to control it, but it seemed best to let it go. I hung it back on the wall with a bit of regret. "You're talking about weapons like they have a conscious, is that true?"

Donavan smiled, "It all depends on what you believe in, my dear."

I sighed and walked to the opposite side of the wall towards the back. The weapons were hung closer together, making them harder to pick out.

"Not sure if any of those weapons will do you any good. Most Raidens find these to be their last choice."

"Why?" I asked, seeing lines of daggers and knives in various sizes.

Donavan shrugged. "They're not the most convenient."

I trusted he knew what he was talking about, but I wanted to be the judge. I froze suddenly as my eyes caught the glimmer of four long knives made of gold. I clutched the hilt of one and sucked in my breath as a rush of heat encamped me. It reminded me of the little knife I had carried with me on my mission to kill the Ascendants. With my left, I took another, and together I jabbed and pierced the air. My body moved fluidly with the motion of the knives. I smiled. "I want these."

Donavan looked at me sheepishly.

"Oh..." I trailed off. "How much, I mean, how do I pay for them?" I haven't heard of any kind of currency in the fifth dimension, there wasn't any in the fourth, but that didn't mean everything was free. "There must be a price for these knives, they're so beautiful."

Donavan's face fell serious for the first time since I walked in. He took a few steps toward me, close enough for him to whisper. "The price in this world is your life."

I locked eyes with him. Physical currency is only paper-thin, but the cost of a life, that is priceless. "So Raidens pay with their blood?"

Donavan nodded. "You are here to defend the fifth dimension and defeat Remnants. That's all you will ever do. Risk yourself every day, and these knives will help guard you. They are by no means free."

I said nothing but looked at the other two long knives on the wall. I took them, carrying all four could be a challenge but I would find a way. "Thank you," I said.

He bowed to me. Another Raiden entered and Donavan turned his attention toward them. I walked to the front counter. The door to the back room was open and I could see Shai examining a longsword. I moved a little closer and tapped the door open to catch his attention.

Shai turned on a dime with a smile on his face, which quickly faded at the sight of my knives. "Long knives?" he commented inquisitively. "Kind of a strange weapon."

"Exactly," I said letting myself in. "That's why I think they are suitable for me."

"You're right," Shai commented as he sheathed the longsword.

I took a deep breath. "Shai, I was wondering if I could ask for your help. I need it, again."

Shai chuckled lowly. "You didn't have to ask the first time and you don't have to ask now."

I couldn't help but smile with immense gratitude. Some people had ways that could make anyone smile even when the world was grim. "What do you know about the Greys?"

He raised his eyebrows. "They are the Herold family. Jerik's mother, Joan, was a kind and caring Herold. Most say he inherited her kindness. Joan was married to a man from the Wayward family, Marwick. He was...well, let's just say we are thankful Joan was the Herold. Jerik had a younger sister as well, Amelia Grey. Amelia and her husband, Evan Wren, were murdered by Remnants, leaving Evanna Grey an orphan when she was an infant."

"What about Jance? Is there anything...unusual about him?"

Shai shrugged. "Not from what I know. He lacks seriousness sometimes. To be blunt, he's not the best fighter, neither is Jerik. But his mother was one of the best."

"Who's his mother? I've been staying in the Herold's House and I've never seen her," I inquired.

"Honoria Grey, previously Honoria Merciless. The Merciless family is known to be some of the fiercest warriors. They are what their name states, no mercy. Honoria was one of the best in the family line."

I frowned. "Was?"

Shai took a deep breath. "She's retired now. She's grown sick with an unknown disease. Jerik seemed unsurprised by it. Honoria has been a mute her entire life."

"Oh, that's sad," I said feeling sympathy for Jance.

"It's alright," Shai commented. "My life would have been more peaceful if my mother was a mute," he said in a very low voice.

Suddenly, something thumped Shai in the back of the head. "Ow!"

"You better think before you speak Shai Cassteel!" A firm voice echoed from the doorway.

I turned to see a very tall woman with dark hair braided back exposing her narrow face. The woman was scowling at Shai, but then smiled and bowed to me. "You must be Natalya," she said, her voice now soft and silky like Shai's. "My name is Ria Cassteel. I'm *his* mother."

I raised my eyebrows and chuckled toward Shai. "Nice timing, she got you good."

Shai bent down and picked up a dull knife off the floor. "She hit me with the butt of a knife!"

"And it was well deserved! Even if I whacked you with the other side, the knife isn't sharp anyway," Ria said jokingly as she strode in the room. Her black skin shined in the light reflecting from the sidereal glass windows and her warming brown eyes made me feel welcome. *I like the Cassteels,* I thought to myself.

Shai put his arms around his mother sweetly. I smiled at the affection. "My mother is the Third Hand for the Herold."

"Oh," I said, I had no idea what that meant.

Ria smiled. "Means I'm right below Ace. The three of us work closely together. The Herold usually has two close advisors, the Right Hand, and the Third Hand. The Right Hand is second in command. In war, if Ace were to die, you would follow me and if I were to die, you'd follow the best Elite."

"And who's that?" I asked.

"Me, or Ronan Surestrike, the sniper is a good shot but

I'm a better fighter when it comes to combat," there was a hint of bitterness in Shai's voice. I got the sense he didn't like Ronan very much, or perhaps it was innocent competition.

"Except for poor Kian, what a shame," Ria said with sadness.

"Who?"

"Kian Gracing," Shai said. "He was incredible. But he disappeared less than a year ago. His family is convinced he's alive. The reality is unlikely."

"Could he be alive?" I asked.

Shai shrugged. "Who knows, there have been countless searches. They never found him."

"I would say I've heard about you Natalya, but I'm sure you get that a lot," Ria said kindly. "It was an honor to meet you. I have to go find Ace." Ria said as she headed toward the door. "Oh," she stopped. "You are very brave. I do not agree with what Ace did. But I have worked with him for years. When it comes down to it, he's done good things in the past." At that, she left the room.

"Perhaps she is right, one wrong doesn't make a person evil," Shai commented. "My mother has a gentle nature behind her titanium domineer, it's what makes her a great leader."

I shook my head. "No, she's right. It's okay, Ace doesn't bother me. It only made me stronger."

Shai beamed. "Do you want to walk with me? I can tell you how to get around here."

"I'd like that," I answered, and my heart thudded with excitement.

CHAPTER TWENTY-SIX

JANCE

The young man tilted his head up toward me with a face full of fear. It wasn't the hopelessness in his eyes that made my stomach turn, it was the scars on his face. This Seer was familiar with war.

"What—" the boy started.

"Don't speak," I said sternly.

I was glad when the boy's lips pierced together tightly.

I can't do this anymore, I thought. *I can't kill him.*

I walked away. I don't care if Ace is out to kill me. My death is coming sooner rather than later. I only took a few steps when suddenly I felt a hand on my arm. I reached for my sword but I was thrown backward with a force that was stronger than my own.

I looked up to see Ace, his breath heavy like an animal. "You do this or I'll do it, *slowly.*"

UNPARALLELED

I shuttered as he released me and stalked away. I turned around, clutching my weapon.

CHAPTER TWENTY-SEVEN
NATALYA

Shai and I walked around the cobblestone paths for hours. It was way past sunset, and Shai talked openly about the traditions and practices of the Raidens. He told me the Black and White Parade trained every other day. Utilizing combat and mind drills that usually involved group work. Scoutings were determined on your skillset and schedules rotated day and night. The Flood trained every day, and the Elites endured specialized training that was classified knowledge.

The youngest Elite ever was Kian Gracing, who Ria had talked about earlier. Even though Kian's family pursued his search, he still hasn't been found and must be replaced. The title would go to either Shai or Ronan. Shai said the Elites are so charming their looks can kill. I laughed. If that was the case Shai belongs with them.

UNPARALLELED

He told me to follow my nose and I will eventually get where I need to go. I frowned, but then I smelled the salty air. I've never seen the beach. I felt my heart surge when the golden sand came into view and the sound of the waves sang into my ears. I took off my boots and ran through the sand in my bare feet, leaving Shai behind. The particles were soft, sticking in between my toes and flying up in an explosion of dust each time my feet left the ground. The ocean tides swashed against my legs as if they were trying to grab my ankles and pull me in. Shai ran up to me and we slowed to a steady walk. For the first time, the fifth dimension felt like paradise.

"I had a nice time today," he said sweetly.

I grinned a little. "Me too."

"What are the rules here?" I asked.

Shai chuckled; he had been patient answering my questions. "There are plenty of rules. Rules you can decide if you want to follow, of course, it is strongly encouraged you follow them. Laws are different, you break them you die, but there are only three."

"I'm not a big on following the rules anyway," I shrugged. "But I'm a law-abiding person, what are the three?"

"First law, every Raiden will treat their fellow Raiden as an equal. Second, The Herold's word will be upheld," he said, walking a little closer to me.

I frowned. "Doesn't sound too difficult. Although I expected you to say no killing, no stealing—"

"All of those fall under the first law. If you treat every Raiden as an equal, you treat others how you want to be treated. Killing and stealing defy those morals. The Raidens have never had issues with the first law because we only have each other. If we destroy ourselves, we will not exist. Humanity, as you well know, struggled with that concept. They kept dividing, never uniting."

I faltered in my footsteps. "You mean war?"

"Yes. I have heard stories of the past earth," Shai said in a faraway voice. "Our world is dangerous. I stand my ground against enemies that threaten all life, Remnants, evil and soulless creatures."

I nodded. "What's the third law?"

Shai's stance suddenly changed, his kind expression darkened, and his voice lost its silkiness. "The third law...kill any Seer on sight."

***

I laid in bed, tossing and turning, waiting for sleep to take over, it never did. I threw the blankets off and got up. I walked to the sidereal window and placed my hand on it, I felt it illuminate to my liking. I snatched my hand off and back away. The damn window could read my mind.

I couldn't stop thinking about the look on Shai's face when he told me what the third law was. The way his eyes glazed over and the robotic way he spoke, contradicting the natural fluidity and gentleness in his voice.

That explains why Jance almost killed me. No wonder he looked so intense and frightened when I first saw him, he probably thought I was a Seer. This also explains what Jance was trying to communicate this morning, that there was something about the Seers I didn't understand. Eve told me Seers can become Ascendants. But she failed to bring up the important piece of information that we are required to kill them. This only added fuel to my angry fire. Why didn't Jance, Eve, or Ronan tell me this? Is that why they quickly discarded my cares for those in the Dead Land? Why, and how, are Seers coming to the fifth dimension? Too many things I still do not understand.

What I am beginning to understand is that everyone is keeping secrets. The idea of killing Seers didn't feel like the correct action in my mind. I understood the Ascendant's threat, the Raidens do not want any more of them. However, to kill the defenseless based on the idea of what they *might* become was not out of protection, it was genocide.

If I were to find a Seer, how could I recognize one? Would I even be able to kill them? The answer was no.

I thought of Jance, I hadn't seen him since our fight. Perhaps some space was needed, but all I wanted to do was bombard him with a thousand questions, which was probably the best way to torture him. His scars formed such beautiful patterns. I couldn't remember all the intricate details, usually, I could snap an image in my mind and remember it forever. But Jance's scars were too abundant to take in at one glance. It would take me a lifetime to even capture one single lacey pattern. Outlined in silver, several shades darker than the average blinding white scars. Was there something shameful about having different colored scars? Raidens always wore long clothes. Except for the one woman who walked into the Merciless house let her crystal skin show without any shame. Jance seemed to take extra precautions to hide. My hand came to the middle of my jacket, *his* jacket, the second one he had given me. He always wore one.

I reached in to touch my wrist. I rolled my up sleeve and my eyes glared at the glittering gold mark along my sepia skin. I took a deep breath and peered at the four golden long knives rested against my nightstand and they echoed a tempting choice. I glanced toward the open wardrobe and the outfit I wore during the race had stitched itself back together. The black and white and the vest had four slits on the back of it.

I jumped out of bed and took my shirt and pants off, I skimmed over my body. The scars I accumulated from the race were still pink and tender, I looked away quickly and slipped into the thick fighting clothes. Then, I picked up one long knife and reached over the back of my neck and slid it into one of the gaps. It fit perfectly. I repeated the action, one knife after the other until they all laid against my back. I went to the mirror and my breath caught in my throat. I barely recognized myself. My face was outlined by sharp angles and my body felt and looked healthier from eating properly. I turned, pulling my dark brunette curls forward so they descended past my chest. The knives against my back gleamed and I felt invincible. I am made of fire and gold, iron, and blood. I've been rebirthed into an indestructible being. Those that knew me before, have no idea who I've become. The perfect mix of something sweet and something ruthless, a river of black honey.

I left my room and urgently made my way down the hall to Jance's room. I brought my fist to the door and banged. When nothing happened, I turned the handle and was greeted by an empty bedroom. There were some books on the edge of his bed and the floor. Curious, I picked one up and skimmed through it. It was about the past earth and the humans that existed there. I turned the pages, revealing pictures of war. The images pulled at my heart and I knew Jance was just as inquisitive as I was about history. I sighed and put the book back down carefully and left the room.

I galloped down the stairs and out the door in a matter of seconds. The air outside was thin, and darkness dominated the fifth dimension. There were shadows of light as the moon tried to fight its way in through the broken sky. I moved with haste down the cobblestone path to see a few Raidens wandering about. I got some strange glances but none of them told me to go back to the house or demanded to know where I was going. I noticed Raidens were incredibly private. They hardly spoke and they never seemed too curious about others. The few that walked the road disappeared suddenly, so quick that it chilled me to the bone.

Still, I held my posture upright and walked with confidence. I marched down the path keeping my eyes out for a white-haired boy, but there was no sign of anyone. When my feet met the grass, I took off in a full sprint, up that stupid hill toward the tree line. I didn't even feel the weight of the long knives on my back. I slowed to a jog, taking only two deep breaths to recover. I can run and not tire, I can be cut and then heal, I can be beaten and stand back up. The idea of what I was made to be, finally hit me. I was eager to discover how powerful I am.

A yell sounded toward the back of Camden. I swung my arms back and gripped the hilts of two long knives and yanked them out as I ran. There were screams and struggles emerging from the fortress, then it was quiet. The silence was more frightening than the screams, panic was rising within me.

My breath stopped completely when my eyes fell on Jance. He was standing with blood-stained his clothes and his sword. I only had to look at the ground to know that the blood was not his own, but the boy who laid dead in the grass. His eyes were open as if he were staring into some sort of abyss, but they were not staring at anything. He had no sense of sight.

A Seer, I thought. "Jance," I whispered.

Jance looked at me with bewilderment and his eyes were shiny. "I *know*," his voice cracked.

For a minute I just stood there. My gaze lingered on the lifeless form and then something happened. The body withered until only bones remained. Within less than a second, the flesh had turned to dust. I did an immediate double-take, my mind trying to deny what I had just witnessed. I put a hand over my mouth to keep from screaming. The grass was already peeking through the skeleton.

Time manipulation. It takes hold only of the dead and of nature. But not to the people themselves. I pondered on this. The way the grass grew, the way the air felt, the broken glass sky. I began to understand the manipulated world. Time was on steroids, making things grow and die all too quickly. But only to those subject to it. The dead definitely, but not the living, no one is growing or dying at alarming rates.

All the remains of the man were now grass-covered. *There's a reason*, I reminded myself. I refused to believe Jance was a murderer. Rage still flooded through me, but I tried to keep calm. The anger I was feeling was not the kind that made me want to scream, it was the kind that made time standstill.

Jance gave me a desperate look. I didn't give him a chance to speak, "What is going on Jance? What is the purpose of this?"

"Now is not the time—"

Time snapped back, my fury released itself and I pushed Jance out of my way. He was prepared for it as he reacted with a sudden solid grasp around my torso.

I looked at him with eyes like a preying hawk. "You better answer my damn questions."

"You don't understand this—"

"Is this all Jerik? I know about the law."

Jance snarled and let me go, stalking toward the Herold's House.

I followed him. "When we get in that house, you and I are going to have a conversation."

Jance trampled the ground as if it threatened to take him under. "Conversation?"

I reached out and yanked at his arm, he spun on a dime. "Not really going to be a pleasant one—I ask you questions and you're going to answer with the complete truth."

Jance looked tired. "Natalya, our conversations never go any other way," he said and shook away from my grasp.

We traveled to the back of the Herold's House. There

was a grey door that blended into the walls to the left, making it not exactly in the center. Strange things like this about this place gave me the creeps. The three and a half chimes on the clock and the sky in pieces, it was weird.

Jance's hands followed the dents and hallows until his finger slid under a hook. He pulled and the door creaked loudly, dark specks flew from the hinges. I slid in sideways, while Jance walked his lanky stature through easily. I came face first with soft material.

"A closet? Really?"

Jance shrugged and pushed the coats out of his way, I could see another door and a winding staircase leading upward.

He opened the door in front of us, and a bright room appeared. I blinked. It was the prettiest room I've seen in the fifth dimension so far. With two large sidereal glass windows, a canopy bed, and a chandelier that held light. What caught my attention was the sporadic arrangement of flowers around the room. Colors that were both deep and bright, petals that were dainty and large.

A woman stood in the middle of the room, she was stunning, with dark brown hair that curled on the ends that outlined her heart-shaped face. She wore grey robes, with sleeves exposing several white scars along her pale arms. Her rich brown eyes locked on mine and she smiled. Strange, whoever this woman was, she was the first Raiden that didn't bow to me as a greeting.

Jance looked distressed. "Natalya, this is my mother,

Honoria Grey."

Of course, I thought. I remember Jerik saying he liked to give his wife flowers; he wasn't kidding.

I raised my eyebrows. Jance had no features from his mother. My eyes traveled back and forth between the two of them, not a single similarity. It was like Jance was created exactly from his father's image. Honoria approached me and suddenly grabbed my hand.

Everything stopped. I had no way to think as an unknown force overpowered my mind. *Natalya,* the voice whispered in the depths of my mind. *I've been anxiously waiting to meet you.*

When Honoria let go, I gasped as my mind returned to its normal state. My eyes went wildly to Jance, who had his head in his hands. "Really mother?" he said with embarrassment.

His mother shrugged and smiled as Jance would. *There's a similarity*, I noted.

"My mother is mute. But she can communicate by doing...that. What she just did, I mean." Jance jumbled his words.

"You can...read minds?" I asked Honoria.

She shook her head avidly, reaching for my hand again before Jance stopped it. "Not read minds," Jance said. "But invade them, and make the mind only hear her voice. That's all."

Honoria nodded.

"Well," I said looking at Honoria. "So, help me understand. Do some Raidens have more abilities than they already have?"

"Oh, this only creates more questions for you, doesn't it?" Jance said with a hint of annoyance.

Honoria caressed his hand. I watched as Jance stood there, motionless while his mother's voice became all he heard. When she let go Jance nodded to her. Then he ran quickly out the door without a single glance at me.

I opened my mouth and then closed it; he was gone before I could tell him to stop. My gaze went to Honoria. I didn't want to speak first, so I let Honoria take my hand.

I know, Natalya Wells, this world never existed in your wildest dreams. All the questions you have will be answered in time. You may have seen things you did not expect to see. You may doubt some of our leaders, you may wonder if all the laws are right and what secrets my son keeps. I assure you; I am going to answer the questions I can and settle your worries. You belong here, please know that. I heard about the race. You proved yourself strong to Ace, who at first thought you were weak. However, the race is only the beginning. You will feel more invincible after your injuries are fully healed. Our scars are alluring and powerful. What was once harmed, can be made indestructible. Take comfort in this. There is nothing in the world like us and there is no one, in any world, like you.

When Honoria finished, I didn't know what to say. My thoughts were cloudy. I took a deep breath and observed the black and white clothing I wore, suddenly remembering it was once Honoria's. "These clothes are beautiful," I started. "It was the original colors of the Raidens, back when the Ascendants ruled over us."

Honoria smiled and took my hand again. *Yes,* her voice echoed in my head. *Now we stand with shades of grey. Black and white were used to symbolize the untamable balance between good and evil. Saying there was no balance, no shades of grey in between. Raiden thought differently. An individual can have good and evil. The truth is no one is good, not one.*

I sighed. "I want to know about Jance."

Honoria's eyes filled with sadness. And something more than sadness, a yearning that I couldn't quite figure. Then it was gone, moments after she blinked.

"I saw Jance's scars this morning. I was mad at him and I think he is still upset with me. They're beautiful, is there a reason he hides them more than others do?" I tried to ask the question as a child would ask, innocent and curious, hoping Honoria would give me an answer.

My son, Honoria's voice sounded bitter in the depths of my mind, *was born with a gift. I think it is a gift, although most think it's a curse. I love my Jansen, Natalya, so you must promise me, you will not speak of it to anyone. I do not want any more questions as to why that is, I just need you to keep it to yourself.*

I nodded anxiously. "So, he was born with it?"

Born with the patterned scars? No one is born with scars; it's the world that scars us. When he was ten years old, he entered the House of Mirrors as all Raidens do, but he healed in silver. He was never let in again. Jerik caught it before anyone could question what happened. Jerik described Jansen as a weak warrior, which is not true. The truth is, he is too strong, he just doesn't know it yet.

My heart thumped loudly in my chest and the golden scar along my wrist throbbed. "So," I breathed out shakily. "A Raiden with different colored scars means they have a certain power?"

Yes, Honoria answered. *It's not normal. Most of them went extinct back when Raiden was alive...*

The voice in my head trailed off. "Why?"

Honoria hesitated. *Raiden might have saved the Scarred Ones from enslavement but that doesn't excuse him of murder. He killed every single Raiden that was marked with different scars, his hatred and vengeance for the Ascendants overrode his motive to protect the Raidens. For those scars only mean one thing...*

"What does it mean?"

It means, there is Ascendant blood in your veins.

If I had any food in my stomach, I would have thrown it up. It was complicated enough to know I was a Raiden. Now to find out I may have *Ascendant* blood. That I could possibly share one single strand of DNA with those murders, the ones who utilize death as a game.

Honoria was giving me a curious look. My horror was probably written all over my face. "Someone in your family hooked up with an Ascendant?" I asked quickly.

It does not necessarily mean that, Honoria spoke with sternness in my mind. *Experiments. Those were more likely the reasons rather than a Raiden and an Ascendant falling in forbidden love. Ascendants cannot have children.*

"Right," I agreed. "And Raiden destroyed anyone who had

Ascendant blood because he hated them so much?"

He wasn't the only one, many of the others did as well. Raidens with the colored scars had no one on their side; the Ascendants rejected them too. Honoria took a deep breath. *Have I answered your question, Natalya?*

I sighed. "Yes..." I trailed off for a moment before launching into another subject, the one clawing in the back of my mind. "Honoria, tonight I saw Jance kill a Seer. Are they really a serious threat to us?"

Honoria seemed to think long and hard before she answered. *They can become our enemies. They are humans with the brain of an Ascendant, stragglers with special minds. I know they may not seem harmful, but we can't risk it.*

My breath was shaky. I decided to test Honoria's patience. "I want to know why Eve was sent to the fourth dimension."

It is between my husband and the Right Hand. I do not know.

I wonder if she's lying, I thought hard. Why would Jerik keep things from his wife? Especially if it was about their niece. It didn't make sense either why Honoria was in this room all alone on the opposite side of the house from her husband.

I looked at the colorful arrangements of flowers surrounding us. Those flowers only made everything appear beautiful, but there was something dark hidden inside the roots.

My boiling curiosity was coming to a simmer. I felt tired. As soon as I think I've figured myself out, I find I am not who I thought I was, and I can't be who I think I can be. The fragments of my being are still scattered, there are more pieces to this puzzle.

I managed to smile at Honoria. "I appreciate what you have told me, thank you."

Honoria returned a grin. *And I can tell you something about my son, he won't sleep until things are set right. I guarantee you he is still awake in his room.*

I nodded and got up from the bed. Glancing back at Honoria who waved. I was about to go out the door, but I paused. "You know, you're the only Raiden I've met that doesn't bow."

Honoria seemed to laugh, even though no sound came out of her mouth. She stood and reached for my hand one more time, and the smile left her lips. *If you bow, make sure your eyes look higher.*

I nodded, having no idea what she meant. I was left mystified at Honoria's words, and why they were still echoing in my head when she let go.

CHAPTER TWENTY-EIGHT
EVANNA

What I've learned about individuals is that everybody has a secret, others lie, and there is always someone throwing knives. In other words, don't trust anyone.

I followed Jance and Natalya. I spent years being a spy, why should I not act on it? Jance killed a Seer, Natalya freaked out and I watched calmly from the sidelines. I saw the guilt wash over Jance's face as he and Natalya lingered over the dead Seer. I could see his sensitive soul ripping apart, and Natalya's anger rising in frightening tides.

They headed toward the back door to the Herold's House that leads to Honoria's room, and I darted immediately to Ronan. His house felt safe; it was made for the Herold's heir, but it seems like Ronan needed it more than Jance. I banged on the door and Ronan opened it a little too quickly. I jumped back.

He wore loose pants and a long sleeve shirt. There was a fire cracking in the fireplace behind him. "I saw you coming," he said sweetly.

"Um," I stuttered as I stepped inside. "Sorry to interrupt your evening—"

Ronan frowned at me. "You don't seem like the type of person to say 'sorry,'" he said with curiosity.

"You're right."

"I see," he said, sticking an arrow into the fireplace. The house should grow warmer, but the air in the Lost Paradise was set at a certain point, nothing could disrupt it. He ran his hands through his red hair. Ronan looked up from his flames. "Are you okay?"

I shook my head. And he dropped the arrow and came close to me. "What's wrong?"

"Tell me what's happened to my cousin since I've been gone," I stated firmly.

"I think that's something you should talk to Jance about," Ronan's voice shot back.

"He killed someone, Ronan."

"Remnant?" Ronan frowned.

"No."

"You know the law—"

"That doesn't make it right," I gritted through my teeth. "You don't understand. I suffered for a Seer—" I cut myself off and my eyes grew wide at the realization I almost spilled my secret. I was surprised how easily my words flowed in front of Ronan, as if I had known him my whole life.

UNPARALLELED

His consistent effort to maintain a controlled stature failed him at that moment. His amber eyes were roaring. "Evanna," he said.

I liked the way he said my name.

"Tell me everything...and I will tell you everything."

I knew what he meant. So I did, and he did too.

CHAPTER TWENTY-NINE
NATALYA

I decided to take Honoria's advice. I came to the end of the hallway to Jance's room and knocked, my heart beating faster than normal.

"Ronan?" he said groggily. He looked up and stared for a moment, then proceeded to shut the door in my face.

"Jance," I said quickly grabbing the edge. "We need to talk."

"I'm too tired," he said through the cracked door.

I maintained my grip. "You're tired, but you won't sleep until we talk."

"You don't know that."

"But your mother does," I said confidently. I heard him groan and felt the tension release on the other side.

I entered, smiling proudly. But it quickly faded when my

eyes fell on him. He was exhausted. His long body was hunched over, and dark circles were forming underneath his eyes. He was wearing a sleeveless shirt. I backed up slightly at his exposed skin. The silver scars took my breath away before I could speak. "Honoria told me about your scars. What they mean."

Jance sighed and looked down at himself. "I'm the first, the only Raiden in the Grey family to have this...disease."

"Disease?" I said astonished. "They're stunning, don't let yourself think that." I swallowed hard, afraid to speak. "I know it means you have Ascendant blood and a unique gift."

His expression contorted and his eyes tore away from mine. "I am a shield," he mumbled.

I raised my eyebrows. "You can make them? That's incredible."

"It's not a gift," Jance muttered bitterly.

"It can only make you stronger," I said. I didn't understand Jance's negativity. Raidens are already blessed with the ability to repel any harm by invincible scars. Let alone, being able to wield something entirely different.

"Stronger..." Jance's voice faded. "I'm not strong, I'm not even a good fighter, then again neither is my father."

I shook my head. "You don't give yourself enough credit, if you put limitations on yourself then you are going to fail. Your mother seems to be on your side. Does your father not approve of you?"

"My father was horrified but my mother showed mercy. They could have rejected me from the family. But they were determined to keep it hidden. Raidens like me are cast into the west. Some go into madness and bury themselves in the Undercity. We are not allowed in the House of Mirrors. I can never access the sister mirror. I can never be Herold..." Jance's words trailed off to a hard whisper.

"Why?"

"Because I can outsmart it," Jance stated. "I have few fears; I know I'm in a mind manipulation. While normal Raidens are hypnotized by the fantasy they see. Some lose consciousness, others who are weak-minded, die."

"Because you are part Ascendant you have the brainpower like them?"

Jance nodded and went on. "I not only nearly destroyed the House of Mirrors itself, I almost died fighting back because I could break through it." Jance cleared his throat. "As time went on, my father encouraged me to make sure my clothes were changed if they were severely torn. Hide myself away and keep my friends minimal."

I made him look at me by the only way I knew how. I put my hand against his face, his eyes widened. I felt his cold skin and the sharp margins of his cheekbones, my thumb an inch away from his lips.

I clung to the hope that I could speak the words as well as they sounded in my mind. "I understand Jance. You hate who you are because you were told to. You feel no one can accept you because you cannot accept yourself. I wish you could see yourself how I see you." I took a shaky breath; his grey eyes were nearly transparent as I spoke. "For some reason beyond my own understanding, all the people I love can't see the power they possess. They cannot break out of the model the world shaped them into. I want to change that. I want to make a crack in the armor and expose the light hidden in the depths."

He didn't say anything, he only traced his hand over mine. His head lowered to my forehead, every little dimension of space that had been between us, was now filled.

"Thank you," he finally whispered.

CHAPTER THIRTY

EVANNA

We were tangled strings of red, Ronan and me.

I struggled to find words. Ronan stood in front of me shirtless. The scars trailing over his body were like fire, a mixture of gentle reds and oranges making jagged, pointed lines like the shapes of flames. "Oh..." I breathed out, "my."

Ronan smiled at me. "I can manipulate fire."

"That explains what I heard before I went in the training room, I heard a crackling like sparks," I said with a low voice.

He placed his hands on the sides of my arms, something that sent a wave of heat over me. "Why were you sent to the fourth dimension?"

My fists clenched suddenly at the bitter memory, but I was finally ready to speak, "I was looking for the one who could *see.*"

Ronan frowned, I couldn't tell if it was out of familiarity or confusion. "*See* what?"

I just shook my head hopelessly. "I don't know. It's haunted me, and it will haunt me forever because I failed."

"Failure is the only word that exists without a definitive meaning. It means something different to everyone. Not even death is considered a failure. Only if you give up and give in, but you won't," Ronan said sternly, then his expression softened. "We know enough," he said moving his hands toward my shoulders. "See something that no one else can see. That can be anyone, a Seer more in likely."

"I thought it was Natalya," I said breathily. "The Ascendant leader, Alda, caught me. I was nearly hung before I was able to escape back here. But I did, I survived."

"And you would have been right about Natalya, but who knew a Raiden was in the fourth dimension," he comforted me as his fingers traced along my face. "You endured a lot of pain Evanna, I can see it in your eyes. The scars from your enemies are not your fault, but your healing is your responsibility. Just know that you don't have to heal alone."

He trailed down my face, to my arm and finally took my hand, I accepted it. "You don't remember anything?"

He didn't answer my question. He didn't do anything I expected, he never did. I hated and loved it at the same time. I was caught off guard when he suddenly pressed his lips to mine.

There ended our conversation. I ran my hands wildly over his skin, his scars felt like I was wrapping my body in burning charcoal.

JENNA HEBERT

I loved the pain.

CHAPTER THIRTY-ONE
NATALYA

I walked back from Jance's room thinking about Eve. I knew my anger wasn't acceptable, it never was. I could beat myself up about it over and over again. Fear is a wicked liar, and anger has no respect. I need to abandon both to become the Raiden my friends needed me to be, who I needed myself to be. I turned to her room, surprised to see the door cracked open. I tapped on it.

"Eve?"

Nothing. I let myself in. The light poured from the sidereal glass windows, shining on the drawings sprawled out on her bed.

I saw an outline of a broken flat shape glowing at the base of her nightstand. I stooped down to see a piece of glass as big as my hand. I grazed my fingers over the reflection. There were dividing lines streaming over the shard. It wasn't cracked like it was broken, because the surface was smooth, warm, and *humming*. I gasped and dropped it instantly, it hit the floor with a clang, and it should have shattered into a million pieces. I don't know why, but I picked it up and threw it back down to the ground. It left a good dent in the wood panels, but it didn't break. I stomped and kicked at the piece of glass. No matter what I did, it remained unbroken.

The clock on Camden rang out, it was morning. I picked up the glass and tried to curl my grasp into a fist. Some odd satisfaction came over me as the sharp edges broke the skin and red streamed down. There was something in it I needed, I *wanted*.

I felt the sting from the cut and my eyes started playing tricks on me. I was seeing the world through broken glass. My vision cracked, spreading into random lines. Something deep inside was awakening, stronger than fear. A whisper in my brain, *destroy it*.

The fifth dimension disappeared as a new scene bled into my consciousness.

I was laying down, all I could make out was the face of a boy with dark hair, barely older than me. I felt a wave of familiarity, combined with a shocking pull of emotion. But I know I've never seen this boy in my life.

"She's perfect," the boy said.

"Yes." Another voice chipped. It was the voice of a man, one I've heard before but I couldn't make out who it was, and I couldn't see him. "She will be made of gold and her unique power could be the destruction of all we know. A catastrophic masterpiece."

The boy's dark eyes glowed with excitement at what the man said, and he smiled.

The vision washed away suddenly, and my body fell forward like a whip. Reality seeped back in. I blinked my eyes, making sure the vision was gone. I was laying on the floor in Eve's room panting, totally unclear about what had just happened. I stood quickly and gazed into the mirror next to me. As my hair fell behind my back, something glittered on my skin. It was like a knife went through my gut; a swarm of horror encamped me. My neck held a star-shaped scar, colored in gold. I yanked up my sleeve and scattered over my arm were golden marks that resembled intercrossing constellations, no one was like the other. My scars from the race were now fully healed...in gold.

She will be made of gold, I thought.

Someone knows who I am.

The unbroken glass laid on the floor. The cut-up reflection of myself staring back at me within the little shard was exactly how I felt. Like scissors had been taken to my soul, and they were scattered among places I could never go. There were parts of me that I could not remember.

My breath came faster as if my body was trying to keep up with my speeding thoughts. It felt so real. Something had been unlocked. Was it a real memory? Or just a manipulation?

I thought of what the man had said to the dark-haired boy. They described me like I could either destroy or inherit the world.

I stood up straight, trying to hold myself together. I felt tears well up in my eyes, my thumb brushed over the original gold scar on my wrist. Silent streams finally fell down my cheeks, I reached down and picked up the glass shard. The little piece of me. It was mine and Eve had it this whole time.

I guess she didn't know. How could she? Unless once again, Eve proved to know more things in her sixteen years than what I could ever know in my life.

A catastrophic masterpiece, I thought. I only had those words. I glanced at the new, glistening lines over my skin. It's hard to put yourself back together when you don't even have the pieces.

I turned and left the room. The unbreakable glass concealed tightly in my grip, with lines always dividing, never uniting.

***

The House of Mirrors came into view before I knew it, it always appeared out of thin air. I almost expected to open the door and find pretty flowers assorted into organized rows like a greenhouse. The truth about the house was, you never really knew what was inside; or how you got inside. You entered and then you were gone. Like the way your brain tells you to flinch when something scares you. You do not even realize your brain made the reflexive muscle contraction for your body to twitch. Just as the House of Mirrors quickly transitions you into its manipulation.

UNPARALLELED

I came alone. I took a slow breath and I was ready for my imaginary horrors.

***

I was falling. Colors and patterns blurred my vision until I decided to close my eyes. Oddly, I wasn't scared, I didn't know the height from where I fell.

These mirrors knew my fears, and yet they were not giving me the chance to feel afraid. Now that truly terrified me.

I landed on all fours, my hands and feet embracing my weight, which felt like nothing. The ground below was hard and wet. I stood up. I had landed on a lonely rock surrounded by the sea.

I swallowed hard. Depth. The waves crashed over my feet, creeping over the rock threatening to wash me over completely. I felt the fear flooding over me as quickly as the water ascended past my knees. I looked around and there was nothing. It was just me and a grey sky, which reminded me of Jance's eyes.

The rock below shook violently. I slipped, barely catching myself in one of the crevasses, the waves roared in response to the shaking. I climbed to the highest point of the rock. My hands scraped across the solid edge; all I could do was hang on.

I should close my eyes, I thought. *I should be afraid.*

And then I remembered.

Rising, I let go of the rock, and the manipulation blurred. I saw the House of Mirrors for what it was. The blue waves faded to clear, the feeling of water dried on my body, the crevasses were my hands held firm, became hollow. The grey sky turned blinding white as if some angelic power were descending from above. My fear disintegrated. I jumped into the water and I ran right across it. I was opened to the illusion and I could see below me. It was glass. Glass that rippled like water and rose like tides, and glass that would consume my mind if I let it. Drawing closer to the sky, the pattern began to disappear into little pieces, fracturing into a broken picture.

The mirrors were filled with sunlight, reflecting from all directions. I muscled my weight against the opposite side of the house. But the mirrors moved with me, it was like a sick dance, and they were leading.

An awful crackling noise echoed within the glass house, and I felt my arm touch its side, it was pinching me into a tight space. They were caving in, the house was shrinking as my body collided with the clear, burning barricades.

Try to manipulate the manipulation itself, I thought.

I closed my eyes and concentrated. *I am not a subject of manipulation*, I focused deep within myself.

Looking down, it appeared like I was running in slow motion, but I knew my legs were going as fast as they could. I reached to my back and whipped out two of the four long knives as a familiar feeling crept over me. A whisper, in the back of my mind, like an animal drawn to prey, *destroy it.*

I slashed at the mirrors and glass exploded in shattering bolts.

***

UNPARALLELED

There was a scream that did not come from me.

My body hit the ground with a thud. It hurt more than I expected because something hard fell on top of me. I scattered for the two knives I dropped in the fall. I eyed them a few feet away from me, I quickly reached out my hand. Out of nowhere, a foot stepped on their hilts. I braced for a Remnant. I looked up to the face of a boy with startling pale skin, contrasting against his straight black hair and eyes dark as night. He had delicate features, except his jawline was broad and vivid. A cloak cascaded down his body, but his forearms were bare and there were no visible scars.

His eyes were mesmerizing. The boy stared at a nearby tree and I saw it bend to his will. A branch encircled my arm and yanked me backward. I fought the resistance of the tree that had been brought to life, but it was no use. I knew what I was facing.

"You're an Ascendant," I said.

The boy cocked his head to the side. "And you're a Raiden," he said as if I were incompetent.

Rage poured through me. I saw his eyes grow wide as I broke the branch. As quick as I was, the Ascendant was faster, I felt roots lace around my ankles before I had the chance to run. He looked at me wildly, not in fear, but amazement. My breath was ragged. "How—"

"It's quite simple," the Ascendant said, cutting me off. "I illegally entered another house, the one in the dimension before this one, wondering why it was forbidden. Well, it seems my question has been answered."

I was speechless at first, I tried to make sense of his

words. "What do mean another house?"

"The houses are everywhere," The Ascendant said casually. "It is said, 'Time moves backward, and it moves forwards depending on the way you want to go.' I wanted to go forward, so I went backward."

I shook my head. "Who are you?"

"Sylas Ascend," he said. "I'm curious about you, I suggest we team up. My life is in jeopardy and you've made a gigantic hole in the House of Mirrors."

"You're damn right your life is in jeopardy—I intend to kill you."

Sylas released his mind hold on the tree. I slid down its trunk and breathed heavily.

"A Raiden boy with red hair came wandering around when we blasted through the house—"

Ronan, I thought. I felt my jaw clench. "What did you do to him?"

"Don't panic, I didn't know if red was friend or foe, so I took precautions. He is behind those trees, although he might appear to be dead—"

I rushed over between two trees. Ronan laid unnaturally still, his pale skin paler than usual, and his amber eyes were open and glazed over. I whirled on the Ascendant. "What did you do!?"

Sylas suddenly became tense and his chest moved in heaves. Suddenly, Ronan shot up like a bullet, and he strung his bow. I yelped and jumped back.

"I—I'm so sorry," Ronan said in confusion. Ronan was a

picture of perfection, so it was odd seeing him stumble over his words. "I swear I saw something—" Ronan turned and stopped his words when he faced Sylas, who wore a precarious smile.

I looked at the House of Mirrors my jaw dropped. The left side of it was destroyed, a mess of broken pieces that exposed a gaping hole of darkness. The broken pieces were splayed among the tall grasses. I glanced down to see my reflection spread along hundreds of fragments.

Ronan craned his head toward me slowly, and the look on his face was one I had never seen before, it was a look of pure fear.

Sylas approached us both a little too closely, he glanced over Ronan. "Surestrike?" Sylas said, he greeted Ronan as if he were an old friend.

I gasped when Ronan pulled his sleeve up, exposing blazing red-orange scars. Ronan was part Ascendant too. I should have known.

Something drew me to the Ascendant, his black eyes connected with mine transcending me elsewhere. My vision was encamped by a black hole and my body felt numb. I felt like I was paddling through black water in a gentle sea. I could see it, and there were crystals glimmering in the sky. I smiled. Droplets of water sprayed on my face, running down into my shirt. Without hesitating, I gently tugged at my collar, the water tickling my neck, and I revealed my golden scars.

My serenity disappeared, and the image of the cloaked Ascendant returned.

"Three," Sylas stared at me for only a moment, before he

recomposed himself. "Perfect," he said.

What happened? I thought. My conscience was in limbo like I was still trying to wake up from a deep sleep.

A curtain was pulled in front of my eyes. I *had* seen him before, in the vision from the glass shard. Like a noose around my neck, the terror choked me in slow motion.

Sylas whipped up his hand and the roots of trees came alive while the glass that showered the ground arose, it looked like raining falling in reverse. A burst of air came behind me, almost knocking me over. Nature had come alive. Then it was gone. I saw the House of Mirrors had been put back together like it was never broken.

"You're welcome," Sylas said sweetly.

Just as I was ready to attack, Ronan reacted. His arrow was an explosion of fire, and it collided with something hard. I gritted my teeth and turned. My heart sped up as I saw the demon coming toward us. Ronan's arrow had landed in a tree trunk and he looked appalled. Sylas's face twisted in amusement.

My breathing accelerated as I planned my next move. I glanced at Ronan, who was still stricken with emotion and then to Sylas who faced the Remnant. Without either of them looking at me, I pivoted slowly to face the impenetrable forest and took off in a full sprint. I heard Ronan start to yell part of my name, then I was too deep in the trees to hear.

I ran impulsively in pure panic, an arrow flew above me, setting the leaves in nearby trees up in flames. I realized I couldn't feel the heat of the fire, the Lost Paradise didn't let outside forces mess with its delicate balance.

Ronan can control fire, I thought. He's going to set the whole forest ablaze. I wondered if Sylas was manipulating him into doing so.

I took an immediate left, avoiding the fire. Craning back, the flames started to fade at a rapid rate.

My feet carried on tirelessly, feeling like I could run up mountains. The light was scarce between the intertwining limbs of the trees. The branches scraped along the sides of my body, I pushed them out of my way, not caring if I gained another coat of blood through it. But I didn't, the thorns brushed against me as if they were petals of flowers, my scars were protecting me. The thicket grew, and a creepy feeling began to slither over my skin. I breathed out and I saw my breath come in visible puffs. It was cold. And I threw myself forward with all my might.

The trees stopped suddenly, and I was encased by a thicket of trees in an unnaturally perfect circle. A white cushion replaced the grass, they were hardened micro pieces of ice. Snow, something I had only read about. I lifted myself, the palm of my hand leaving an imprint in the whiteness. I shivered; the coolness felt foreign to me, the fifth dimension's manipulation didn't work in this small place. My eyes landed on the tree in the center. It was nearly turned upside down. The leaves were emerald green, like my eyes. They kneeled forward, touching a trunk that was black as night, as if it were bowing. There was something wrong here.

I walked around the back of the tree and gasped. Four long knives penetrated the trunk. Three of them looked like mine, but the fourth did not stick out as far as the others.

Curious, I kneeled and wiggled the short one. I couldn't feel the end of the blade, it was broken.

Not four, I thought. *Three and a half long knives stabbed into a bent tree.*

Without warning, a sharpness grabbed my shoulder and I was thrown back. My superhuman genetics kicked in and I was back on my feet faster than I fell. I withdrew two of my long knives and whirled toward my enemy. A Remnant stood in front of me. His hair was white, and red veins were distended under his skin. I felt a sensation like the tracing of nails scraping against my conscience.

No, I thought.

I focused on the knives in my hands. I met the pools of blood that flooded his eyes and he attacked again. I was quicker, I made a slice across the Remnant's torso. A scream exploded from his mouth, but the wound didn't slow him down. With a force beyond anything I knew, I was punched, the long knives fell from my hands as I crashed into the bowing tree. I gasped for breath and it hurt. I hadn't been punched; I was impaled. Blood was pouring out my side quickly and the Remnant was crawling on all fours. It crouched low, preparing to charge at me again.

I twisted to one side and yanked another knife from my vest, just as the Remnant pounced—and it dove through my weapon like a thread through a needle, in slow motion then all at once. I saw the pointed edge of the knife appear through the Remnant's back. Screaming at the sight, I jerked it out. The Remnant fell on top of me, I pushed the weight off and scrambled away, wanting to get as much space from the body as possible.

I fell in an attempt to stand. I crawled toward the bent tree. I tried to take deep, slow breaths. And every time I breathed, I felt like I was being pierced over again. If I survived this there would be a wicked scar, but that was a good thing, nothing else could ever hurt me there. I tried to keep that in mind as my vision started to dim. I didn't know how much blood Raidens could lose and still survive, or how deep of a wound we could endure. I debated if it was worth it, pain raked me with every breath.

I laid there under the tree, it covered me like a blanket. I don't know how much time passed. I began to feel oddly peaceful and I adjusted to the pain. Pain always turns numb after feeling it for too long.

My eyes started to close, and then a light like fire came through the thicket. Ronan stood, bow at the ready. I was fighting against a sleep that felt too overwhelming, a sleep I didn't know if I would wake from. Gathering all the energy I had left, I forced myself upward and groaned. Ronan was at my side and moments later I was in his arms. He took off running, I could hear him speaking to me, but I couldn't make out his words. I wondered where the Ascendant had gone. Sylas was my last thought before I was pulled into blackness.

***

In my dream, a girl was running through the forest. No older than fifteen, her streaked blonde hair was cut short. I could see it starting to curl at the ends giving her an innocent appearance. She was panicking as a boy chased her. His image was clouded, and I couldn't quite describe the boy, aside from blue eyes. They weren't a bright blue that shined like light or a deep blue like the sea. But blue.

The girl stumbled and fell, landing beside a tree. Her sleeve slipped up her arm, revealing green scars, her skin was a painting of nature, intertwining leaves and branches coated her body. She was gripping the roots in the earth like how a child would hold a blanket.

The boy caught up with her, he held a set of long knives in each of his hands. His eyes were gentle; they didn't look good or evil, only lost.

He raised a knife, drawing closer to the girl like he was going to stab her. Suddenly, he took several steps back. He hesitated for barely a second, then he threw the long knife. It landed in between her shoulder blades.

Long knives were not meant to be thrown, they were too heavy, but he was close enough that the force pierced the girl. I felt my heart break as the girl screamed, and screamed and screamed...

But she didn't die.

The boy's breaths became ragged and uncontrollable. He threw another knife and it landed slightly below the other one. The girl leaned on the tree harder, and her screams turned to grunts of pain.

She was still alive.

The boy turned from anxious to angry. He threw the third knife, this time harder and faster. And it landed in her lower back.

She let out a breath, and continued to breathe.

The boy suddenly spun on his heels and threw the fourth knife toward a tree as he let out a cry of frustration. The boy shook himself and ran to pick up the weapon, and when he did, he found only half of the blade still attached to the hilt. The long knife must have been weakly made, the impact from the tree had shattered the top half of the blade. A look of shock passed over his face as he stared at the broken long knife.

He paced toward the girl robotically, standing in the same place he was when he threw the other knives. His face was emotionless as he threw the shattered weapon. The girl made no sound when the jagged edge of the broken blade joined the others along her spine.

The girl rose to her feet and faced him.

I hadn't seen the girl's face until now. The hair trimmed just below her chin was tipped with red, outlined by lovely heart-shaped features. Her endarkened expression was filled with something more than just physical pain, it screamed a different kind of torture.

The girl was no longer crying. Her body was bent forward, the hilts of the three and a half knives protruding from her, and she *smiled*. Her left leg crossed behind her right, she bowed low and stretched her arms out like wings. She held her head high and her dark green eyes locked on the boy.

The grin on her face widened as she spoke, "*Mendax, Mendax.*" And she collapsed on the ground right beside the tree, dead. The tree started to curl over her and wrap her in an earthly embrace.

The boy began to scream. He clenched his fists into his hair, and it fell out. His skin turned ghostly pale as the vessels began to boil above his skin, blood pouring out of the exits. His thick chest caved in, his arms and legs became thin sticks. His strong youthful body deteriorated.

The boy, now turned creature, ran away. The only remnant he kept from his old self were those blue eyes. They were still beautiful.

***

I woke up screaming. Slowly, my mind settled into reality as I looked around a familiar room. I was in Ronan's house. I immediately got up. I felt a slight soreness in my side from where the Remnant had pierced me, I shivered, not wanting to look at it now. I charged out the bedroom door.

I entered the small living space and expected to see Ronan, instead, the Ascendant stood in front of the fireplace. He seemed to have made himself at home.

"Did you have a nightmare?" he spoke to me with his back turned.

I opened my mouth and then closed it, hesitating with my words, "How did—"

"I know," he finished my statement. "I know the story of the Bowing Tree and now you do too, it gives everyone nightmares." Sylas faced me, his expression calm. "There is more than just time manipulation at work, there is also the manipulation of words." He paused and walked closer, reciting the words of a poem.

"If I bow while standing strong

Know it is because you were wrong

It is time to live with your hypocrisy

When I take my bow, it will be in mockery

As I bow down, my eyes will look higher

With a grin of vengeance and a voice like iron

Mendax, Mendax

Liar, Liar"

I locked eyes with him. "*Mendax*...liar. She called him a liar?"

Sylas nodded. "A lie...and a symbol. You hate the way the Raidens bow to one another. Closing their eyes and lowering their heads as if they are giving themselves to a higher power. Nicoletta defied that." He moved toward the fire and extended his hand into it.

My eyes widened, I opened my mouth to tell him to stop, but he retreated his hand from the flame, there were no burns on his skin.

Sylas examined his hand as if he expected it to be damaged. "Letta's bow was a farce, not only to the boy but the whole system. At the root of that story, there's more than a girl, a boy, a lie, and three and a half knives. Revealing the truth hiding in the shadows will cause even the ones who once loved you, to drive knives into your back. Cast you away like you mean absolutely nothing..." he trailed off. His voice was passionate like the story meant something to him.

"Get out," my voice was tense.

"I thought you wanted to kill me, here's your chance," Sylas said casually. "You cross me as rash, but not unwise. You, the Herold's son, and Surestrike all have unique abilities."

I suddenly went numb. "I'm not going to ask how you knew that..." my words drifted. I thought back to the peaceful ocean where I saw the stars. I had been imprisoned in a daydream and I revealed my scars to him. He was a manipulator, and I was his subject. I spoke carefully, "I was in the House of Mirrors to find out what my...gift is. I do want to kill you. You destroyed humanity, and your cruel manipulations, *experiments*, in the fourth dimension—where did those children come from?" I buried my eyes into him trying to stare down into his soul if he even had one.

Sylas searched me, which sent fear through me since I knew what his eyes can do. "No Natalya, not my manipulations. It's the higher elites of my people. They are the reason for the experiments. But I am glad you asked because I want you to help me—those children can be saved. And I mean *all* of them, even the ones you think are dead. They are not. The elites are reversing time."

My heart skipped a beat, I knew they had control of time. His eyes glistened. What if he was lying? What if he was a part of it? "I don't think I believe you."

His arms went up and back down in a quick motion. "I have been everywhere. I've seen the darkness of hell, the hope of heaven, and all the worlds in between." Sylas paused, and he looked down at the floor as if he were reflecting on a bad memory.

UNPARALLELED

I heard a sound from outside Ronan's house, I flinched.

The Ascendant whispered to me, "I am the greatest manipulator, and I hold the strings."

He turned toward the fire, and it exploded like the sun itself had burst. When flames settled Sylas was gone. Just seconds later, Jance and Ronan walked through the door.

CHAPTER THIRTY-TWO

JANCE

Terrified would be an understatement of what I felt when I saw Ronan running with Natalya bloodied in his arms.

I don't know what happened. Ronan had found her by the Bowing Tree along with a dead Remnant. I don't know what madness drives her to be so stubborn to go that deep in the forest alone. Why she didn't think to invite me along?

I shuddered at her screams. When Ronan and I returned to the house Natalya had been standing in the living room, her face pale and full of emotion. She looked like she wanted to tell us something, but Ronan ushered her to go rest. A mix of panic and despair came as she dreamed, waves of cries came from her. This was a normal occurrence, all Raidens have nightmares from that tree.

Ronan sighed deeply annoyed. "What is going on?"

She screamed again. I bit my lip, "Everyone has ways to deal with the nightmares."

My best friend regarded me with a sulk.

I held his gaze. "Do you remember the cerulean, Ronan?"

Poison was hard to come by, but it existed. Most Raidens were not a fan of cerulean, but some considered it a good time. It was a deep blue liquid that made you feel a thousand senses. Like dragging ice over the skin, it gave you stimulating sensations. It was pleasurable because it made the body feel warm or cold and it gave the mind a clean slate. Cerulean was made by the Ascendants long ago and they used it to de-stress. It was easy to get high on. You felt everything all at once, then nothing at all.

A few years ago, Ronan and I found a stash of the blue liquid in the Herold's House. I remember feeling blurry like I could swim in mid-air. It did something different to Ronan. I remember his hands shaking. The nightmare that plagued him took over the moment he lost himself. He began to grow wild and it started with the screaming. He inflicted himself with a knife that I wished I could have stopped. I just watched as my best friend became subject to the drug.

Ascendants manipulated off emotion, and for some people, emotions are displayed more violently than others. There was already an internal battle raging within him, and the drug just put it on stage. Ever since then, he and I avoided it altogether.

No one can understand why individuals respond the way they do to certain stimuli. They only see the tears and hear the cries. People who judge will stare at the scars on your body and peel at them, making you bleed again for their own pleasure. Never taking the time to understand who birthed those scars and why. When people shame you for your reaction, they refuse to acknowledge what they did wrong. People will blame the spark for starting a fire and declare that it wasn't rational. But when the tangled roots arise, the fight to hide them will fail. Our masks, our composure, will be lost within an internal madness. Even Raidens lose themselves. We can conquer the Remnants by building our invincible exterior and shielding our minds. But we are all subjects to our own doings. The most difficult task in life is to kill the demons within yourself. There is no physical escape from mental torment.

Ronan exhaled. "Reliving the past won't solve the problems of our future."

"I agree," I said, scanning his face. I knew my best friend. I could tell he wanted to tell me something.

Ronan's voice slid through his lips like breaking glass, "Jance, I need to tell you something about Natalya."

***

The Black and White Parade ran the race again this afternoon. Natalya was determined to run. Eve, Ronan, and I insisted for her not too, but that only made her want to do it more. She was suddenly different. She seemed harder, walking like she had an unknown power. It only made my eyes linger on her longer than usual. Natalya gave me these complex emotions.

She still came out more cut up from the race than everyone else, but she won again. I could tell she felt a slight sting in her side when she moved quickly but she was training herself to ignore it. After the race, I watched her as she headed toward the training room in the Herold's House. Of course, Shai had come up to her. I couldn't help but feel a twinge of jealousy as he put his hand on her side where she had been hurt. Natalya shook him off, I felt a bolt of victory go through me. Then I asked if she wanted to spend time with me. She said no, and my victorious mood faded.

I decided not to take it personally. I understood wanting time to be alone. Still, I went to the training room. Even though she wanted to be alone, I didn't want to.

Natalya whipped her long knives about, slicing at an invisible enemy over and over. The more she practiced the more her body adapted. Her speed and strength increased along with the natural fluidity of her movements. She smiled as she tossed a long knife in the air and then caught it by its hilt. I let myself out, I don't think she even noticed I had entered the room. It was intriguing, seeing someone who was not only content but so happy, being alone.

I headed to the kitchen. Eating was a struggle because my stomach kept churning. The fifth dimension had perfect food. I took a bite of a carrot, it was crunchy, sweet, and strong. My face puckered.

I gazed out a window and saw the sun begin to move over the house and near the forest. As I walked out of the kitchen, I saw Natalya lingering on the staircase. Her arms held her head up. She looked to be in deep thought, her angled features were pressed together in hard lines.

"Jance," she said as her face spread into a smile.

I grinned from ear to ear. Suddenly, I had an idea. "Are you busy?"

She shook her head, curious.

"Follow me," I said, darting up the stairs to meet her. I took off in a fast walk and turned left, she followed me, keeping up with ease.

The house felt uninhabited; I heard nothing but our footsteps echoing in the halls. I turned around the side of the training room down a hidden hallway, at the end there was a miniature door, not even big enough for a coat closet. I opened the door that exposed the twilight sky above. We raced up the stairs to the rooftop outlined in white stone. The walls were delicately carved with stories. Images of Raidens raising their weapons to fight, some wore their bloody wounds like streaks of pride leaking through their skin, knives deflecting off crystal marks. The details always took my breath away. Artistry was rare, the rooftop was the trademark of self-expression, allowing a little bit of humanity to shine through.

There was a fountain standing tall in the middle of the roof. The sea was visible from the north, a blue blanket coated the edges of the valleys. The setting sun was fading in the southwest, parallel to the fountain. The white stone glittered in the remaining light. After staring at so many shades of grey it was refreshing to see white, like the heart of heaven itself.

Natalya gazed into the view, I heard her whisper, "It's enchanting up here."

"I'll show you something even more impressive," I said,

offering my hand.

She hesitated but took my hand and flinched. I knew what she felt on my bare skin, my scars gave people chills. Then she stroked my hand a little, feeling the engraved silver scars on my wrist and the thin bones underneath. As much as I was thinking about her touching me, I tried not to make it obvious. I lead her to view of the sea, but she was still looking down at the walls.

"Look up," I said.

Natalya shifted her focus and her jaw dropped as she saw the fifth dimension in its entirety. I smiled as I lifted my gaze beyond. The rolling hills with little houses perched inside them. The tall cliffs that outlined the ocean, climbing up each other. I never really thought how amazing the view was until I saw it through someone else's eyes. The Raidens below looked small, making these invincible superhumans look completely vulnerable. And it was all enclosed by the broken glass that kept the warmth of the sun away from us.

The Lost Paradise indeed, I thought to myself. The Divided blocked out everything people in the past earth had once taken for granted.

"What's beyond the glass Jance?" She asked in a low voice.

I leaned down, close enough that our arms touched. "The rest of the dimensions I suppose."

Natalya tore her eyes away from the rest of the world and looked at me. "Do all the dimensions look like this?"

I shrugged. "Don't know, we'll never know."

She paused for a moment, and then shot her next question. "Explain the Remnants then. What are they truly?"

I retreated my weight off the wall. "The Remnants are their past mistakes. Lost pieces of people who are too far gone to be saved."

Natalya didn't say anything, she looked distant.

There she goes, again, I thought. *Far, far away from here. Where does her mind take her?*

"My nightmare was a story," she mumbled. "The girl with the three and a half knives who died—is the girl the bowing tree?"

I nodded.

"She turned and gave a bow of mockery in the face of her greatest betrayer. I only hope I can be as brave and strong as she was if things go wrong."

"I can assure you," I said looking at her intently. "Things, always go wrong." I smiled.

She smiled back. I grazed her arm suddenly, which made her jump. My hand was wrapped gently around her bicep. I wanted to snap her out of that demented dream, the story of the bowing tree is the secret behind the manipulation of words. "I didn't bring you up here to talk about Remnants, or stories, or for you to ask a billion questions," I said franticly.

Natalya laughed. "Is there any other way you and I talk?"

I laughed as well. "Not so far."

She turned her attention to the sea. "I wonder," she said, "how far you would have to sail to touch the Divide."

"Far," I said. "I told you how I saw it from the sea, but no

I never came close to touching it. Many Raidens have tried, but none have succeeded."

"That's disappointing to just give up." Natalya turned around, so her body faced the darkness of the forest.

I turned with her. "There's no point. Why go searching around for something that's the same on all sides. It doesn't matter where you go, it keeps you in."

She dragged her foot across the white marble floor. "Have you ever asked your father about the way out?"

I froze. It was one of the first questions I asked as a child. Along with where did the others go if they failed the manipulations in the House of Mirrors? I never got an answer, only a punishment. Some of my invincible scars are from my father, and they still hurt. "No," I lied.

"It's the strings," Natalya spoke slowly. "The cosmic strings, the world is bigger than what our eyes can see. I wonder how the Ascendants blew them up and made them real parallel universes."

"Science, belief, and a little bit of magic," I commented. "The Divide is invincible. It's why the sun cannot be felt and why rain doesn't fall. Everything grows rapidly because it was manipulated to be so. The Ascendants wanted the fifth dimension to be paradise until they poisoned it themselves by their failed manipulations."

"Remnants," Natalya said, her body bending slightly against the wall.

"There's more to it than them," I said. "The idea of being so close to perfection, then for it to be slaughtered by evil. The

Ascendants wanted to rule the world, they manipulated the strings and humans, destroying a paradise. No matter what world you live in, nothing can be perfect. People who want power are prone to destruction."

"I think there is beauty in lack of perfection. It's people's broken hearts and the scars on their bodies that tell their stories. The determination and refusal to succumb to any standard. The brave that fight against the corrupt. The need for power stems from the need for control. I even have to remind myself that the strings of the world are not in my hands," she said with fire in her voice.

"You are humble," I said with a hint of admiration behind my voice. "It's like you've lived a thousand lives."

She looked down. "I feel something Jance, like parts of me, are not with me, my memory is wiped. I remember nothing before the age of seven. I could have come from anywhere. Just like the rest of the children."

"Except you are not like the rest of the children," I confirmed. "You are a Raiden."

Natalya inhaled sharply. "I know," she hesitated before speaking again. "Do you think the Ascendants and Raidens could live in peace again?"

I raised my eyebrows at her. "Make sure that comment never leaves this rooftop. Nobody else thinks that way."

"I'm not asking anybody else—I'm asking you," Natalya said crossing her arms. "You are different Jance."

There was determination through those green eyes I had come to know so well, they echoed an underlying hope. "I believe it's stupid to go look for the people who enslaved us, let alone trust them. Do you think we can all live in peace?"

Natalya dropped her gaze to the stones. "I don't trust them but are all of them bad?" her words came out in stutters.

"I can't answer that because no one is good." I breathed out the words.

"I've heard that a million times. But you have a kind heart Jance, don't let anger pierce it...like I let it take over mine. Don't fall into self-destruction, we all have regrets. I see the weight you carry. It's not right that the Seers are killed. We need to remake this world. It was created, wasn't it? It can certainly be destroyed."

It's like she can read me, I thought, *like there are words, not scars, on the surface of my skin.* "I understand, and I want to forgive my father, Ace, and myself. I feel as if I'm not allowed to fight against it."

I saw her take a shaky breath as she hesitated. "Why does Ace want you dead?"

Her question didn't surprise me, but it was time I spoke the truth. I nodded, "Because Jerik wants me dead, discreetly."

"How do you know?"

I looked at her, I tried not to let my eyes fill with tears. "Because I have Ascendant blood—"

She laid her hand on my arm gently. "Jance..."

My name had never sounded more beautifully broken.

I rubbed her arm. "He has yet to kill me," I said. "I am part Ascendant, maybe that comes with the perk of defacing death. Maybe I can't be killed," I joked.

She stepped away from my touch. "It amazes me to think someone could have an endless life. Who would want to live forever?"

I shrugged. "Maybe not in this world."

Natalya said nothing as she inspected the wall, last names of Raidens were engraved in small black writing.

"Camden?" she questioned.

I looked to where she was pointing. One name was in white and it would have blended into the white stone if she hadn't grazed over the word with her fingers. "Yes," I said. "It's a tragic story. Camden is a dead Raiden name that's why it's white. White meaning oblivion or nonexistent."

"A dead name? How can that happen?"

"It is rare. When you marry you can choose a name, there is great honor in both. It's very hard for a name to not be carried on."

"When I first appeared in the fourth dimension, there was a list of names on the wall. My eyes fell on Natalya Wells, and I knew that was me, even though I had no memory of who I was."

I glanced where the Divide ran all the way around, a never-ending waterfall that faded to the clear sky. "Names are written on the walls here as well. I think names are more important than labels, those are words that inflict emotional wounds," I said, kicking my heels back against the wall.

Natalya crossed her arms and looked beyond. "Depends on how much you let those words define you, don't let anyone tell you who you are."

"Ronan always managed to direct my thoughts away from the opinions of others," I spoke with grace as thoughts of him encircled my mind. "He talks about his unmemorable past as if it didn't bother him. Perhaps, there is a way to deal with an unknown past, or a past you wished never happened. He accepted his life with courage that even I do not possess, the courage to forget."

"Ronan is extraordinarily brave." Her expression was glossed with hesitation, she cleared her throat. "I know about Ronan's fire."

I gave her a comforting look. "I know, he told me."

"It wasn't exactly subtle. He shot a flaming arrow above my head."

I smirked. "Why'd you go there by yourself anyway?"

Moments passed before she answered. "I wanted to find out who I truly am," she said tugging the hem of her sleeve down. The motion was all too familiar to me.

"I've spent years trying to figure it out..." I trailed off. "Years trying to discover why I am the way I am. I've always ended up running in circles."

Natalya sighed. "Just when you think something connects to something else, you get lost in a tangled loop." She paused. "I remember the open strings and closed strings my teacher, Mr. Barnes, had talked about. How some go full circle and others are left open."

My eyes wandered around the rooftop. "Sounds a lot like life, one big messed up loop. Everyone comes from somewhere and everything comes from something." I took off my jacket, removing it was like shedding a fake skin, I knew I was safe on the rooftop. I darted toward the fountain and scooped up a bit of water in my palm. I strode back to her, caressing it in my right hand.

I smiled as I spoke, "It is impossible to come from nothing. From the air we breathe, to the reason we are on this rooftop tonight, it is not without purpose." I threw my arm straight up in the air and the water expanded in the atmosphere. Slowly, the droplets fell, showering Natalya and me in white crystalized pieces, they bounced up slightly when they collided with the floor.

Her jaw dropped. "How did you make it snow?"

My smile grew. "It's not *really* snow."

I held out my hand, when the frozen water touched my fingertips, they exploded in little shatters. I had manipulated the water to form tiny shields, and they were as breakable as I felt right now.

I noticed Natalya staring at me. My silver patterns on my arms stood out against the whiteness surrounding us. She was observing them, my scars intertwined themselves into various circular and diamond appearances, like snowflakes. I was never fooled by their radiance. A beautiful sight most likely conceals an underlying danger.

"Jance...I want to see what you can do."

I decided to trust her fully. I jolted my hand upward. With a whip of wind that came from me, a thick glass barrier appeared between the two of us, building itself out of nowhere. She put her hand over mine, but we were not able to touch. It was cold like ice, yet unbreakable. In my glass there were no cracks, it formed a solid, clear shield. I could see Natalya's eyes dancing on the other side.

"What is it?" she said through the glass.

"A shield, at least that's what my mother tells me." I lowered my hand, and it was gone in a matter of seconds.

"Jance, that's unbelievable," she said breathlessly.

"I'd like to think so too, but—"

"Stop that!" she exclaimed. "Stop acting like you've got a curse on you. What you just did was phenomenal."

I didn't oppose her. "Thank you," I said shyly.

"You're welcome," Natalya smirked. "About time you take a compliment."

I glowered down at her wrist. Natalya was admiring the last of the manipulated snowflakes falling gently to the ground. I wrapped my hand around hers, my fingers grazing the hem of her sleeve. She relaxed, and my breath shook as I suddenly flipped her palm over, a strange gold scar was embedded along the inside of her wrist.

She snatched herself away from me. Her eyes blaring, she only stood still for a second before she turned and stalked away.

"Natalya, wait!"

To my surprise, she listened. I didn't know any other way to do this, it seemed the only way she was going to open up is if I exposed her secrets myself. "Look, Ronan told me. He saw your scars when he carried you out of the forest."

Natalya's voice was grazed with anxiety. "That's why I went to the House of Mirrors. But something happened and I—"

she choked. "I *broke* through it."

I frowned. "That happened to me as well," I assured her, but she did not look assured. "Gold scars," I said. "Just know, that no matter where you are hurt, like all Raidens, once you have been scarred, nothing can ever touch you there again."

Her furious face softened. "I'm happy I'm here."

"Really?" I said, surprised at the sudden change in her mood. "Why?" I said curiously.

"Life is alive and worth living. Knowing that there is something to fight for gives me hope." She looked down, and then back up at me slowly. "No matter what scars heal over my body, white or gold, I'm here for a bigger purpose. I just don't know how to be a Raiden, let alone part Ascendant."

I shook my head. "You are not alone," my voice was a blanket of empathy. "I will help guide you through this. And you are right, there is hope."

"Hope," Natalya confirmed. "I confused my feelings for vengeance. For a long time, I wanted to murder the Ascendants for taking the only person in the world that mattered to me. But now I have Eve back, plus a whole other world. This is what I've always needed. I think that was what humans needed too. It's not materialistic, it's created and tangible. Ideas can be made into something real. I feel sorry for the people who never look beyond the world they live in for happiness. If they did, they would discover how exceptional life can be beyond their own lenses."

"I guess I don't quite understand," I murmured. "The Lost Paradise is not the first place someone would go to find themselves or find something better."

"To me it is. It is something more than where I came from," she said. "Wherever I came from..." Natalya's attention drifted to the walls, some words were drawn within the details of the carvings. I saw her eyes were starting to blur, melting into the images. I shook her shoulder.

"What do they say? The words," she stammered.

"Don't read writings on walls," I said with a stern voice.

I glanced where her eyes locked, paralyzed by the words on the wall, I swore I saw a carving of a Raiden raise its knife. I gasped and averted my eyes. I know she saw the same thing when I heard her suck in her breath.

"Got it. Don't read the writings on the wall," she shivered. "Word manipulation?"

I nodded. "Wall Readers. They are people who become addicted to staring at the words and spending their lives deciphering what they mean. They go insane, that's what happened to my grandfather."

Natalya frowned. "Are the words, *Mendax*, *Mendax*, a part of this language?"

I snapped my neck toward her furiously. "How do you know those words?"

She raised her hands innocently. "Stories. The girl with the three and a half knives."

I sighed. "Don't go around using those."

"It means 'liar, liar.'"

"Stories make reality interesting. But what you'll find is that reality is stranger than the stories. In the end, many turn out to be true."

I walked back over to the fountain. The sound of the running water was always a tender noise. Natalya followed. She breathed slowly. I watched her chest rise and fall and her eyes peered at mine. My heart tightened at the intimacy. I gently grazed my fingers over her throat, my hand finally resting on the back of her neck.

"Are you searching for more scars?" her voice purred.

I opened my mouth and then closed it. The moonlight began to shine over the fifth dimension, the sky had grown darker. I could see the light reflecting off the white stones surrounding us. They gleamed at the sight of the moon, giving them a bluish tint, catching Natalya's eye.

"Moonstone," I said inadvertently. "It glows blue when the moon comes out."

I wrapped my arms tightly around her. Her eyes closed halfway. My heart pounded. I couldn't remember the last time anyone made me feel like this. She hugged me back and leaned into my embrace, her hands nested in the middle of my chest. The frigidness of my scars did not seem to bother her. Her fingers gripped traced the silver patterns that replaced my skin. I knew that I was invincible, and nothing could damage me there, yet her touch had the power to go directly through them. My hand came under her chin, forcing her head up, our faces only inches away from each other.

A stupendous roar came from behind us. I snapped toward the forest to see a mass of Remnants running wildly out from the trees. Their humanity entirely stripped from them, eyes so intense and red that they appeared faceless, creatures moving like shadows that danced around the trees like bloody ghosts. They charged like an organized army, barely a second passed until I heard the first dying scream of a Raiden.

CHAPTER THIRTY-THREE
NATALYA

We almost kissed. It felt like forever ago, yet only moments had passed. I was numb, I barely felt the grasp of Jance's hands as he dragged me from the rooftop. I practically tumbled down the flights of stairs, running down the hall to his room. He let me go, grabbing a thick jacket and swinging it on. He scattered for every weapon he had, yanking them into his long pockets and belt.

He looked at me with shocked eyes. "Stay here. Do *not* go outside. Do *not* leave this room."

I opened my mouth to protest but he closed the door violently behind him before I could say anything. I was alone, and everyone I loved was going to war against hundreds of mind manipulating demons.

CHAPTER THIRTY-FOUR

JANCE

I sprinted down the corridors of the mansion. The doors of the house burst open; Raidens were pushing their children and elderly through faster than I could move. The Herold's House was a secondary safe place if Camden wasn't accessible. Cursing under my breath, I made my way out the back.

I was instantly faced with a Remnant as I exploded out into the battle. It bared its teeth, pointy black shards encased its mouth, and a trivial amount of fading red hair descended against its slumped shoulders. I could see through the demonic appearance that it used to be a girl. The creature did not attack. I jabbed with my sword, feeling my scars ignite in correlation with the adrenaline pulsing through my blood. The Remnant sunk to the ground. I frowned, it barely defended itself. I crouched down by the house and observed the scene. I've never seen this many

Remnants attack all at once. They were not bred to be an army.

Someone organized this, I thought.

I quickly looked down at my feet as the earth shook beneath me. Without warning, the ground ripped beneath me, like someone had taken a huge knife and cut through the dirt like butter. I dashed, but something wrapped around my ankles and snaked up to my wrists. It was so tight I turned away, afraid to witness my hands and feet being severed off my body. Dark roots pinned me to the earth. My heart began to pound as I struggled against the force. I saw a black cloud appear in my peripheral vision.

The shadow loomed over me. It was a Remnant Ghost. I never believed they existed, yet in what might be my last moments, I am proved wrong. They moved like wisps, impossible to kill, with power like the Ascendants and minds sharper than sidereal glass. I accepted my time was up.

I turned to my right, my short sword inches away. I saw tons of Raidens lying in a blanket of crimson that covered the grass. This was beyond a few of my people dying here and there; they were being slaughtered before my eyes.

And I'm going to be one of them, I thought, *if I can't reach my sword.*

I tried, but all the roots restraining me were far too strong. I kept my eyes wide open just like I was taught. Stare at your enemy, show them you are not afraid of death. The Remnant Ghost stalked around slowly; it was making a mockery of me. I barely had time to take my final breath when a flicker of dark red twirled beside me, and a short sword pierced the creature from behind. It screeched, then dissolved into shadowy ash. I smiled as I met the familiar dark blue eyes.

Evanna pulled me up and we sprinted to the opening under the Herold's House that leads to the sewer. I shielded her against the chaos as she slid down first; I followed swiftly behind. Our feet landing in the green, mushy water. Gasping the fowl air, we looked intensely at each other, thankful we were breathing at all.

"What is happening?" I asked with urgency.

Evanna shook her head. "They came out of the forest in dozens. The Flood is already out there, and Ace is with the Elites. Where's Natalya?"

"Locked in my room."

My cousin closed her eyes as if she were in pain. "She won't be for long," Evanna's breath was shaky and her voice trembled. "I've seen so many of us die in a matter of seconds."

"The Ghost—"

"I killed it," Evanna said. "I don't know Jance...this is a massacre. But who—"

I rested my hands on her shoulders. "Fight now, figure out why later."

Evanna nodded in response. And then I felt my heart suddenly clenched in my chest, "Ronan?"

Evanna's eyes went wide. "I—I don't know."

I was climbing out before she could finish those three words.

CHAPTER THIRTY-FIVE

EVANNA

I watched my cousin rush out of the sewer. When we were little, we would come down here and look around. One time we found a body. It was the first time either one of us saw someone dead, and very dead at that. Usually, flesh deteriorated to dust and bone quickly, but the water had preserved this unfortunate person. I remember thinking it looked like a giant worm. I didn't ponder on it much. Jance took it a little differently. Soft-hearted as he was, he paled at the sight. That dead body became more to him than just the trauma of seeing someone floating down the sewer below our house. It lingered in his mind because he never stopped questioning the reason behind it.

I stood paranoid in the same spot where we found the body. My feet sunk a little lower than they did when I was little, signaling that the earth down here was slowly rotting away. Even in the fifth dimension there were dirty and ugly places.

I took a breath. The Ascendants never manipulated me, they enslaved me, but they failed to take hold of my mind. I knew how I could use my connection to the Remnants to defeat them. But everyone will see.

Be seen or be dead. Be exposed or be killed. It's going to come down to my choice.

CHAPTER THIRTY-SIX

NATALYA

"Like hell I'm staying in here," I mumbled to myself.

I extended my arms over my head and gripped around the hilts of two long knives. I pulled them free from the sheaths in my back. I stared at their stunning gold complexion and contemplated.

Can I do this? I thought. I remembered how fast and terrifying the Remnants were, how much they resembled people, the fact that they had been people, and could enter your mind if you let them. But I clung to the fact that my friends are in danger, and I forgot fear.

I could hear several voices coming from below. I galloped down the stairs, the mansion was filled with children, who seemed to look neither scared nor sad, but emotionless. There were elder Raidens as well who held the same expression. Peeling my eyes away, I ran to the front door and charged into the night.

I saw red. The flashing weapons of Raidens cast beams into the night, it was iron mixed with stardust and death. I felt stunned. I took a step toward the chaos and tripped over a body, and what was supposed to be a slow decay, happened in a few moments. I watched the body change to grey as the skin shriveled, the teeth deteriorated into chalk, and the eyes melted from the sockets into a strange liquid. Finally, the entire being sprinkled into dirt, exposing the bones. Death, if it were to have a proper definition—something invisible is coming after you.

I was forced out of shock when a Remnant appeared, excessive curling red veins shot out of its skull. It reached out its long hand and I stabbed it. It retreated and stared at me. I felt a scrape against my mind.

No, I thought to myself. "You will not take over my mind," the words flowed out of my mouth with a murderous tone.

I do not take over minds, the Remnant responded.

My face twisted, and I ran my long knife into the chest of the demon.

Something knocked me off my balance and all I felt was a heaviness sink into my chest. I don't think I screamed. I felt a pool of warmth underneath me. My face turned to the side, and I saw my long curls splayed over blood-soaked grass. There was blackness...then light.

CHAPTER THIRTY-SEVEN

EVANNA

If I could describe the worst thing that ever happened to me, I couldn't. I could only visualize it. There she was hovering around a Remnant; I was waiting for her to kill it. Finally, she did.

I darted in Natalya's direction, then three Remnants surrounded me. Well, three and a half, one didn't have any legs. I felt one Remnant run its long black nail down my sleeve, it was strong enough to tear my clothes and pierce deep below my skin. I only winced a little, it should have hurt a lot more, but I was born for pain and bred not to feel it. Undoubtingly, everyone is susceptible to a certain kind of pain, mine was just deeper below the surface.

They were clawing at my mind. I pushed into their nightmares with a force.

Visions invaded me. A performance of scenes played in

my head. I saw a woman with knives laced through her. I saw a girl drugged and left at the side of the street. I saw men abruptly blown to pieces.

The Remnants are people from the past world who did horrid things, and so they became the evil they were, and their victims lingered in their minds.

They screamed, pursuing my conscience even farther.

I will not let you in, I thought. *My mind is mine.*

They scattered. I saw a flash of light, but my eyes were squeezed shut. My conscience produced a force that rebounded into the minds of the Remnants, I made them relive the reasons for their existence. I did this by letting them in me and then shoving them out. I watched them shiver, then fall to the ground.

I did to them what they do to their hosts, make them die from the inside out. It was a manipulation, a power that I had gained from living among them. I didn't know of anyone else who can do this. Then again, I never told anyone. Perhaps I had a niche, or perhaps I was special.

With power, comes sacrifice. Now the memories are mine and the images are tattooed along the walls of my mind forever. I do not know what is going to happen to me.

Suddenly, I felt another Remnant push me from the back and dig into my chest. I felt its nails nearly clawing at my heart. But it wasn't happening to me, it was happening to her.

I didn't hear her scream. I didn't hear her suffer. I heard myself yell and I bolted. Again, I was blocked by Remnants tearing away at my body. One succeeded by scraping down over my eye. I swung my sword toward its face, an eye for an eye. The remains dripped off my sword.

There was one thing about finding out someone you love was dead, it was another thing to watch it.

We're all going to die, was my final thought.

CHAPTER THIRTY-EIGHT

JANCE

I ripped myself away from the war like a coward, but I would abandon the world for my best friend. I tore through the trees and found Ronan; his back was bloody. He stood in the part of the forest were the trees didn't grow and the temperature was freezing. The place where the only tree without thorns bowed in the snow.

I watched him put his knife back in its sheath, Ronan's hands were shaking, a dead Remnant by his feet.

"Jance," he spoke with his back to me. "I remember the hopeless feeling—a bloody knife in my hands and only a name was left in the hollows of my mind...Ronan Surestrike." He finally met my face. I was surprised to see tears in his eyes. "I'm inflicted with nightmares and flashes of a place with red skies and clear skyscrapers. The grass that grew instantly died, animals were scarce and when it rained it poured with violent thunder, lightning, and wind. Sparks ignited engulfing fires—everything *burned*."

I frowned at him. Why was he ranting about his past in the middle of a massacre? Then it occurred to me, there were more details he knew. There was a way to retrieve memories or piece back a broken mind. But it was far, far too dangerous. It's amazing the lengths people will go to remember or forget. "Ronan," I said. "Is there something you want to tell me?"

He stared at me and I saw the golden shield in his eyes start to break.

"Here at the end of everything?" my voice enforced.

There was shuffle coming from the trees. A sinking feeling came over me that my soul could be sucked into the depths. *Remnant Ghosts*, I knew.

I held my sword upward while Ronan stood motionless.

"*Ronan!*" I screamed at the top of my lungs.

They poured in like buckets of black ash from the trees. Then when they came to the tree line, they stopped. I lowered my sword. They were afraid of the Bowing Tree, but they still lurked along the edge like they were going to swallow us up at any moment.

My hands started to flex in little seizures. I've never felt such a draw to my power, it was whispering in the back of my mind. I couldn't hear words, only feel the desire. I jerked my hands forward and the glass shot up at my summoning. The hollowed eyes of the ghosts grew wide with shock. They spasmed and twisted like tornados in the sky and flew away.

I breathed hard, realizing the power within me. "Ronan?" I said with a little fear.

Ronan stood behind my shield. I saw my friend smile, but his face was whipped with a pang of certain guilt. "Secrets have divided us Jansen," he said simply.

I frowned. Ronan never called me by my full name unless something was wrong. "What are you talking about?"

He came close to me. "Tell me everything in this place that everyone avoids. Did your grandfather really go insane? Or could he not handle the memories that plagued his mind, like I can?"

My eyes narrowed. "You're a Wall Reader?"

"For a purpose," Ronan said. "It was easy because I had no memory. I can take hold of others because I have none. I was just hoping—"

"You were hoping," I cut him off. "That you would find out about the place you saw. You don't remember Ronan, but I heard you screaming at night when my father brought you back. You talked about a place with the red skies—"

"I've found nothing!" he barked furiously. "No trace of anything related to the place I see. No fragments of memory line up with the words I've read." He walked away. His breath ragged and his eyes changed to a tarnished shade of amber.

I swallowed hard. I've seen this kind of madness before. My grandfather pacing through the Herold's House mumbling about words and the power they possessed.

My mind went back to the past. I was four years old and I couldn't sleep because someone was stomping up and down the hall. I was too afraid to step outside the safety of my room but brave enough to take a small peek through the door. I barely opened it, and I saw my grandfather trotting along the halls with his hands outstretched, rubbing the sides of the walls as he moved. His eyes were vast like a wild animal. I heard him whisper things, about how the Undercity soaks in blood and scripted words would appear on the wall that displayed stories of the victims.

My grandfather had lost himself in trying to bring back someone else. My grandmother, Joan, had been Herold. She was unusually kind and had a knack for whipping young Raidens into shape. She died of natural strain; the mirror took its toll on her. When a Raiden passes, they are buried in the Death Meadow. It is rumored that the flowers and earth absorb the remains. In the Lost Paradise, nothing is ever fully lost. In a way, it can preserve someone's memories. But anyone who has tried to dissect the secrets in that underground cavern hardly ever come back out. My grandfather swore that Joan had communicated to him in the Undercity by writing on the wall. Words that screamed without making a sound. The greatest power in the world is held by those who can manipulate words. They can live forever.

I snapped back to reality and my eyes latched onto Ronan. I felt like my heart was about to burst. "The manipulation of words," I said. "My grandfather talked about it all the time. Blood memories, items, and places manipulated by superhumans who have a power that is unbound from this world. It's extreme Ronan, and anyone is susceptible to the trap, do not think you are invincible to it."

He reached for his knife again. "But *we* are invincible. It begins with us Jance, the Raidens with Ascendant power. Some things don't make sense about us, and the Seers. We have been taught that the Ascendants created us by torture and manipulation, took humans against their will, but that may not be true—"

"You're trying to tell me," I said angrily. "That everything we know is a *lie*."

Ronan grew quiet. "Not all of it is a lie, I believe there is a very misunderstood truth."

"Then what is the real story? Who told you this? Ronan, I'm afraid I'm going to lose you—"

There was a universal scream coming from the battlefield. My heart screamed with it. I *hoped* Natalya stayed in my room, I *hoped* Evanna's cunning brain kept her safe. The odds against me are ninety-nine percent, hope is constantly clinging to that one percent.

Ronan took off and I staggered after him. Mad or not, he was my best friend till the end.

Running through the thorns seemed easier than ever but time was moving slowly. We finally came to the edge of the tree line, and the Remnants were gone. The evidence of death was all that remained.

CHAPTER THIRTY-NINE

EVANNA

I woke in the infirmary. My injury was covered with gauze. I felt tears spring up in my good eye, I wished the Remnant took them both out.

My good eye traveled to Ronan and my cousin. Ronan's hands rested on Jance's shoulders. They were both drained of life. But Jance; he was drained of all heart. His grey eyes were nearly white from the tears. He looked at me and laid his head in my lap, heaving in a silent deadly cry. I curled my fingers in his hair. Ronan didn't look at me, his head was bowed, refusing to show any sign of emotion.

I didn't know if it was night or day. The days to come would pass without purpose. When I met her, I thought she was the one who could *see*. Now I realized, I was both wrong and right. She was the one to be seen and never silenced, her anger came from the need for justice. Natalya was the voice of those who had none.

"Has anyone tried to find her?" Ronan broke the silence.

I wanted him to look at me, but he kept his head to the ground. "There's no point," I responded. "If she's out there it's impossible to identify her bones."

I felt my cousin wince in my arms. He moved his torso up. "So much death. I have never seen Remnants like that...the ghosts are real."

I barely remember anything after I saw Natalya...*die*. I struggled to decide if I wanted to fight or be killed right then and there. The moment before I wondered if I could cheat death, a Remnant came at my face. I saw torn skin and black teeth before I fell into unconsciousness. I don't know how I wasn't dead. A part of me wanted to know what the rest of my story looked like—if I had any words worth living for.

"They were working together," Ronan said, finally looking at me. "Remnants are not a united force, somebody rallied them to destroy us."

"Not even Ascendants can control Remnants," I said meeting his eyes before he diverted my gaze again like he was hiding something.

"I know," Ronan confirmed. "That means we're dealing with something much worse."

"What's worse than an Ascendant?" Jance inquired bitterly.

I sighed and touch the bandage on my eye. It felt odd, I never liked things to be bandaged up, Raidens hardly did, except if the injury was truly awful.

Ronan kicked something on the floor and cursed. Jance and I jumped.

"What's worse than an Ascendant!?" Ronan's voice fired at Jance. "Someone like us..."

Jance looked terrified.

"Tell her Jance," Ronan ordered.

My cousin didn't say a word. He simply rolled up his sleeve and displayed his arms, which were patterns of silver. I couldn't help but touch the lovely design. Family is love, not scars. "I don't care what's on your skin. You are my cousin, one of the few people I have left."

Ronan spoke on his behalf, "Jance creates shields, he's saved my life multiple times."

Jance didn't smile. "And I will do whatever it takes to keep saving your life. *Both* your lives."

I looked at the boys. "No more secrets?" even though I still had them. I was a hypocrite.

They both nodded. I continued to stare into the swirls of Jance's scars. Ronan was right, someone with Ascendant blood was far more powerful than a normal Raiden or Ascendant. There is likely an Ascendant blooded Raiden that assembled the Remnants to kill us. But who and why?

Revenged flooded through me and it gave me scary strength. I stood slowly from the bed. I felt Jance put his hand on my shoulder, I pushed him away. Heading toward the mirror, I tore the bandage off my eye and threw it on the ground. I kept it closed, and with my other eye, I looked. There was a nasty, flaming red scar that started at the edge of my eyebrow and stretched to my temple. It looked worse than it felt. Slowly, I opened my injured eye and blinked a few times. By some impossibility, I could see.

My fist went to the mirror and it shattered into hundreds of pieces. Broken glass spread on the floor as I fell on top of it and burst into tears. Jance and Ronan looked at me, agony was painted over their faces.

"I—" I struggled to speak through panting breaths. "I don't want to see the world without her."

CHAPTER FORTY

JANCE

Pain, like everything in life, is a pattern. It repeats itself for as long as you continue to let it. I refuse to lose Natalya. Her death carved an inescapable labyrinth of darkness that is going to break me. There is no way to bring people back from the dead, not in this dimension, but there is a way to find them again.

The fire flickering in Ronan's living room was mesmerizing. Ronan kept throwing arrows into it, his eyes dazzled morbidly as the arrows caused a shower of flames. "Are you sure this is a good idea?"

"No," Evanna cut in quickly. "It's not a good idea, it's a very bad idea. That's why we're going to do it."

I grinned a little. Evanna was fearless and full of brilliant bad ideas.

Ronan's knowledge about how to navigate the Undercity

was about to be our saving grace. Now, once I lost someone I loved, I'm fully embracing my grandfather's insanity. Most importantly I understood his suffering.

Ronan and I told Evanna about Natalya's scars. I think Natalya would have wanted her to know. Evanna didn't seem surprised at all, she just nodded, I wanted to know what she was thinking.

When I mentioned my grandfather I saw Ronan's eyes burn with fear as they darted toward Evanna. He must not have told her he was a Wall Reader. I sighed internally, so much for no more secrets.

Ronan glared at me. "I don't like this."

I glanced at my cousin, who was lost in thought. She was smart enough to know that Ronan was hiding something. From what he told me, he's only searched for memories of himself not someone else, we were taking the risk of having our minds become subject to whatever memories we may come across in the Undercity. We all knew what could happen. At the same time, Natalya had a gift, and we are all determined to find out what. There is no doubt the dead have answers.

"Ronan," Evanna said approaching him. I wanted to look away, but I didn't, she took his hand. "Please."

I rolled my eyes and gagged.

Ronan ignored me and let out an exasperated breath. "How are we going to sneak out of here?"

I smirked at how easily he was convinced. "I wouldn't worry," I said, "everyone is trying to recover. No one will be watching us."

"This is the fifth dimension," Ronan said. "Someone is always watching."

"Jerik is locked away in his room as always, so is my mother and neither of them have seen me since the attack. They probably don't even know if—" I cut myself off, feeling my anger rising.

Evanna came close. "Jance," she said sympathetically as she squeezed my shoulder. "We love you."

"I know Evanna. Just forget it," I said with irritability.

"I think the best way is through the meadow," Ronan continued. He didn't understand how it felt to have parents who didn't care about you. I don't know which is more painful, to know you are not cared for at all, or to never know if anyone ever did.

Evanna shifted her attention to the fire. "I'm afraid of the meadow."

The Death Meadow was beautiful. It grew above the Undercity in countless rows of all kinds of flowers that contained nightmares of their own. Evanna and I ventured there once when we were kids. She had picked a bright red rose and instantly screamed. She claimed a girl had dropped dead in the meadow. I didn't see anything. Evanna ran forward as she clung to the flower. There wasn't a dead girl, but the stem of the rose dripped with blood. We never went back.

"Those flowers have probably grown, with thorns," I said. "We'll have to be careful."

"Okay," Ronan said.

"Fear is all in your head," Evanna added nonchalantly,

sounding like she was talking more to herself than us.

We left, rounding far away from the Herold's House. As soon as the grey building started to fade behind us, we took off in a full sprint. Raidens are fast but our speed is nothing compared to our endurance. Luckily, the fifth dimension wasn't a gigantic piece of land. We approached the Death Meadow in half an hour.

The overarching hills of flowers nearly blinded me, like a rainbow had fallen flat on the ground. They came past my knees and scraped the top of my thighs. I sucked in my breath. My vision was filled with the endless galaxy of unique hues. As I stared at them, I began to feel drugged and dizzy. The flowers reached Evanna's waist, making her petite frame look even smaller. She walked straight ahead keeping her eyes sharp. I could tell she was scared and refused to show it. Ronan seemed to care less, but I know he's walked through the meadow countless times to get to the Undercity.

Something sharp pinched my finger. I lifted my hand to see that a thorn pricked me, I sucked the blood from my finger, annoyed at it.

We continued in silence. A few hundred feet later my vision started to twist. Up ahead I saw a shadow start to emerge over me. I froze, Evanna and Ronan stopped and turned. The shadow moved fast like a Remnant Ghost.

I heard a voice, *"You can't feel."*

I thought of the Seers and how many I have delivered to death. "No," I said.

It came again, this time louder as the sky grew dark, *"You can't feel."*

"No!" I screamed.

I felt someone shake me, I jerked away and shut my eyes. I heard something different, "It's not real!"

My eyes shot open. Ronan stood beside me; his hands grasped my arms. "Jance, it's not real."

I inspected my finger. "A thorn poked me. Damn flower."

"Be careful," he said, pushing me away. "Don't let it in so easily."

Evanna gave me a comforting smile. I gave her a small grin back.

Just because it was a manipulation doesn't mean it wasn't wrong. I thought.

Finally, I saw the lines of flowers descending. At the peak of the downturn, there was a small hill with a strange entrance on its side. We hurried to it. An eerie feeling hovered around this place. A looming fog layered over the entrance and I heard a strange sucking noise coming from inside, like the cave was taking in a huge, ghastly breath. Ronan's pale face had a new green undertone like he was going to throw up. Evanna stood strong, ready to kill whatever crossed her path.

Ronan hesitated, but went down first, disappearing into the blackness, followed by Evanna, neither of them took a single glance back at me.

Words of Raiden I learned in school echoed in my thoughts, *Always keep moving forward, don't look back, not even at the ones you love. You just have to believe they will follow you.*

Those words were demented. I always looked back.

UNPARALLELED

Taking a breath, I slid into the darkness where we were created.

CHAPTER FORTY-ONE
NATALYA

I was surrounded by dead trees and iron bars. The sky was no longer broken, it was a hazy orange. I was back in the Dead Land and free of any injuries. A pair of black eyes leered over me. "Eve—" I started.

"Your friends are alive," Sylas cut me off.

The Ascendant stood in the same place where the Divide had shattered when I entered the fifth dimension. That felt like a different life. The glass split the tallest tree, which was half dead, but the other half was alive beyond the mural.

"I can see it now," I said, staring through the glass.

"You always could see it." His voice was coated in confidence.

"What happened?"

"Here you are alive, but in the fifth dimension, you are

dead. In the same way, humans existed in the fourth dimension, except I didn't have to pull your bones from the earth, you're not being played on repeat. I possess one of the many fragments of you. You have one as well."

"I can exist in more than one place?"

"There are many places where you do exist. No one is ever given the freedom to choose. You have a choice. There are parts of you throughout all worlds."

My breath caught in my throat and something hummed against my leg. I reached into my pocket and took out the shard of glass. With every breath I took, I felt it thud against my palm. It had its own heartbeat that matched mine. I stared at it in disbelief.

"You were made to be the undoing of all the dimensions," Sylas began. "You have capability beyond your control. It is unparalleled to anything in this world, and the worlds beyond." His black eyes suddenly had light in them. "That is what you are."

"What?" I whispered.

"Unparalleled," Sylas said with admiration and an echo of fear. "If you would let me show you."

Sylas's eyes never left me. I studied myself as I pulled up my sleeve, baring my glistening scars.

I looked around the fourth dimension. The naked trees, the pink houses, the grassless dirt, it was all the same. But there were no teenagers, no children without parents or purpose, no Mr. Barnes. This dead world was no more, and I felt just as dead inside. I didn't know what was going to happen or if I was even alive at all, this could be a dream.

I figured if it's a dream there would be nothing to lose. "Show me," I pleaded.

Sylas gave a stiff nod and held out his hand.

I ran my eyes over the spider-webbed pattern on his palm. I grasped his hand and I saw the world through his eyes.

CHAPTER FORTY-TWO
EVANNA

I could barely see. I knew that Ronan was in front of me and Jance was behind. It was pitch black, but the tunnel expanded as we walked farther down. My feet slushed in the muddy ground. At least, I hoped it was mud.

I heard a sound like a thousand threads tearing, I could see the outline of Ronan rubbing his hands together. Suddenly an orange-red light appeared. His scars glowed in the dark in the shape of flames. I pulled my sleeve up, my scars were bright white like diamonds sparkling within the cave.

"Well, well, I hope you know that you are nothing but a monster Surestrike," a silky voice came from behind us.

Everyone pulled out their weapons and turned in less than a second. The light coming from our scars revealed the smooth figure of Shai Cassteel.

Ronan looked at him, his arrow still locked in his bow. "I am trusting you Cassteel."

Shai ducked his head and bowed. "You have my secrecy. Although I was not referring to your scars."

Ronan seemed to hold his breath. Jance scowled at Shai as he looked down at his self to be sure he was fully covered.

I frowned. I had no idea what he was talking about. "What are you doing here Shai?" I asked curiously.

"Same as you, looking for Natalya. If you think you are the only ones that care for her, you're wrong."

I saw Jance glare at him. I bit my lip.

Ronan put his bow away. "We do need help," he said, but his amber eyes glowed with caution. "Who better to join? We need the best fighters."

I raised my eyebrows, I never heard Ronan be so humble. They both were neck and neck in becoming the next Elites.

Nothing else was said, we moved forward with Ronan's flaming scars leading the way. They were not really *glowing* or shining in a literal sense, it's just a manipulation. Our scars are the opposite of darkness, a trick of the eye, simply made to look brighter in dark places.

Jance's light grey eyes were just as easy to see in the cave. I tried to imagine how his silver linings would shine, the snowflake patterns would be the most alluring of them all.

I was too thankful that he was still breathing to be angry at him for keeping this secret, and Natalya's as well. When it comes to life and death pettiness tends to deteriorate. It's not until there is a present threat, people begin to understand life is hanging by a string that could be cut at any moment. No one is safe from it. What a shame that it is death's responsibility to make us truly care for one another.

The walls were decaying, and the tunnel was starting to curve along the corners, forming a square. Our footsteps changed from dragging through the slop to making small splashes the farther we went. I glanced down at my feet and I wished I hadn't, part of it was mud mixed with thick scarlet liquid. I swallowed the bile that had risen in my throat. It's strange, I should be used to it by now, but the more torture and death I see the more it threatened my sanity every time.

Everyone else stopped in their tracks at the realization of what we were walking in.

"Well," Ronan said lightly, "we tried," and he started to walk the other way.

Shai grabbed his arm. Ronan gave him a death stare as he snatched himself from Shai's grasp.

"I was only joking," Ronan sputtered with a tone opposite of joking.

"This is no time for levity Surestrike. What's wrong with you?" Shai questioned with frustration.

Ronan's breath was coming quick. My face creased. I hadn't seen him like this before. He was usually fearless, and now all I could see on his face was fear.

"We don't have a choice," Jance said looking nervous. "This is for Natalya."

Shai gritted his teeth.

I looked at him sympathetically, I twisted the ends of my

hair, a few strands falling in the bloody mud, standing out like little crimson waves. "We won't give up Shai," I said lowly.

Shai nodded and followed behind Jance. I took a deep breath, the air tasted like sulfur, similar to the Ascendant's hold. I covered my mouth with my arm and tried not to look down as the smell grew stronger.

Suddenly, Jance fell. I barely had time to react as the ground seemed to disappear. I heard Ronan scream. One by one we were all falling in midair. My shoulder slammed against something hard as I toppled down a slope. I was dizzy, but I could see light spilling from different directions.

I attempted to stand as my head cleared. The underground city was a chasm of empty halls lit with strange glows. The slope I had crashed into was backed up against a high wall. I startled when I saw a woman sitting at the top. She had an ancient face with a wispy body. Her black hair was cut at her cheekbones and it was turning white at the roots. Eyes like hallowed clouds stared at me, making goosebumps appear on my skin. My shoulder ached and I rolled it back. The girl jumped at my movement. I instinctively began to reach for my short sword. I felt Jance's hand on my arm as he stopped me. I turned to see Ronan was on his feet and Shai was struggling to get up. When I looked back toward the woman, she had vanished. I resisted the urge to scream. Jance's face narrowed into a mysterious glance, he had seen her too.

"As we go on there will be traps," Ronan's words came out with his panting breaths. "This place is meant to consume you. There are rooms, with...things."

"What things?" Shai questioned; his voice went up an octave.

I glared at Ronan. "Yeah what *things*? And how do you know this?" *No more secrets?* I thought. *Apparently, I'm not the only one full of shit.*

He cleared his throat. "I've been sent down here on scoutings before."

Liar, I thought.

Shai snorted. "Sounds like a mission that's only for an Elite."

"Exactly," Ronan said smiling sarcastically at Shai, who rolled his blue eyes.

"Why would Jerik send you here?" I asked, my voice on edge.

Ronan was silent. Suddenly, random flickers of light sprayed from above, followed by the sounds of dripping liquid too thick to be water.

Shai cut in, "Sometimes to learn about the future, you first have to discover the past."

I sighed in his direction. "This isn't the time for your poetry Shai."

"No, he's right," Ronan said looking downward.

"Grey, have you ever looked at the positive side in life?" Shai questioned.

I raised my eyebrows. "Abundantly, I'm a ray of optimism. Now let's move on before we get killed by something in the shadows."

"We need to find Natalya," Jance said slowly.

"We need to find *memories* of Natalya," Ronan corrected.

"Then lead the way Ronan, since you seem to know so much about the Undercity," Jance said in a bitter tone.

Ronan stepped forward and authority flooded over him. "Follow me."

I put one foot in front of the other and I tried not to look at the red scars lighting our way. I distracted myself in thought. The torturous acts of our creation still lived in these dark halls. When we die, our skeletons disappear into the ground and we return to dust. The Lost Paradise is heavily manipulated to retain, regrow, and reproduce all that happens within it. That's why this place drives people mad, it enforces the denial that death had won. My grandfather, Marwick Wayward, was a sorry witness to the Undercity's manipulation. I'm convinced, Jance and I are way more intelligent.

I lifted my gaze as the halls expanded into an open region encased by tall columns. Our footsteps echoed in the underground fortress. Ronan led us toward the left, near a collapsing archway, looking like it could crumble at any moment. Chills crept down my back as the dark caves turned into blinding white walls. Our path changed from mud to a silver sheet with old crimson stains. I was walking the history of my people.

The sounds of metallic echoes bounced off the walls in the Undercity as we walked. I felt like we were screaming our presence to whatever else may be down here. I became preoccupied with the writings; strange inscriptions traveled along the passageways in red, standing out against the whiteness. I felt a shoulder bump against me. Jance looked at me intently. "Do not read the writings on the walls," he whispered.

I nodded. I knew better. Jance was going to be the most careful, he remembered our grandfather more than I did. Wall Readers are the worst subjects, filling their heads with memories that didn't belong to them. It is a sweet torture and I could feel the temptation rising—probably from all the memories I already carried from the Remnants. *In fact,* I thought to myself, *it is the same thing.*

We came closer to a barred door, suddenly the tunnel started to shake and ear-piercing screeches were coming from the opposite end.

"Remnants!" I yelled in warning.

We ran with a sea of red eyes chasing us. I had faced death too many times to believe I was going to die. I am brave. I turned on a dime and faced dozens of demons coming straight at me.

Then the walls caved in.

CHAPTER FORTY-THREE

NATALYA

A long aisle led to an altar with an odd cross shape around it. "A church," I said in confusion, observing the sanctuary filled with dated pews.

"Yes," Sylas answered calmly. "This is a part of you—"

"Stop it," I said, my voice on edge. "Stop manipulating me. I don't know this place."

"The breaking of your conscience is never forgotten when you're physically in the memory. You are terrified of manipulation, so don't become subject to it. Think Natalya and *look*."

I slowed my breathing and investigated the church. I walked in between the pews. I heard a voice singing in the distance. My eyes diverted to the altar. A little girl about the age of seven stood in the center singing hymns of praise to an empty crowd. Her face was glued to her songbook. As I came closer, I noticed she was transparent like a ghost. The girl met my gaze, she had lovely green eyes, like me.

The little girl was me, she held eye contact for a second, then out of nowhere her figure disappeared, like a breeze had washed her image away.

My hands were shaking, and I felt my head being flooded with memories of this church. Like a curtain being lifted from my eyes, all that was forgotten I remembered. I used to sing in here.

I turned to Sylas. "I saw," my voice cracked. "What does fear of manipulation tell you about me?"

"Your ultimate need to have control, which is deadly."

"Height, depth, manipulation, and betrayal," I uttered.

"They all are connected to you."

"What do you mean?"

Sylas cleared his throat and his footsteps made different noises, like crunching over grass. "Some people have fears about losing the ones they love."

"Is that your fear?" I asked curiously.

His face lowered. "It was," he paused. "I ran out of people to love."

I swallowed hard. "Do you know who is behind the attack?"

"No, but I have a feeling it will be revealed soon," Sylas answered. "I don't want to speak on it unless I know for sure."

I looked away from him. I could see through the windows outside the sanctuary. I saw the cloud that encamped the fifth dimension, letting no one see what is on the other side. A wave of relief washed over me. "The fifth dimension."

Sylas laughed. "Of course, the Lost Paradise. We are in a paradigm shift. This is how Seers enter the dimensions, their past experiences combined with their sight."

If this is how they enter, and I existed in a world outside the dimensions that only means one thing, I thought. My glare burned into the Ascendant's black eyes. "You know who I am. Tell me everything. I was a Seer, wasn't I?"

"Yes. You were once a Seer, most of your memories were stolen from you."

I tried to exhale but I couldn't find any air left in my lungs. "By you. I saw you! In this—" I whipped out the piece of sidereal glass I took from Eve's room.

Sylas came closer, casting his eyes over the glass. "It's one of your many pieces." He smiled. "The Herold wants the Seers to die because they could become Ascendants. But it is *not* just Ascendants."

"Wait," I said exasperated. "The Seers could be Raidens? Like *me*?"

"Raidens, Ascendants, or traces of both like you, there is still so much you don't know, and my time is limited. The Seers utilize paradigm shifts as ways to go from place to place, they are prominent among ley lines in the past earth."

My hands clenched into fists. "The past earth?"

"Think about the Remnants. They are people who have done horrible things—" Sylas ended mid-sentence; his face turned grave. "Hell resides within our worlds. You become what you have done."

My thoughts drifted to the words Sylas had said to me in Ronan's house, *I have been everywhere. I've seen the darkness of hell, the hope of heaven, and all the worlds in between. I am the greatest manipulator, and I hold the strings.* I was just beginning to understand the power that rests within the dimensions, and Sylas himself. I returned my mind to the present. "The past earth...it exists?" I asked softly.

"Yes, it is a time manipulation, and there are many different timelines. The elites, they have an official title, but I don't know what they call themselves, are messing around with time. This is the bigger picture Natalya. The Lost Paradise has its problems, but we need warriors like you to save the earth."

I could only imagine the thoughts living in the brains of those Ascendants. World domination, controlling others, and the endless desire to defeat death itself. They had cracked the code by discovering death is not the taker, time is. This all started as visions and ideas that eventually made these worlds come alive and then they created the Raidens. If we are capable of imagining such things, then we are capable of doing them. Both the good and the evil. Anything is possible.

"How?" I questioned.

"One individual, the one who can *see*, is the key to them all. Someone with great power. That is who Evanna Grey was searching for in the Dead Land," Sylas said, tracing the edge of his blade.

I closed my eyes, it all made sense now. "But the Raidens are killing Seers, what if this person is already dead?"

Sylas shook his head. "No. I can assure you, this induvial is not dead."

I frowned. "Sylas this all seems so hopeless—"

Sylas came close to me. I startled as he pressed forehead to mine. Being touched by someone who held the strings of the world in their hands was like resting your body against the sun. All the strength that lights the universe was in front of me. But I too had some of the universe in my blood, the stars. And then I remembered that the sun was the king of all stars.

"The Seers are still subject to the past earth," I could feel the coolness of his breath as he spoke. "The Remnants are as well, but they are too far gone to be saved. But for us, the Ascendants and Raidens, are subject to nothing. We rule the dimensions and we could rule the earth. Its great man-made cities, its billionaires, its governments, and all the humans that inhabit it." He pulled himself away from me and placed a hand on his long sword. I squirmed as he gripped the blade and blood trickled down. His face showed no pain.

"I do not want that," Sylas continued, his voice genuine. "There are some that do, and the key is the one who can *see*. It's nothing poetic it's literal. This person can see all things in the dimensions and possibly the earth. Help me find the Seer."

I swallowed hard. "How do I do that? How do I believe your intentions are good? And you are telling the truth?"

"No one is good." His voice loomed with sadness.

I sighed inwardly; I was sick of hearing that phrase. "And you expect me to believe you are good?"

He looked at me with honest eyes. "Of course not. I want

you to believe my choices are good."

My hand clenched the glass tighter, I barely felt a tingle when I saw blood running down my hand. "Where could this one Seer be?"

He let out a loud breath. "If I had any idea, I would have found them by now." He spun away, the bottom of his long black cloak swept over the marble floor, which looked to be growing flowers.

I let my hands ease on the shard as I finally began to feel pain. The white walls of the church were beginning to melt like wet paint sliding down a canvas. I could see the broken glass sky. The paradigm was disintegrating. As the walls flaked away, I saw a shattered mirror showing my reflection in broken pieces.

"What do you see?" he whispered.

"I see me as I am, broken."

"Look harder."

I did. I noticed my eyes were dark like his. I sucked in my breath and looked up; the ceiling was breaking.

Sylas whipped me around, gripping my shoulders. "Two should be enough to return to the Lost Paradise. *Don't die again.*" He smirked. "I'm going to rescue your friends from something stupid they decided to do. I'm sure we'll meet again." He released me.

Before I could ask any questions, Sylas vanished into thin air. There was a flower at my feet where Sylas had been standing, it was white with petals sharp like knives. I picked it up and my vision blurred with the image of the church. An odd feeling passed over me that this memory is one I would rather discard.

I didn't know if I wanted to acknowledge the demons that ruled over me in another life.

I lifted my eyes above and embraced one of my long knives, ready to shatter the glass ceiling and enter the world once again.

CHAPTER FORTY-FOUR
EVANNA

The ground below was still shaking. I saw a flicker of red, a Remnant was speeding toward me. Someone grabbed my shirt and threw me backward. I stood up rapidly and spun near the demon—only to see that it was already dead. I looked up, expecting to see Jance, Ronan, or Shai.

But I didn't see any of them.

One came to me, it felt familiar.

Eeeevvveeee we meet again, it slithered in my mind.

Ah, I thought. *That one, how did it get here?*

It pounced. I felt its claws digging into my shoulder and I jerked. The Remnant bowed its head and I felt something like a thousand tiny knives enter my leg. I screamed.

In my pain, I saw the Remnant smile. *You have something missing from your pocket.*

My breath deadened. *The glass,* I thought.

My hand immediately went to my side, but I forgot that I never had the sidereal shard, it was still in my room. That would have come in handy right now.

The Remnant did a perfect job of distracting me. My eyes widened as pain shot through my leg again. My body went limp, I saw its red eyes glare up as its body curled over me. The mouth of the creature opened, just inches from my face—and it flopped on top of me, the weight knocking the breath out of my lungs.

I shoved the Remnant off. Ronan hovered over me; panic displayed all over his face. I reached out my hand expecting him to help me to my feet. Instead, he kneeled and scooped me up in his arms.

There were monsters everywhere. Ronan held me in one arm, the heat of his skin burning me.

Suddenly, a fire erupted. Jance and Shai stood unharmed as a path made of blue and orange flames lit the Undercity. I heard the Remnants scream. The fire was under Ronan's control, I felt the pulses of his heart mimic the ebbs of the blaze, rising and falling with wild speed. I was sweating in his arms. Whatever power that existed under his skin it was unlike anything I had ever seen.

As fast as it ignited, it burnt out. The Remnants where now piles of ash and black powder floated in the air.

I looked into his eyes; they were a light gold. And then I felt a new kind of fire that burned even brighter as he tenderly pressed his lips to mine. It was him and I, and a fire that could kill.

We separated. I was breathing harder from the kiss than from the times when I thought I was going to die. He smiled and tucked his head down on my neck. His breath was cool, which felt odd.

I looked down at my leg, it was already healing but it still hurt.

Ronan lowered me to my feet. "Can you walk?"

I nodded, not trusting myself to speak yet.

Jance was streaked with blood that wasn't his own and Shai seemed fine. There must have been dozens of Remnants that came through that tunnel. Jance approached me slowly, I took two quick steps and threw my arms around him.

"What happened?" Jance questioned with force.

"I don't know, so many Remnants," I whispered as I retreated from the embrace.

"Not *that*," Jance spurted.

I looked toward Ronan, who didn't make eye contact with Jance. "He—I mean. You don't need to protect me Jance, not like that."

My cousin didn't let me go; he spoke with intense clarity, "You don't know everything about my best friend, Evanna."

"*Idiots!*" Ronan shouted abruptly.

Shai whirled on him. "What?"

"We locked ourselves in," Ronan said annoyed.

"How do you know?" Jance asked, looking confused.

"Because I *do*—" Ronan irked.

"Okay, okay," Shai said with irritation. He went to the door and yanked it, nothing happened, he began to pull harder and it still didn't budge. He finally slammed his fists to the door.

I groaned. *Boys*, I thought, but even my patience was thinning by the minute. The Undercity drained energy fast. I tried to assess the situation. We were in some sort of prison, the room was divided by two jail walls, a drastic change from the metal floors and white walls. The Undercity was filled with odd shifting scenes that went from one to the other dramatically. "What do we do now?"

Jance was laying on the dirt-covered ground. "I don't know," he glared at Ronan, "how do we get out of this?"

Ronan leaned against the cell, keeping his head against the wall unable to look at any of us. His hands were wrapped tightly around the jail bars as if he were trying to break them. "This place has a history that exists inside the walls, the ground, and all that surrounds it. It will re-live them over and over."

"What is this game?" Shai asked. "It wasn't a manipulation Ronan. I felt the ground shake; it was real."

"First, don't read the writings on the wall," Jance cut in with a firm voice.

Ronan ignored him. "There's a reason the words are written in blood that sinks deep into walls." Ronan gripped the Surestrike knife in his belt protectively.

"Blood memories," Shai whispered. "How do they manipulate?"

"Like the flowers," I answered.

"This is dark stuff." Jance's eyes flashed.

"Well, we knew we were doing something dark and forbidden," I reminded.

Ronan took a short glance at Shai. "Words warped with *Cruentus*. The word bonds blood to another item, it can be anything. But we are nowhere near the place we need to be to dig up blood memories."

No one said anything. I couldn't help but stare at Ronan. He had withdrawn into himself which frustrated me. A passionate moment between us had passed quickly into more continuous moments of silence. I glared at him before I turned away, he was just another truth I would have to figure out on my own.

"I know," Shai complained. "My mother is the Third Hand. We need to get to the heart of the city."

"Yes," Ronan commented. "It's gold, a pretty place."

Something passed between Shai and Ronan. An untold truth behind the two of them. I knew very little about our direct destination, other than it was the heart of the Undercity. But by the looks of it we were in for a long road ahead.

I sighed as I dusted off my clothes. I felt a thud on top of my head. I glanced up, the dirt fell from above and hit me in the face. I wiped it off, I wondered how far down we were. There was a possibility that it all might cave in.

The boys wandered around the enclosed cell. I glanced through the bars. I could make out a large lump in the corner. I wrapped my hands around the bars and tried to squeeze my face through. I could make out the body of a boy about our age. He was broad and muscular with beige skin and wavy hair. He was laying in the dirt stained with blood, I couldn't tell if he was breathing.

I backed away from the cell. "Guys, there's someone next to us," I announced.

The boys spun and marched to the cell. Jance peered through and frowned. "Probably was tortured and then thrown in here. Maybe a traitor?"

"He's not moving," I observed. "He looks harmless."

"Looks can be deceiving," Jance said walking away, Ronan followed wordlessly.

Shai stared curiously at the slumped body. "Is he alive?"

I shrugged. "I can't see."

Shai grabbed the bars and shook them. "We should find out." He jolted the bars even harder, I heard something pop. "Aha!" he exclaimed.

I turned to see that the bars had risen from the ground. Shai tugged once more and the whole jail wall moved.

I smiled. "You're brilliant Shai." I walked to the other end of the bars and snapped them out. Shai and I slowly lowered the left side of the cell to the ground.

"We're in an underground prison; don't waste your time on a worthless life," Ronan said glaring toward the body.

His words were cruel, this wasn't like him at all. I gave Ronan and obscure look; his porcelain face was the whitest I'd ever seen, and his gold eyes were shaded brown. "Worthless life?" I questioned. "If it was you lying there, what would you want someone to do?"

He said nothing and I proceeded toward the disheveled body. I felt Jance put a hand on my shoulder as he knelt over me. He hesitated slightly and then rolled the boy onto his back. I heard Jance take a sharp inhale. "Kian Gracing."

Everyone else's eyes went wide, I just stared.

He looked just as I remembered when we were kids, but older. A handsome wide-set face with thin delicate lips. His body was dense, he looked perfectly healthy for being missing for so long. His caramel-brown hair was longer in random places, looking like a child had cut it, and his narrow eyes were closed.

Jance pressed two fingers under his jaw. "He's alive, unconscious, but alive."

"I honestly thought he was dead," I said bewildered. "We have to take him."

"Strange, he looks no different from when he disappeared," Jance said frowning.

Ronan was suddenly looking over my head. I felt like turning around and punching him, but I held back. "It looks like he's been frozen in time," he said.

I noticed some dirt falling on Kian. I glimpsed overhead; dust was sprinkling down in puffs. I saw some trickling onto Jance's shoulders and sticking in Shai's hair.

"Something's happening," Shai whispered.

"It's going to cave in!" Ronan shouted.

There was a sudden vibration and this time it wasn't the ground below; it came from above. Larger clumps of earth fell rapidly.

"What is that?" I asked, coughing.

A blinding white light appeared under the doorframe, blowing it completely off the hinges. I squinted my eyes to see a black figure in the doorway.

"You Raidens get yourselves in all sorts of trouble," said a smooth, casual voice.

I knew them anywhere, it was an Ascendant. Mysterious dark eyes blankly stared down at us. He held out his hands, his palms were streaked with white lines, the same scarred look that resembled the Raidens.

"What are you all doing on the ground?" He asked curiously.

Jance and Shai looked petrified.

"Sylas," Ronan said.

I froze when Ronan said the Ascendant's name like he was an old friend. *Sylas*, I thought. *I know that name.* It sounded so familiar, yet I couldn't pinpoint it.

I had no time to react when I was forced against a wall, my breath instantly left my lungs. The land above started to fall at the speed of light. The earth fell on us with the violence of everything held above it and the sprays of dirt made breathing difficult. I coughed and started to panic. Suffocating was not the way I wanted death to take me.

There was a motion that set time apart from reality, the falling earth slowed to a near stop. Clumps of dirt bounced in midair and the dust danced in low vibrations around them.

The Ascendant stood unblinking; he jolted his head toward me. "*Go!*" he screamed.

Ronan and Jance took off, Shai and I locked eyes and we staggered back toward Kian. When I tried to get closer, my body flew backward by what felt like an invisible whip. I cried out in pain. My body crumpled at the impact of the metal ground. I was shaking as I stood, and then my heart dropped at the sound of an avalanche falling downward, blockading the way.

For a second there was only blackness and sounds of heavy breathing. Then I saw the mound of earth move from the inside out.

I felt a pair of arms bring me to my feet, I turned to see Shai. We jumped at the echo of a deathly scream.

The Ascendant broke free from the mountain of earth with Kian in his arms. "The exit!" he shouted, his eyes looking furious.

I blinked and then shook my head, there was a gaping hole in the side of the Undercity that I swear hadn't been there before. Light poured from the outside. I got on my hands and knees and crawled, the smell of fresh mud and blood filling my nose. I peered down at my hand, it was stained freshly red. I went deaf, hearing my heartbeat rebounding in my eardrums. I moved faster until I stumbled onto a blanket of flowers. I began breathing the air that was too crisp. It was the closest thing to fresh air I had ever known; the Lost Paradise had bitter oxygen.

I half opened my eyes, the brightness of the broken sun felt almost foreign to me, I felt like I had been underground for days. I heard Shai come from the tunnel, his sounds went back and forth between a scream and a breath. The Ascendant came out after carrying Kian in his arms, and he laid him down in the bed of flowers. I frowned, I didn't think an Ascendant could be so calm, so gentle.

Ronan was halfway to the top of a hill; his pace gave the impression he was trying to get away fast. My heart hammered at the sudden realization that Jance was nowhere in sight.

CHAPTER FORTY-FIVE
JANCE

I escaped the torrential downfall in the Undercity and looked back to make sure everyone made it out then I ran to the forest. I finally collapsed in a heavy gasp.

My knees were sinking into the tall grasses. I took off my jacket, exposing my silver scars, intertwining like delicate snowflakes. They looked beautiful to the naked eye, but all beautiful things have an ugly side. I always felt the need to constantly cover my body. What it represented, what evil it took to create something like me.

I had always seen the disappointment in my mother's eyes when she met mine. Like this person was not her son. I was not meant to have those grey eyes. Regardless, I was destined to be the Herold. To endure the misery of seeing all those fears. My grandmother, Joan, held the images so tightly in her mind and helped Raidens overcome their fears. She raised the greatest generation of Raidens to ever exist, Jerik's generation. Our people are weak because my father is unable to handle the heavy responsibility, his fear had consumed him. I didn't have to guess my father's fears because they were obvious. It was a fear that was shared by only one other person I knew—the fear of manipulation.

A Remnant's memories could easily enter the mind if it is not well guarded. Evil may not always have the upper hand, but it only takes a little for it to win. Only a few Raidens had strong minds. Ronan is one of them, having a shield around his mind for years to barricade the memories he couldn't touch, and ones he soaked in from the Undercity. I couldn't help but revisit the conversation we had during the Remnant attack. He told me that everything we know about our existence is a very misunderstood truth. When he had said the name of the Ascendant in the Undercity, I knew there was something deeper at work. I couldn't help but think the Ascendant was manipulating my best friend into believing something unreal. Since Ronan had no foundation, his mind was a clean slate to become the perfect subject. No matter how dense his conscience is, an Ascendant's manipulation can penetrate the strongest minds. This possibility terrified me. I'm half Ascendant, I figured I was next on the list. I ran away from them as fast as I could.

We are all subjects of manipulation, I thought.

I was the most vulnerable and submissive subject to ever exist. I felt the weight of my father's mistakes. My guilt was the worst burden. I killed those that did not deserve to die. I feared my power, I feared *myself*. This curse is within me and I cannot escape myself. However, my power exists outside of my mind and body. I had shown Natalya on the rooftop how I could manipulate all the molecules, how I could get them to bounce off one another. I can create energy faster than time itself, producing an invincible shield.

I held my ground as my first subject approached. The Remnant tried to invade my mind like a knife cutting into my consciousness. In that instant, I threw my hands up and the glass formed together. The Remnant's weight crashed into my barricade and it quickly retreated, letting out a shrill as it ran into the distance.

A smile spread over my face. I felt powerful. The glass shield continued to rise out of my hands, it was almost to the sky.

And then it fell. A horrible feeling washed over me. I turned and looked through the tree line that overlooked the fifth dimension, and there was a war unlike anything that's ever happened before.

I saw Raidens fighting one another.

CHAPTER FORTY-SIX

EVANNA

I watched the boy I loved play with fire. "Ronan," I whispered.

He turned to me. Shai, being the saint that he was, took Kian to the weaponry hoping Ria could find a way to wake him. The Ascendant vanished like they always do. While Ronan owed me an explanation, he hadn't said a word on our way back to his house. And Jance had run off. I was worried about my cousin. I felt like he abandoned me. I'm sure he felt betrayed by Ronan as well, however, he shouldn't have disappeared like that.

I felt incredibly alone.

Ronan's eyes glowed as they examined me. I tucked my knees up under my chin as if I were trying to close myself in from being hurt by whatever other secrets lingered between us.

"I've been working with the Ascendant for a long time," he started. "When Natalya went into the House of Mirrors, they both exploded through it, and part of the house shattered into hundreds of pieces. The Ascendant was able to repair it. That's how no one knew what happened and no one will ever know."

A wave of resentment went through me. "Why didn't you tell me she went into the house and destroyed it? Why didn't you tell me you've been in cahoots with an Ascendant?"

Ronan stood quickly. "You haven't told me anything, Evanna!" he yelled with frustration. "I did not want to tell you about Sylas because I didn't want you to jump to conclusions based on your experience with Ascendants. Everyone is programmed to remember the pain of their past—"

I shook my head slowly. "I am not like that," I said sharply, cutting him off. "Don't you dare for one second think I wouldn't have heard you out. Do you want to know what happened to me? Fine, I remember everything I endured. I wasn't touched by the sidereal glass until my last minutes in the fourth dimension. I nearly got my head cut off when I was a child by Jerik, as insurance I would survive the Ascendants beheading. Severed to the point to where my Raiden blood took over, but not enough to prevent me from healing slowly and painfully. My greatest pain was not from my enemies, it was from someone I *loved*." My breath was shaky, and I felt a tear fall down my face.

I couldn't believe I admitted it. This internal pain was worse than the Remnants' memories and the Ascendants' abuse combined. It goes back to that experience in my childhood. The biggest scars, the nightmares, all of it grew as I grew older, but I never healed the hurt of my child self I left behind. Not even going to a different world changed that.

Ronan laid his hands on my shoulders. At first, I didn't know if I should embrace him, push him, or remain frozen. Like every time he came close to me, I couldn't find it in my heart to disregard his comfort. He wrapped his arms around me. I uncurled my body and rested my head on his chest. His heartbeat was strong and loud.

"I am not sure," he said lowly, "what Jerik is capable of. There has always been something strange about him I do not trust."

I kept myself tucked against Ronan as tears slid down my face in a silent cry. "He loves Honoria, all the flowers—"

"That's a facade, but what is truly at the roots—" he stopped his words suddenly.

I frowned at him. "What do you mean?"

"Evanna, I'm sorry," Ronan said stroking my hair. "I want to tell you something."

I unwrapped myself from him.

"I'm a Wall Reader," he said as he pulled out the knife, coated in a red tint with SURESTRIKE printed down the blade. "The knife that came with me from wherever I was before contains blood memories, like the flowers in the meadow and the walls in the Undercity. I can hide from Jerik in the House of Mirrors because I can repeat the nightmares of others and present them as my own. I've gone to the Undercity many times and I read the writings. The manipulation of words, the one kind of manipulation that is underestimated, is the most powerful of all."

I was suddenly terrified of him. And yet I couldn't make

my body move away from his touch. "How do you—"

I didn't finish my sentence. The house shook, we both reacted in seconds and sprinted out the door.

I saw a shield rise to meet the glass sky. At the same time, there was blood on Ronan's doorstep as my people drove blades into one another.

***

Ronan bravely entered the fight as I scattered up to the Herold's House.

When I reached the door to my uncle's room I hesitated. He was talking to someone. I peered through the crack in the door and saw a Raiden woman, who talked to him in a soothing tone. Her eyes were wide in awe.

"I'm fast," her voice cooed. "In motions that can make me almost unseen. I can move my body in short bursts of speed like lightning. Evading enemies or tricking people to wonder if they saw me."

I watched my uncle with pain. The mirror behind him showed a sea of blood with the image of the Raiden woman drowning in it.

The fear of bloodshed, I thought. *What an awful fear to have as a Raiden.* She had long, bolt-like scars that were blinding white, a little too bright to be deemed common.

"Then," Jerik spat. "You are no longer any use to me my dear. I am looking for the one who can *see*."

Jerik did something that I did not expect. Taking out a

knife, he cut the throat of the Raiden with a quick motion. Her body hit the ground like a giant sack and blood spilled into the room.

Jerik turned, I followed his gaze to the black and white flowers on his desk, suddenly growing intense in their colors. The black into feral darkness and the white reflected a dangerous blare.

I thought of all the kind things I had seen Jerik do and the sacrifices he made. The way he took me in when my parents died. How he treated Honoria, filling her room with almost magical flowers. He was tied to the mirror, a subject in his own way. I did not want to disappoint him, I wanted to fulfill my mission in the Dead Land despite the fact he had nearly beheaded me. But if he hadn't the Ascendants would have succeeded in killing me. He sent me to find the one who could *see*, and he instructed the Raidens to murder Seers. Now, I see how he's using his people as pawns in a game of seeking one person that I don't think will ever be found.

Ronan was right, it was all an image. It was not real. There was something about the flowers that flashed as a warning, something I should have figured out before.

I felt myself breaking. I couldn't cry anymore, my sadness turned to rage. No one was safe, Jerik had lost it. All those who are half Ascendant are now targets; all the ones I loved.

Very few Raidens survived the Remnant attack, my mind raced quickly. *Except for the ones who may have had an extra advantage,* I thought.

Our race was near extinction and now we see the need to

kill each other. No matter how far manipulated, no matter how close to perfection we may get, no matter if you inject starlight into someone's veins, humanity falls into the same wicked trap. The habit of self-destruction was too great to ignore.

Except there is still something good worth fighting for.

I saw Jerik turn to the mirror, and my eyes were suddenly locked on a series of fears. Violent seas, giant creatures, animals with large teeth and claws, and even people. Rolling tides of fire, being burnt alive, knives, choking, hanging. I saw the fears of Raidens, and Jerik was playing them in reels. His breath came hard.

I stormed into the room. Jerik collapsed to the floor shaking like he had been swimming in a frozen river. He mumbled a list of fears. "Fear of height, fear of depth, fear of betrayal, fear of manipulation."

I paused. "Those are the fears of Natalya Wells." I knew her fears. I've known them all along.

Jerik shot up and grabbed his sword in a panic. His grey eyes changed to metallic and his hair wasn't blonde but blinding white. Jerik stepped forward in a frightful blaze, then sword clattered to the ground and he fell back down.

I rushed to his side, "Uncle?"

Jerik looked at me, breathing intensely. "Evanna Grey. There is something I have to tell you before my time is up."

"Are you dying?" I asked, my voice trembled.

"I'd rather be dying," he choked.

"I agree," I said, not knowing if I meant it or not. "What is happening?"

"Jansen is not my son. He is not even a Grey. Don't trust him, don't trust Surestrike." Jerik paused, his eyes gaping from their sockets. "I didn't want you to become Herold. I didn't want your life to be full of fears."

I grimaced. *Too late uncle*, I thought.

"You are the only blood Grey, and I am so, *so* sorry, but the enemy lies within our own family. Do not trust any Raidens with Ascendant blood."

A loud bang echoed behind us. Ace Huntington bombarded through the door with a sword in hand. Something dressed in darkness followed behind him and suddenly drove a knife into Jerik's side. I lashed out at Ace, but he tossed me against the stone wall, holding up his weapon against the mysterious figure coming after Jerik. I let myself fall into blackness.

CHAPTER FORTY-SEVEN

JANCE

I tried to stop. I leaped into action when I heard a cry of pain, only to realize I had caused it.

The Raiden was on me, her cropped brown hair was now blood-soaked and her blue eyes empty, that matched her sparkling scars like waves. When I ran out of the forest something was drowning me as if I had been submerged underwater. My shield rose, I don't remember reaching for my power, regardless, glass sprayed from my hand diagonally into the girl's body. I stared down at her lifeless form in front of me.

The gifted Raidens were fighting with the powers they had kept hidden for so long, they finally found their opportunity to shine. I saw one Raiden teleporting from one place to the next, like lightning across the sky.

I saw Ronan stringing his bow and releasing arrows

engulfed in flames in between fights, aiming to break them up. The eyes of the common Raidens filled with fear. They all seemed to be watching from the sidelines, not attacking or being attacked. A small girl raised her heavy sword and swung at a man twice her size, knocking him out cold. She had strength like no other, her scars a shimmering bronze.

I saw my people in scars of red, blue, yellow, maroon, and colors my eyes couldn't take in. One man with yellow scars was approaching me. I yelled as my eyes burned. A power to blind.

Through the chaos, I struggled to seek out the ones I loved. I tried to find Ronan's fire again.

Anger rose in me, and so did something else.

Suddenly, the fifth dimension shook like an earthquake. I collapsed on my knees.

All was quiet for a moment. Someone stood over me. I saw the tip of a dark brown robe. I shook my head and surveyed above to see a shadowy version of my mother.

Jansen, I heard in my mind. *My son, I need you.*

I barely had time to regain myself when I felt a hand around my neck.

I coughed up blood and felt the tightness increasing on my throat.

Her grip on my mind was like a noose. There was a forced image placed inside my head and I was blind to everything around me. Enclosed in her vision, I was a child again. I was running to my mother, she was cloaked in brown, her face emotionless as she stood solid like a tree. I reached for her, but she did not pick me up. Instead of looking hurt, my child-self turned to stone. Not literally, but I could feel my heart hardening.

The scene shifted to Jerik walking along the cobblestone path coated with broken glass. I sucked in my breath when I realized it wasn't Jerik, but me as a man. I watched my elder version raise his hand and swipe the air. And the glass rebuilt itself into a crystal castle, with a raging sea and dark skies surrounding it. I smiled, my eyes were clear and my hair white as snow. I walked up the path toward the castle. The ones I loved outlined the path, Ronan, Evanna, and the Raidens living in this dimension. Their heads bowed forward, hands folded in front of them, and their eyes closed as I flowed by. I was gliding over the ground like a ghost.

The grip on my neck loosen. Honoria was showing me a future. A future in a new place, where I ruled and that I *created*.

Nothing matches my regret, Honoria's voice flooded my mind, *I was never there for you when you were a child. I cannot undo the past Jansen, but we can build the future. Your power is something you cannot control alone.*

I gasped as my body slid to the ground. The fighting stopped, everyone was staring at Honoria, the Ascendant blooded Raidens stood behind her, their faces filled with pride and loyalty. I felt a kick behind me. I turned my head to see Ronan point an arrow right at Honoria, and a horrid, incomprehensible scene lingered in the sky.

The white scarred Raidens were hovering above the ground, mouths gaped, eyes wide open, they were screaming silently. I saw Shai, his body nearly being pulled apart, blood sprouted from his wrists and his eyes stared into oblivion. They all seemed to be hanging by strings like pale snakes slithering down from the broken sky.

I looked desperately at Ronan; crimson spots stained his pale skin. I examined my sleeves and I saw red droplets fall on me.

The gifted Raidens remained on the ground, suddenly they placed their hands on their temples. I saw Ronan drop his bow as he fell. I felt it, there was a great pain pulsing within my skull. I screamed. She was invading all our minds. Honoria's voice permeated the glass walls of the fifth dimension.

Your minds are not easily manipulated, not like the ones that are stunned in the sky. What you have been told about who you truly are, is wrong. Stop fighting among yourselves, that is what the Herold wants. He is killing you all. I offer you a new world, a world we do not have to hide in.

It sounded so good, although deep in my heart I knew something evil was brewing and the gifted Raidens were believing her. I fought against her utterance but it was too strong. Who would have thought someone without a voice could have such powerful words.

You are all under the manipulation of your leader, Jerik Grey. He murders us for the color of our scars. Honoria took a few steps back and her eyes locked on Ronan and I. *Jansen and Ronan, abandon Jerik. He will kill you both. He is weak-minded because he cannot handle the fears. Follow me, we will not hide our scars. I will help make your minds as invincible as your bodies.*

UNPARALLELED

Honoria paused for a moment and turned her attention to the tribe of colored scarred Raidens behind her. She glanced back at me lovingly and ushered me to come next to her, but I was steadfast. She continued her speech. *Together, with my Jansen, and myself. We can create new dimensions; and we will find the one who can see.*

I felt the release in my mind, and my breath echoed within the chorus of all the others. I looked around wildly. Create dimensions? My mother has just crossed a new bridge of insanity.

One Raiden, the man with the yellow scars who nearly blinded me, looked at Honoria like he was hungry for power, her words entangling him into a trance. All the Raidens behind her came forward, attracted to her temptation.

I glanced at Ronan; his face was painted with a stirring rage.

I met Honoria's eyes. "Create new dimensions?"

Honoria smiled. *Just like you, Jansen. You were not born, you were created. I took you long ago and brought you to life.*

The bitter air was sucked out of this dimension, I tried to take a breath and it left me choking.

Created? I thought. I recalled Honoria's vision of me building a castle from broken parts, and my loved ones bowing to me. My heart started to beat differently. I felt a new pulse within my body.

I can build *worlds*, not shields. I can create dimensions.

I looked down at my palms and then back at my mother, her features were poised like a queen. My brain raced with a maddening idea. "Honoria," I said in awe. "You finally gave me the answer I needed."

I felt her scrape my mind like a Remnant. But I raised my hands from the ground to the crackling glass sky. I could command pure sidereal glass. My scars, in the end, were the stars.

I heard gasps of wonderment. I met Ronan's eyes and he read my mind. He began pulling the Raidens trapped in Honoria's strings down from the ankles. He started with Shai, who looked disoriented, but he joined Ronan in rescuing the rest. They all held the same delusional expression, trying to shake off the trance. My shield cut off Honoria's manipulation on them.

The Ascendant blooded Raidens were frozen, they were looking to Honoria for guidance. I did not want to wait for her next move.

I closed my eyes. I envisioned a safe place and a glass dome fell around the people I wanted to protect. I thought of an opening to another world, and it parted like a giant riptide falling over us.

Ronan smiled and jumped through, followed by the white scarred Raidens, one after the other.

I felt myself weakening. My body shook. My eyes fell on the Raidens behind Honoria. "*Go!*" I screamed.

But they all stared at me like I was the enemy. I could see Honoria's hand was raised, ordering them not to attack. Their bodies stood too still to be subject to their own free will. Her eyes burned into me.

UNPARALLELED

My parents are tyrants, I thought to myself, *and I can't save everyone.*

I held it for a few more seconds. I lingered into blackness before I knew if I saved anyone or if I had sent them into a manipulated abyss.

CHAPTER FORTY-EIGHT

NATALYA

I rose to my feet and ran out of the forest. Bending and twisting to dodge the large thorns. I grazed my hand over a thorn as I ran, but it didn't impale me. When I reached the edge, the fifth dimension was extremely quiet. I darted around Camden, staying close to the Divide. No Raidens were on the cobblestone path. A horrible feeling crawled over my skin. I crept along the hillsides, coming closer to the Herold's house.

The sidereal glass windows illuminated my way. I jogged to the side of the house and slid down the wall. My eyes were half-closed, trying to see through the window but its brightness made it impossible. I listened, what came behind the window was muffled and unclear, but it didn't hide what the sound was; a series of screams came in unison, the terrors flowed like music.

My hands went to my back, I gripped two long knives

and snatched them out, then abruptly felt a hand on my shoulder.

"What are you doing?" A narcotic voice blurted. "I didn't bring you back for you to die on me again. I only have one flower."

I whirled on Sylas; his black eyes were sinking pits. "What's happening here? Where is Eve—"

We both turned as another scream arose. I whipped my long knives in front of me, clinging to them as if I would never hold anything again, and I might not.

Sylas gave me a smile of encouragement. "We'll do this together."

I nodded. We darted toward the front of the Herold's House. I saw the doors had been blown off their hinges. There was light everywhere inside, like the sun itself had bled into the house. The Raidens and their defenses all aimed at Sylas, I jumped in front of him. At that moment they deemed me as an enemy too.

I reacted to the need to survive. I screamed as a girl, no older than myself, pointed a knife toward my chest. I dodged and held one of the long knives forward, the girl spun for a counterattack and her body rammed into my blade. She fell to the ground.

My mouth gaped as I stared at the body. My eyes took in the girl's torn clothing, exposing a series of deep purple scars. I wondered what her power was. How long had she kept this secret? Did anyone that cared for her know she had Ascendant blood? But my questions will never be answered, I hadn't even known her name. I didn't mean to kill her, she turned too fast and plunged right into my exposed blade. She didn't know I was trying to right the wrongs. In my best attempt to do good, I do evil. I will never have the chance to tell her that we are the same, we are not enemies. If only I could rewind the clock. Death likes to mock its victims, as does time.

Another Raiden was on me, a middle-aged man raised his sword. I lowered my knives. He can kill me; it was well deserved now. As his arm came forward, I saw a glimmer of blue like the sea. I dove immediately. It felt more automatic than voluntary, like something internal was trying to protect me.

"*Stop!*" I yelled. I took the edges of my sleeves and yanked them off, exposing my series of patterned gold scars. I held my arms up in front of the man and held my breath.

He froze, his sword hung in midair.

"We're all on the same side," I said gesturing to myself and Sylas, who was defending himself poorly by the sword, but well with manipulation. A Raiden girl stood frozen in his trance. The other Raidens seemed to calm their chaos, their eyes trailing to me.

"You say," the man said breathily. "We are all on the same side, and you stand with a mind manipulator?"

Sylas released his subject. The girl sucked in her breath and fell to the floor, making the other Raidens raise their weapons again.

"*Monster,*" the man grunted through his teeth.

"No!" I yelled.

Sylas regained his composure. "I'm not the monster

lining you up in my own home to kill you."

The man did not have time to answer. An arrow went through his back, sticking out of his chest. The Raidens scattered like insects across the floor, I've never seen Raidens in such vulnerable terror.

I looked up, Jerik was on the floor bleeding with Ace standing at his side, a black bow in hand.

"Natalya Wells," Ace's burly voice called.

I glared at him, that was the first time he said my name. Anger flooded through me. "Now, you call me by my name?" I said in a frightening whisper.

I took off up the stairs, pulling out my long knives. I was going to kill him.

CHAPTER FORTY-NINE

JANCE

I did not kill anyone, nor did I create the dimension I envisioned in my mind. I did, however, hold a shield that encamped half of the fifth dimension. I saved the Raidens from Honoria's manipulation. The shield had fallen away when I did, perhaps my mother had been lying.

I woke on Ronan's couch. For a moment, I pretended it was all a dream. I clung desperately to the past when it was just Ronan and me. My days passed with scoutings, training, and the occasional murder. I shivered. I hated my past as well, so why was I wanting it back? I could see every Seer's face I had killed. The dismay in my father's eyes as he glared at my scars. The past can be sickening, but at the same time comforting and familiar. I took a shaky breath, no matter what, there is no going back.

Ronan was next to me, he smiled. Shai stood behind

him.

"You've been holding out Grey," Shai said with his arms crossed.

I shook my head. "Where's Honoria?"

"Gone," Ronan said simply. He grabbed my hand and pulled me from the couch.

Shai nodded. "The Raidens she had a hold of are safe at my family's weaponry. But something is going on in the Herold's House—"

"Let's go then," I announced as I grabbed my sword from the floor. Ronan and Shai nodded, they always looked ready to fight. I never did, I wasn't a good soldier whatsoever. But I will willingly leap into death's arms if it means protecting the ones I love.

We reached my home in seconds, the bolted doors had vanished, the house was filled with cries and struggles. We walked into a war. My home, the place where Raidens came for shelter and safety was now a battleground. The grey stone was masked with Raiden blood.

I saw the Ascendant trying to calm the Raidens. I could hear him saying that they all had a gift. But my eyes were drawn to the stairs, I froze. I heard Shai and Ronan gasp. Natalya galivanted up the stairs with a wicked look, her side was bloodstained. She was charging toward Ace, and a wounded man cowered beside him with light hair that resembled my own, my father.

I screamed and Natalya turned. Her green eyes met mine, and in an instant, I felt like everything might be okay. She was alive. I wanted time to stop so I could run and take her in my arms—but time was not my subject of manipulation.

Ace beat Natalya to the attack, I yelled her name a split second before Ace sent her flying down the stairs. I ran and caught her, she struggled to get away from me and back to Ace. For some reason this made me grip her tighter, unable to let go.

"Jance—" she started. "I know I'm alive."

I released my hold as Ace descended toward us. I felt helpless, I saw my father raise his head. I sucked in my breath. His hair looked whiter like mine was in Honoria's vision.

Ace was suddenly above us, I tossed Natalya aside, trying to protect her.

Suddenly a flaming arrow appeared, clipping Ace's arm, I could hear the incineration of his skin.

I saw Natalya's eyes linger toward Jerik. And behind him, Evanna was creeping from Jerik's room.

For a brief moment, my heart was whole. Everyone I loved was around me and breathing.

I returned my attention to Ace, who stood growling. I heard Ronan string another arrow. I clung to my short sword, trusting Ronan to injure Ace just enough to stop him. I needed to get to my father and find Honoria. I reached out to touch Natalya's shoulder, just to know that she was there. My priority is, and always will be, the people I love.

CHAPTER FIFTY
NATALYA

The instant I saw all of them this broken world felt like it had been put back together. Jance, Ronan, and Shai looked extremely weak but their eyes had fire behind them. I could see Eve in the background, her blue eyes held mine for a split second, a flood of emotion was exchanged between us.

There was blood coming from Shai's shoulders, but his face was filled with joy. Ronan looked at me amazed, but not surprised, as he strung his arrow. And Jance—he looked like he had a reason to live again. His embrace on my shoulder was almost painful, I could feel my veins pulsating under his grip. His face was fixated with a deathly glare toward Ace.

Another arrow flew in the air landing in Ace's shoulder. It occurred to me that Ronan was not trying to kill Ace. I'm sure he could tell us things we probably needed to know. I felt he wasn't worth it. Whether you held a knife to his throat and threatened him lies could still come from his mouth.

Ace fell down the stone staircase and Jance leaped to his father. Ace's body tumbled right beside me.

Time slowed down. When Ace slid by me I didn't notice the knife he held in his right hand. I didn't have time to react when he raised it in front of my face. His hand came down and I closed my eyes like a coward. I heard someone fall, followed by a cry of pain.

A heap of curly hair laid on top of my body. Shai had thrown himself in front of me and Ace's knife was embedded in his chest. My eyes went right to Ace, one of Shai's knives protruded from his side as well.

The crowd of Raidens was flooded with anger and confusion. Pointing fingers at each other, they fought with their words mercilessly. Ronan approached the crowd and I had to hold my breath as a knife almost went right through Ronan's chest, and Eve bounded down the stairs toward Ronan. Sylas wrapped an arm around Ronan's chest as the Raidens continued to argue.

I jumped, feeling helpless. Shai was leaning his weight against me. I met his fading eyes. "Natalya—"

"Shh," I said trying to control my shaky breath. "It's okay, you'll be okay—"

"Natalya," Shai cut me off. "I want you to stand with those that can take you to new worlds. Question when you need to question, but also listen when you need to listen. Promise me you'll never lose your spirit." He smiled.

I managed to smile back, tears forming pools in my eyes. "I promise."

Shai's face grew serious. "And be careful who you trust. The company you keep holds many secrets."

I hesitated, but Shai's eyes were looking at Jance, who was kneeling over his father. Jance did have secrets, but Shai didn't know the weight he carried. "I know," was all I could say.

I felt Shai stroke the side of my face. "It's not the end," he said.

I felt tears slide down my cheeks, not sure if it was weakness, or if it was the slight aspect of being human I was desperate to hold on to. I had formed new bonds with people I never thought existed. Now, they were my world, and to lose someone made me question everything. "I am at the end where it should have never begun."

And then his hand fell, his body felt heavier. Shai's eyes were blank and lifeless and his chest no longer rose and fell. I sucked in my breath repeatedly, feeling like I was suffocating.

Above me, there was Jance and his father; Jance's face twisting with a mix of shock and disgust. Below me, Sylas and Ronan were still trying to gain control of the Raidens, who all seemed to have calmed down. Eve stood protectively beside Ronan, but I could feel her eyes lock on me. In front of me was the dead body of a person who I had grown to love, and beside him, a man who I wished was dead.

I stood and Ace managed to stand as well, he pulled out Shai's knife from his ribs. Remorse filled his eyes and then he dashed through the doorway into the night.

JENNA HEBERT

I took off after him, working my way around the Raidens, stumbling over the injured and deceased. My eyes grazed over the stone floor and my feet left bloody footprints behind. Nothing was stopping me, when I felt a hand grab my arm, I yanked it back. I saw it was Eve out of the corner of my eye.

Ace had vanished, but I could see a gory red trail. I followed it, leading around the house and it disappeared. I yelled and slammed my fists against the house then I fell forward. My head shot up to see that Ace had entered through the hidden door that Jance showed me, one that led to Honoria's room and the rooftop. I followed the crimson tracks up the winding staircase.

CHAPTER FIFTY-ONE

JANCE

My father was smiling. "She's *alive*."

I saw Natalya disappear after Ace, I wanted to dart after her but my father was gripping my shirt like it was his last thread of life.

"You," my father choked, "were created, not born."

In a matter of seconds, I discovered my whole life was a sick, twisted lie. My father was never my father. My cousin was never my cousin. I didn't have a father or a cousin. Or a mother. One parent has been out to kill me my whole life, while another wants me to create new worlds while holding strings around my neck.

Jerik's grey eyes were now swarming with a clear tint. "You were placed here as an experiment, but there is someone who has been manipulating me into other thinking. Like a force

I cannot see Jance. Something that moves like a shadow in my mind. I swear it's real."

"A Remnant Ghost? If you let them invade your mind, they will win Jerik." I said quickly, unable to call him father.

"No," Jerik said, coughing, a little blood coming from his mouth. "A Raiden, someone with a unique power, something wicked." His eyes met mine. "I hoped Ace would kill you because I did not want to do it. I need Natalya. She shattered the House of Mirrors. Even though the damn Ascendant wiped it away, but nothing gets by me."

The look in my father's eyes told me he wasn't lying. "Why do you need her?"

Jerik's eyes went wild. "The one that's been plaguing my mind, the shadow. I sought to clean our race away from the Ascendants. Someone I once loved has betrayed me. And Ace has betrayed me. He decided the side he's taking just seconds ago," Jerik's voice was cracking. "They all want something... someone," he spoke breathily. "Yes. The one who can *see*. Must. Be. Found. I will find it before *her*."

"The one who can *see what*?" I begged.

"Look at your eyes, Jansen Grey. They are pale and your hair lacks color. It is the sign of someone who has been heavily manipulated. The whole Grey line is finished," Jerik spurted. "*She* will not be more powerful than me, the sixth dimension will be the unbinding."

I stuttered at his unexpected words. "The sixth dimension?"

Jerik nodded, taking shaky breaths.

I gritted my teeth. "What do you want with Natalya?"

"Her power...will destroy—" Jerik choked.

I couldn't breathe, I was almost tempted not to, wondering if I even needed to, can an experiment survive without air? I didn't even know if I wanted to be living at all. "I want to know one more thing—"

But my words were cut off as the man who I thought was my father, plunged a knife in between my shoulder and chest.

With amazing speed, Jerik darted to his room. I could see him through the entryway disappear as he walked through the mirror, into the nightmares it held.

I roared as I pulled the knife out of my body and stood.

CHAPTER FIFTY-TWO
NATALYA

Ace was kneeling on the fountain, the same place where Jance and I almost kissed. He was mumbling to himself. "Where are you?"

I walked slowly toward him. I didn't see anyone he could be speaking to.

He cut himself off, grunting in pain. His hands going to his head.

My heart surged, I reached for my long knives in my back. "Ace!"

He spun on his knees and smiled. "Are you going to kill me Natalya?"

"You killed Shai..." I said fighting tears.

Ace laughed again, and then he was suddenly thrown backward, knocked unconscious.

Something dark whipped past me, casting the long knives from my grasp. I fell to the ground, the white stone illuminating brightly in my eyes. A mix of shadow and human. I had seen Remnant Ghosts, their scary figures and narrow faces, what stood before me was nothing like that. It was a dark blot cloaked in a remote brown and it cascaded downward like long hair.

I pushed myself upward to find my long knives. My hand met the hilt of the first one as the figure stomped on the blade. I gasped. It shattered into pieces. I felt my heart break with it.

Natalya Wells, what kind of poor manipulation are you?

That voice. I've heard it in my head before, I met a pair of dark brown eyes.

You have made a mistake. I am the greatest manipulator and I hold the strings.

"Honoria Grey," I said with shock. She was an earthy shadow, like tree roots that had dissolved into brown air.

Honoria seemed to laugh at the name. *You don't know anything do you? My name is Honoria Merciless.*

"Names are earned," I said. "Merciless fits you well."

I felt a strike against my side and a cut along my arm. Honoria held a longsword like the one Sylas carried. Red seeped through my skin and then it healed, replaced by gold. That was the quickest I've ever seen scars layer over skin. The shape of stars outlined with curved designs covered the wound.

Honoria's expression was full of amazement. Ghostly arms traveled up my spine as she continued to bury her voice deep into my consciousness. *You have no memory of where you*

came from. You grew from the age of seven in the Dead Land.
The Divide did not part for you, it broke, and sidereal glass did
not touch your skin beforehand. You impossibly entered the fifth
dimension. The only reason it was not shattered entirely was
because you were blindly unaware of your power, and you still are.
You can do something that absolutely no one else can do.

I reached for a new long knife. "You know my power?"

I do, Honoria echoed in my mind. *I am giving you a*
choice. You were born a Seer, and you can go back to your original
life. Free of Remnants, free of terror, you will have no memory of
this. Truthfully, I do not want to kill you.

I didn't understand her words. "There is no going back—
"

Are you sure? You died here girl, and you were supposed
to stay dead, but the time manipulator was on your side.

She was talking about Sylas. "Time manipulation..." I
said. "The fifth dimension, it's as far as you can go without going
back?"

Yes. This is the total and complete future; it's called the
Lost Paradise for that reason.

My grip on my weapon tightened. "Does this have
anything to do with the one who can *see*?"

Everything.

"See what?" I asked.

Everything.

I had enough. I threw my knife in Honoria's direction, a
poor attempt, she diverted it effortlessly.

She remained calm. *Natalya do you want to know*

yourself wholly? Or continue to be broken? You do not know how dangerous you are. Part of you wants to see this destruction. You will not be able to begin again if you make that choice. I am giving you your only chance. You are designed to be the downfall of all the strings that hold the dimensions together. You, destroy.

Honoria's voice echoed in my mind and it couldn't be blocked out. The Remnants can scratch the surface, but they can be conquered if you learn to guard your conscience. But Honoria, her voice, her *words*, were hypnotizing. She didn't say anything unique; she didn't use big words and she didn't have too. I had learned about the manipulation of the body, the mind, and time itself. I knew there was the manipulation of words. I remembered how Sylas had spoken about it after my nightmare of the Bowing Tree. It was the only time Sylas looked truly heartbroken.

I watched Honoria's hand, it was coated with dark brown strings, like spiders crawling around in her palm. "Your power," I said, "is words. You're a word manipulator like the Bowing Tree."

Honoria looked obliterated at the mention of the story. *She was my ancestor and a fool. She had the gift of words and she never used it. When she finally did, she cursed herself and her lover, who did nothing but lie. Played her and many others like puppets on a string.* Honoria's words seemed to weaken in my head, I noticed tears forming in her eyes. *For making me love and thinking I am being loved in return, is the ultimate manipulation.*

I finally understood the story of the Bowing Tree, *Mendax, Mendax,* Liar, Liar. I took a shaky breath and concluded what happened to Honoria, and Nicoletta, the past had repeated itself.

I swallowed hard. All wrongdoings should be brought to justice, but vengeance can be a prison. I understood wanting to be heard, especially when everyone refuses to hear you. But true power doesn't live in revenge and I learned that the hard way. I cannot fix this. Honoria's pain is not mine to endure. Regardless, she told me what I needed to know. My direction is forward, and I must fight for who I am. It's too late for her, but not for me.

I took advantage of Honoria's emotional weakness. I leaned down and wrapped my hand around the knife she had broken. I was the storm and the sea. I could sway the waves, but not calm them. I unraveled from the seams where I am barely stitched together.

My hands seized with tremors and the gold shined on my skin. I threw my long knife and it soared into the sky as a crackling echo mimicked the familiar voice in my head, *destroy it.*

I gasped and looked up. I could see the blood sun rising behind the Divide and I thought I heard thunder for the first time. I realized suddenly that it was not thunder; it was the sound of the sky breaking.

You are just what I thought you could be, and more, Honoria's voice rang in my mind.

"You don't know me," I said, reaching to my back and then froze, I was out of long knives.

Neither do you.

I gritted my teeth. The sidereal glass shard was still hidden under my armor. I am a catastrophic masterpiece. The image of the church Sylas had shown me was contained in the flower in my pocket. Honoria was referencing my memories in my past, my creation, and my true purpose for my existence. I had two pieces of me, I do not know where the rest are. Pain and death exist here, and everywhere. But I have friends, I have a power I have yet to discover, and most of all there was something to fight for. Save the Seers, save the world that still exists if someone can go back far enough. This world is inescapable. The dimensions, the worlds in between the real world, gave the escape that humanity will always search for. And some find it, only if they can *see* it.

"Honoria, you're right. I do not know myself," I said as I looked the word manipulator in the eye. "But I will not go back to find it. I am not my past; I am the future. I have a gift beyond the natural world and I will embrace my power." I took a shaky breath, but my voice came out like iron, "I am *not* a subject of your manipulation."

I threw the broken long knife and it struck Honoria's arm. She glared at me in shock, not pain.

I lowered my body, my right leg crossing over my left, and my arms expanded out like a bird. I kept my eyes high, just like the girl with the three and a half knives. "There's your goddamn bow," I said with fire.

Honoria pulled out the knife and screamed. Her body suddenly caved from the inside out, shrinking to a shadow. Her eyes remained the same and they were looking at me with an endarkened threat.

Honoria wasted no time; her whole being went through

me. I screamed, feeling sickly blood race down the side of my face, my vision blurred, and my body went cold. I dodged out of the way before Honoria could strike again. She moved like the Remnants, overconsumed with manipulation.

Suddenly, two figures erupted from the attic entrance. I jerked my head to see Ronan and Sylas.

Honoria seemed terrified at Sylas, his black eyes fixated on her, and she fled like a ghost in the sky, washing away into the new sun rising. My mind finally felt at peace.

"Natalya!" I heard Ronan shout.

There was a hand on my back. The last thing I saw was the magical eyes of Sylas.

CHAPTER FIFTY-THREE
EVANNA

I walked out of the Herold's House. The Raidens seemed to be in a daze, unable to comprehend what exactly was going on. Although I didn't know what was going on either. Shai was dead. Honoria and Jerik were gone. Ace was under arrest and may be executed. Jance could create new worlds. Ronan was with an Ascendant named Sylas, who apparently, brought my best friend back from the dead. And to top it all off, there was a ginormous break in the sky and the Divide might crush us all any second.

I kept my ears open to gather information as I walked the cobblestone path. I spent half my life on this path and the other half in the labyrinth of the Ascendant's hold. And one year with my best friend. I heard talk about the Unparalleled. The word becoming the universal statement for ones with Ascendant blood. But I heard the tone of the voices speaking, saying 'unparalleled' like one would say alien, with fear and a hint of curiosity. Something that wanted to be shouted, but everyone still whispered. I listened as I walked.

"Natalya Wells, the one that came through the Divide."

"She has gold scars, *gold*!"

"She's a hero, she saved us from Honoria."

"She could be behind it all. She's one of the...others."

"I saw her being carried down from the rooftop by that Ascendant, and Ronan Surestrike. What happened to her long knives? The fourth was broken. Doesn't that remind you of a story? The girl with three and a half knives."

"There are rumors about the ones that could find the sixth dimension. She could be the one, and we would be out of this prison forever! Look! The Divide is breaking!"

"Do you think she could set us free?"

"Jansen Grey created a new sky!"

"He shielded us. He protected us from Honoria."

"Ronan Surestrike, the boy with no memory, he can manipulate fire."

"Can we trust those with Ascendant blood? Honoria had them all lined up as her subjects."

"It was our leaders that betrayed us. We were hanging on their strings."

"Jerik Grey was trying to kill the Unparalleled ones. I do not understand, it's like what is happening with the Seers. Do we continue to murder? It doesn't feel right."

I stopped walking when I heart my name.

"Evanna Grey returned with a disaster right behind her.

Whatever stupid decisions she made that brought this upon us...I wonder if she has regrets?"

This made me burst into laughter. Perhaps I shouldn't regret; all those stupid decisions made me brave. Be brave or be stupid? They are one in the same.

After I laughed, I cried.

The words I heard from the Raidens were not all that bad. I kept my head and eyes forward, not feeling an immediate need to escape the crowd. I embraced it. When you've been scarred in ways you never thought humanly possible, torn and betrayed by those you expected to be your leaders and loved ones, and witnessed the death of your best friend. You learned that being talked about was the least of your concerns. I let the whispers and words fly. I even met the eyes of some of them, who quickly looked away.

When I circled back around to the Herold's House, I saw Jance and Ronan in the distance, they noticed me immediately. Ronan came running and scooped me up in his arms like I was weightless. I got lost in his breathing for a second, and then I forgot to breathe as he kissed me. I smiled as he lowered me to the ground with care.

My cousin approached me slowly, he cleared his throat. "Evanna, I'm not—"

I cut him off by throwing my arms around him. "I know. I know, and I don't care. You're my cousin, my brother, my family. Nothing will ever change that."

He embraced me back. "Natalya is alive."

I smiled as I breathed into his shoulder. "I know that

too."

***

Since the sky was about to fall, Ria ordered all Raidens to retreat to the Undercity. Everyone was quickly gathering belongings and shouting about, still in dismay of the past events.

I walked the halls of the Herold's House for the last time, collecting a few sketches in my room. I realized the glass shard was nowhere to be found; I knew exactly who had it.

I headed into Honoria's room and was welcomed by the rotting smell of the once beautiful flowers. I scanned the room in disbelief. I picked up a rose, its root had turned black, the petals were shriveled, and only a slight blood color remained. Suddenly, it started to feel like granules were shedding off it then it turned to ash, slipping out from the spaces in between my fingers. I was hoping the blood memories they contained would give me some information. It was hopeless now.

I dusted off my hands as I heard footsteps approaching. Ronan's broad figure came into view. My eyes met his and they filled with tears. Ronan's arms wrapped around my torso, trying to comfort me.

Water slid down my cheeks as I pulled away from him. I will never forgive my uncle. He will pay for killing Raidens and Seers, my soul was hardening and echoing the need for justice. All the torture I endured was not in vain. Pain can cripple some people, they shut themselves out and refuse to fight back. While others use it as a weapon and harnessed it to increase their willpower. You can wear pain like a noose or carry it like a ball and chain.

UNPARALLELED

I took a final look around the decapitating garden through blurry eyes and left. I carried my pain with pride out of the house I grew up in.

CHAPTER FIFTY-FOUR
NATALYA

I opened my eyes and narrowed them due to the brightness. I was in a white room. I was barely strong enough to walk and I stumbled when I tried to rise. My vision finally cleared, and I saw blood streaked along the walls.

My breathing increased as my legs finally allowed me to go forward. I maneuvered down the halls and the steel floors echoed against my footsteps until it changed to red dirt. I felt better instantly, and I started to run. Then I collided with a cloaked figure, I shoved against him, knowing who it was. "Where the hell am I?" my words tumbling out of my mouth.

Sylas didn't budge against my weight. "The Undercity, follow me," he said, nearly disappearing as he blended into the darkness.

I jogged up to him. "The Raidens—"

"Have nearly destroyed one another. To ease your concern, your friends are safe."

I felt comforted. "Good."

Sylas said nothing but continued down a path that grew broader as we traveled. The Undercity was a labyrinth of tunnels that all looked the same. The outline of Sylas sunk deeper into the shadows until I could no longer see him.

"Sylas!" I called out.

There was no answer.

I stopped, there was no sound of movement like he suddenly vanished into thin air. I was alone.

I fell to my knees and screamed, a scream that could shatter the world. I felt foolish to trust the Ascendant. I was so confident. I wanted to believe in him so badly. Only to find out I had been on his strings all along.

We are all subjects of manipulation, I thought. I felt both manipulated and betrayed. I'm losing control. The ability to see beyond a manipulation was something I pride myself on, the House of Mirrors couldn't fool me. In the real world, I had been terribly wrong, I made the perfect subject.

I felt the halls narrow, and the walls began to slide closer together, causing it all to shake.

Did he bring me here to be crushed to death? I don't understand why he didn't kill me a long time ago.

Because, I thought, *like all Ascendants they want not only physical but a mental death.*

My self-esteem plummeted from his betrayal. Rising

anxiety whipped through my mind like a Remnant. What if Eve, Jance, and Ronan were behind this? Why else would they allow me to go so easily with the Ascendant when they thought he was our enemy? I spiraled from one horrid thought to the other.

I stood and screamed even louder. My vision was tipped with dark edges, like ink bleeding into my eyes. *I will not die a subject of their manipulation!* I screamed in my mind.

I ran toward a wall, feeling the solid space, I felt curves like the side of a mountain. I pulled my weight up, lifting my feet off the ground.

The scene shifted.

Water was falling on my face and lightning bolts flashed as a sky opened above. I was on a cliff. Below was a raging sea and the edge was high above me.

It's not real, I thought. But the rock became slippery under my fingers as the thunder came with a piercing crack. The more I told myself it wasn't real the more real it became. The rain fell fast, I was losing my grip in the crevasses of the rock.

Here were all my fears at once. Sylas had betrayed me, what lay below was the depth of the sea, and above was the height of the cliff. Feeling all my fears at once made me feel nothing at all. My physical body was failing, and my mind was urging me to let go, and let the deep take me.

I looked up for what I thought to be the final time. Then something triggered me, an impulsive feeling, like a volcano beginning to erupt when I saw the broken glass sky was so close to the top of the cliff. It was electrifying, the pieces had light shining through them.

UNPARALLELED

I climbed. My mind not thinking of the height above or depth below. One foot, one hand at a time, and I didn't stop. The thunder and lightning turned into a gentle thud and barely a flicker.

I reached the surface of the cliff, hoisting my weight up and I stood victoriously. I touched the sky, seeing the whole picture but feeling each piece, reminding me that in the end it was not meant to be whole, only pieced together.

Destroy it.

I reached back and grabbed one of my long knives, and by chance, it was the broken one. I stepped forward preparing to throw, then I saw something peculiar on the rocky ground, it was the shattered pieces of my knife. For a second, I thought I wanted to collect them, so I could repair it. But I stopped, taking a long look at the shards. The pieces paralleled the brokenness of the sky.

My foot went back, and I kicked the pieces over the edge, I watched them fall into the sea.

I'd rather carry three and a half knives proudly instead of mending a broken blade. Because no matter if it were back together or not, it would never be the same as it was before. To be shattered into pieces one must embrace being broken. Then, only in time, it will begin to heal.

I faced the sky, and my arm went backward as I launched the knife with all the force I had, it struck the sky like lightning against a tree. It exploded in slow motion. The sky fell and a red sky appeared behind the drips of shattering glass. My gold scars glittered in the new light. For the first time, I could feel the heat of the sun and the naked wind against my face. A red bird flew across, matching the color of the sky.

Destroy it, I thought as I smiled proudly. The knife fell back down, and I caught it in the air.

"Natalya Wells."

A familiar voice echoed behind me. I turned. He still had the same domineer, except he looked shiny, more superhuman than human.

The broken long knife fell from my hand. "Mr. Barnes?"

"You were listening that day in class?"

"But how?" I asked.

"You were brought into this manipulation for a reason. Sylas did not betray you, but he did test you. Indeed, you are the Destroyer."

I hesitated. "The Destroyer?

"Yes," Mr. Barnes said. "First of all, my real name is Eroe Bending, I am an Ascendant. A very old one. I can manipulate my way from the fourth dimension to the fifth, but I am unable to bring myself back to the real world anymore."

I came closer, approaching him like I would a ghost.

He moved like he was pacing around the classroom, he gazed into the blood-filled sky. "I was against it—I held my ground against the violent manipulations that turned humans to Remnants, but others with power recruited more Ascendants to their side. Alda is forever my enemy. When the experiments got out of hand, the Remnants kept breeding underground where we buried them, they came back with an avenging spirit we could not conquer."

I choked. "Mr. Barnes...*how* did humans turn into such demonic creatures?"

"Call me Eroe," he said calmly. "The Ascendants took the humans who performed evil acts in the world. Their intentions were like this, if they took the bad people out of the world, they were doing the world a favor. Before they were Remnants, they were known in the world as criminals and murders, horrible people of all kinds. They did not know what to expect. When we tore open the minds of those who had chosen evil, they were rebirthed into demons of their own feats." Eroe seemed to look distant, his mind lost in the past.

"What happened?" I edged him on.

Eroe took a deep breath. "When the Ascendants realized what had become of their failed manipulations we feared for our race. We, being myself and a few others, created another superhuman phenomenon that stretched the boundaries of imagination and physical capabilities. We called them the Scarred Ones."

I nodded. "Raidens, after the warrior who set us free."

Eroe raised his eyebrows. "So it is said. Originally you were already free."

"That's not the story I heard."

Eroe's intense green eyes locked on me and he walked with a certain grace that was older than time. "It was my idea. We wanted to connect the human mind to human pain. To scar someone over and over, to heal stronger and faster every time."

My face twisted. "*Your* idea?"

Eroe raised his hands, I saw the same webbed pattern

over his palms just like Sylas's. "Raidens are not descendants of humans, but Ascendants. *Willing* Ascendants who wanted to give up everything, their mind, and immortality, to become what we envisioned."

"You're saying that we are descendants of Ascendants?" I questioned.

Eroe nodded. "You *all* have Ascendant blood...the story you know was greatly manipulated. Question everything Natalya, think for yourself. Some Ascendants were indeed afraid of the Scarred Ones, but not all of us had evil intentions."

"But why?" I probed.

Eroe flinched. "When I presented the Scared Ones to the Ascendant leaders at the time, they were like you. Colored scars and magnificent abilities. My leaders felt they were *too* strong, *too* invincible. They were so blinded by their fear of being overpowered, that they wanted to alter my experiments—" Eroe choked, running fingers through his hair in frustration. "It's been countless years...and it still sends anger through me. I'm afraid I'll never be able to overcome it."

"What did they do?" I asked.

"They tortured them...after that my precious creations came out different. White scars, with the colors and gifts, stripped away. When that happened, my friends and I were banished from the fifth dimension while the rest of the Ascendants enslaved the Scarred Ones. There carries on the tale that is told by the Raidens today. They all know the story, but no one knows the prologue."

I was speechless. My mind was racing as I struggled

for words. "There's nothing wrong with us? We *all* have Ascendant blood. And the white scarred Raidens are just further manipulated?"

"Correct, Miss Wells," Eroe said in a voice that sounded like I was back in school.

"How can the ones you created still exist? Raidens are not immortal."

"The lucky few who still had the DNA started spontaneously emerging from some Raiden families, proving that my experiment was stronger than I imagined. I created three uniquely gifted Raidens, hundreds of years and countless failures eventually lead to something unparalleled to all creation. That's what I called them, the Unparalleled, one that I kept close, one that was stolen, and one that is lost."

"Am I—" I choked with a mix of astonishment and denial.

"I kept you close, Natalya. You were born a Seer. The only time I was able to enter the real world was when I came for you. I remade you." Eroe said with a passion that had a hint of love behind it.

I never thought about having parents. I had no memory to fill those human emotions or desires. I was a blank piece of paper, but I'm discovering the invisible ink all over me. I gazed at Eroe's face, I felt I was looking at the only version of a father I would ever know. "I'm your catastrophic masterpiece. I heard you say that in this—" I whipped out the shard. "Did you create me to be so broken on purpose?"

Eroe looked at me sympathetically. "I eliminated

your previous life from your mind. I had to put the memories somewhere—it was also insurance if you died, you would be able to live on. Everyone wants to be undone from what they are, which is impossible, but not for you."

I observed the sight beyond the cliff, my eyes followed down to the ocean where I had discarded the shards of my broken blade. Knowing I had already made a choice, but still, something deep down in my heart was calling to my worldly life. I felt anger rise because my curiosity demanded that I know; I had to have all the answers. "Why am I not allowed to remember?"

Eroe hesitated. "I will tell you the truth. The shard and the flower are parts of your memory to keep you alive. I made sure they were in the hands of someone I trusted, Sylas. He gave the shard to Jerik Grey, who gave it to little Evanna Grey, as a key to come back to the Lost Paradise. It was no coincidence Natalya, that you and Evanna arrived as a pair in the Dead Land. I put you there, and Sylas helped Evanna crossover. Sylas kept the flower. I abandoned the rest of your memories in unknown places and took out my memories of where I sent them."

My heart thudded with a sudden flow of rage. "Why the hell would you do that?!"

He shook his head. "Natalya, if you are determined to put those pieces together you will lose everything that I designed you to be. To destroy, one must *be* destroyed."

I was shaking, my hand enclosing around my knife I dropped. I embraced my broken knife and the shard against my shoulder, wrapping them in a tight hug. I was clinging to my existence and it was cutting right through me. I felt blood trickle down my neck.

Eroe's face was painted with empathy as if he felt my pain. "Other worlds exist outside these glass walls, now you must shatter the sky. I know what you desperately desire, to save the children, along with the Raidens and Ascendants. We *all* came from humans, the Seers. They grew to Ascendants, please understand not all of us are like the ones you've come to know. The good ones are magicians, and some sacrificed themselves to be bound to the magic in the stars and they became Raidens. Your scars will illuminate in the dark because you are made of starlight. Think about Raiden himself, names have power. Radiant is the word his name diverged from. Whether we be Seer, Ascendant, or Raiden, we all have a heart that beats, a body that bleeds, a mind that envisions, and an everlasting soul."

"Save the Seers, make the Raidens understand that not all Ascendants are evil, and take down the ones that are. Unite the Raidens by telling them we all have Ascendant blood...we are all one." I trailed off and took a large breath. "I have to rewrite the story of the world."

"The world has many stories. You will find light and darkness in all individuals. The one thing you can count on is the existence of polarities. But you are not alone." Eroe comforted.

I scraped my foot against the rocks, watching the pebbles fall into the sea. "You said there are three Unparalleled?"

"You know another one," Eroe said.

Deep in my heart I knew the answer. "Jance," I whispered.

"He is the Creator," Eroe said slowly. "He was stolen from

me by another great manipulator."

I narrowed my eyes. "Honoria Merciless."

Eroe nodded. "She brought him to Jerik Grey under disguise. She is a master of manipulation with a talent for taking over minds with words."

I couldn't comprehend her power. "Honoria is a Raiden—"

"Is she though?" Eroe interrupted. "She has fallen into the depths of dark manipulation. And no matter what she has designed herself to be, we all fall under the category of superhuman. But there is one part in that word that is more important than the other."

"Human..." I trailed off.

Eroe nodded with a tender smile. "The shields Jansen can manipulate are not just a glass protection. He can create new dimensions. Honoria wanted to save him and destroy you. Jerik wanted to save you and destroy Jansen. They both had evil intentions working against each other," Eroe said heavily.

I frowned. "Why would Jerik want to save me?"

Eroe glowered. "The man was obsessed with dimensional travel, he wanted to get to the sixth dimension. There's some rumor that retreating to a new dimension can separate the Herold from the mirror, and he would survive the process. The same way you appeared in the fifth dimension with no evidence of your injuries from the massacre in the fourth. Jerik stuck his nose in places it shouldn't have been. He saw you explode through the House of Mirrors and assumed you were the Destroyer. He was threatened by his wife and he made many mistakes in trying to escape his hell. But his biggest mistake was going up against Honoria. She also knew about you and wanted you dead or sent back into the past. Jerik sought to destroy the rest of the gifted Raidens because he wanted to bring her down. He was old fashioned and wanted to keep the Raidens pure and protect the Grey line."

"Wow." I stammered. "You should have seen all the flowers in Honoria's room."

Eroe's expression turned sad. "Every rose has its thorns and some of them have knives. Deception is a learned traumatic trait that can easily blind truth, especially when the lies are good. What you have been told from the very beginning is true, we are all subjects of manipulation. Everyone is subject to something, and sometimes someone." He sighed. "Honoria shares the same power and made the same choices as her ancestor Nicoletta did. Talk to Sylas about the girl with the three and a half knives and the Remnant with blue eyes, he knows the untold details."

I nodded. Sylas seemed to be personally connected to the story. "There was no forgiveness," I commented.

"And no escape," Eroe continued. "Honoria stayed in the comforts of the Herold's House, mute and alone creating a bitter plan. She wanted to rule, she never agreed with Jerik's thoughts on Jansen and she wanted to use the powers the gifted Raidens possessed. In the end, both Jerik and Honoria failed in their endless desire to become all-powerful. They've vanished." Eroe came close to me, putting a hand lightly on my shoulder. "Know this, they both saw you as an average Raiden with a different past, but you are so much more than what they believed. You are not a subject on their strings. You proved that in the end."

I swallowed hard and gripped his hand on my shoulder, a wave of impenetrable faith washed over me. It was the belief in myself. I rose from the depths where they tried to bury me and I'll let them sink in quicksand, along with the death of my doubt. "They both wanted something that could make them powerful. It's the one who can *see,* isn't it?"

"The third, the last, the one I lost..." Eroe faded.

"Where are they?" I urged desperately.

"It's complicated Natalya," Eroe said.

I felt he was withholding a secret. "You were my teacher. I am not just your creation, you *know* me. You can trust me," I said with certainty.

Eroe took a sharp inhale. "Above all else, I should trust my creations..." he trailed off, his voice shaking on the words.

I winced at the term creations. I had a heartbeat and I breathed. I was invincible and alive. My face contorted into a determined frown. "Are they in the fifth dimension?"

Eroe looked mystified as if he had forgotten where he was. "No, he shouldn't be...could he?"

Eroe grew fearful. I let out an exasperated breath. If Eroe fears this individual, who knows what they are capable of. As Eroe's anxiety accelerated, the sky grew darker, like deep blood pumping through a heart. He flexed his hands.

My own fear gripped me. A manipulator should always be feared. I am afraid of the binding strings, the inability to breathe, and becoming subject in the presence of another.

No, I won't allow this, I thought. My eyes flared. The sky was under my command as it swarmed dark green.

Waves came rolling in high like a flood, threatening to take me under. And I smiled. It was my quiet storm. I could scream without making a sound. It was written on my skin and painted in the sky. Just like the art on the graffiti wall. "No strings bind me. I hold the strings," I whispered.

Before I knew it, a void was plastered over my mind. An abyss fell like a black screen over my eyes. I no longer felt the sun.

CHAPTER FIFTY-FIVE

JANCE

One by one I murdered them. The souls of the Seers turned into demons haunting my dreams. Killed for their ability to see the little blanket of glass that covered the sky, to see things no one else can. The bodies piled around me. I screamed with the pain I caused them and the pain I caused myself.

My eyes blared open from the nightmare. I heard the ragged breaths of Evanna and Ronan beside me, lost in their dreams.

Ronan's body flared like he was battling an invisible enemy. "I killed him! I killed him!"

I sucked in my breath, recognizing the familiar words of his nightmare. I crawled to his side and shook him. "Ronan, wake up."

Ronan shot up like a bullet, his amber eyes watered. He

took several deep breaths. "I'm okay."

I nodded and pulled him to his feet. Evanna lay quietly not too far away, looking pale.

Ronan knelt beside her, pushing her hair out of her face. "Evanna," he said sweetly.

She opened her eyes slowly. "Morning already?"

Ronan smiled. "A new dawn."

"Indeed," I said.

What lies ahead is a mystery. Humans always talked about how life was unpredictable, I never thought that. Life can end suddenly. I had witnessed death's game too many times. I've even played the role of the murderer and guilt will always be heavy in my heart, never letting me forget. Being close to death doesn't equal unpredictability, it means predictability. We will all come to an end, but it is the timing that no one knows. I always thought this made life predictably unpredictable. I stiffened as the wound in my chest pulsed, I will be feeling this for quite some time. I almost wished Jerik's knife had aimed more toward the middle and killed me. I do not know if I want to find out what's going to happen next.

Ronan told me the Ascendant took Natalya to speak with somebody important. He assured me she was safe. I tried to have faith in Ronan, if he trusted the Ascendant I could only assume he was on our side.

Ria's guidance was accepted with grace, she was the only one holding the Raidens together. We were now barricaded underground because the Divide was cracking. A few of the gifted Raidens remained among us because of family ties. The ones in the Herold's house had fled. They could still be in the fifth dimension, but all we know is Honoria had rallied them to follow her. The Raidens without gifts made most of our remaining population and tension was growing by the second.

I wasn't sure how I was going to rewrite my identity. I grew up telling everyone I was Jance Grey. Realistically, I have no title to the Grey name. I wasn't born into the family; I hadn't been born at all. Despite that fact, they were my only family and I was proud to be a part of it, even knowing their weaknesses. Jerik fell into a disturbed fate and he wanted to escape. I have no idea where the mirror took him. I'm glad he wasn't my biological father. I had to accept Jance Grey was not a part of the Grey line, but someone who was brought to the family for a reason.

I looked at my friends. "I'll kill my parents, though they are not my parents. I wish Jerik had told me more, I wish I had answers. Who put me here and why?"

Ronan looked surprised. "Jance—"

"No, Ronan!" I snapped. "My whole life has been a lie, Honoria was never my mother, Jerik was never my father. I have no parents, I was never born, I was *created*." I repeated my words manically, running my hand through my hair that always blocked my eyesight. I felt like it was getting whiter. "I feel like I am unreal."

"No," a voice ascended behind Ronan. "You are not unreal, you are Unparalleled."

My eyes darted to see Sylas standing next to a man. Another Ascendant, but my eyes didn't linger on him for long. Ronan went to Sylas and they hugged. I watched them, Sylas caressed Ronan like they had a special bond. I will not question Ronan right now about the depth of their relationship. I will find out one day if Sylas is worth trusting.

I couldn't tear my eyes away from Natalya. She looked beat, her face reflecting a blazing bronze glow and her long dark curls were streaked with blood. Still, she managed to smile at me. Her eyes a shade of green that I could only envision when there used to be seasons, they matched the color of newborn spring leaves. A fresh hope.

Evanna ran to her first and they embraced, Natalya held Evanna tightly. I saw Natalya pull out a random shard of glass. I watched something pass between them that did not require words.

Her eyes fell on me. I came closer and put my arms around her carefully as if she were as breakable as glass. She stroked my back gently. Her scars were not cold like mine, or hot like Ronan's, they were electrifying and flowed over her skin like liquid gold.

She retreated from my arms and raised her glass shard, she seemed to breathe a little stronger when she gripped it. I also saw a white flower peering out of her pocket. Natalya slid the shard inside her black and white clothes. She looked intently at all of us then turned to the man beside her. He had brown hair and green eyes that stared at me compulsively.

I tore my eyes away from the Ascendant as a chill went down my back. He looked at me like he wanted to hug me and then kill me. Then again, almost all Ascendants gave me that feeling, I could never tell their intentions.

"There's so much I have to tell you," The man said.

***

Eroe talked with me privately. It began with my parents. Honoria wanted me to be her accomplice, basically her slave. She stole me from him and kept me asleep until it was the right time. She knew I could create dimensions. She wanted me to build a new world for her that would be under her control and cast Jerik away.

I stared at the Ascendant as we walked along a white hall in the Undercity. Someone I didn't even know was telling me the story of my life. He knew my secrets that I didn't know existed. I felt sick.

"Honoria had been pregnant when she decided to bring you to life," Eroe said, lifting his arm around my shoulder. "She replaced her child with you."

I stopped. The sudden halt of my feet echoed within the halls of the Undercity. "What happened to the real Herold's heir?"

"If I knew I would tell you Jance. I honestly have no idea what happened to the Merciless child. Honoria never took the Grey name she only identified with it for the sake of politics."

I didn't want to think Honoria killed the child. *No,* I thought. *I would know it in my heart if she did. My brother or sister is alive.*

"Eventually, Jerik caught on. When you entered the House of Mirrors and came out with your ability that was all the evidence he needed. You were not his son and he despised you because of it. He despised Honoria even more. He wanted you dead because he pieced together Honoria's plan."

I couldn't believe it. There was only so much I could take right now. I wanted to know how Eroe created me and how was Honoria able to bring me to life?

Out of darkness, a voice whispered in my mind. *Honoria was practicing forms of dark manipulation. For something to come into light it must first be made in darkness.*

I decided to save that conversation for another time. I couldn't let my own mind become my enemy, but I felt like my hope was one in a million forces of evil chalked up against me. I must accept what has taken place. It's funny, the truth is supposed to make you feel better. Now that I have heard it, it only enforced the evidence that my life is nothing and I belonged to the shadows where I was made.

Eroe sighed. "Jansen, what's important now is our future not our past," he said passionately like he was reading my thoughts. "Put those negative thoughts out of your mind. There is something more important I must tell you. It's about Natalya and the fate of you both." Eroe's voice had a transcending pulse, "but you have to promise me you will keep it to yourself."

I nodded.

"Your powers are the same, as far as altering the dimensions to your will, but they are opposites in that manner. You were created, never born. Natalya was a Seer, and her past soul is scattered in unreachable places. The shard and flower you saw earlier are two pieces from her lost life. If she were to find the others, she would return to her past self. But she will not do so. She can destroy and you can create, those do not parallel." Eroe shuttered and his gaze diverted, he couldn't look at me. "You and Natalya are a combination that will lead to an unconquerable evil. The Destroyer and the Creator, only one can live."

I was on the floor unable to cry or scream. I refused to believe his words.

I carry a new secret now and it is a death wish hanging around my neck. My heart wanted to stop beating on the spot, but it still thudded with Eroe's words resounding in my mind.

CHAPTER FIFTY-SIX
NATALYA

I collapsed in tears in front of Ria and Donavan. Saying sorry would not bring Shai back, or make the pain go away. But sorry was all I could say.

I did not feel comforted when Ria put her arms around me and told me it was okay; it was not okay. Hearing her say that Shai would have done it for anyone did not make it okay. Nothing would.

I was just honored that they wanted me to be with them when they buried their son. I was dressed in royal purple. Ria had loaned me some clothes for the ceremony. I had never seen Raiden women in dresses, clothing here was made for fighting. The dress clung to my figure, framing my open shoulders, and exposing my scars. She told me a Raiden's scars should be visible when they lay their dead to rest. Ria said nothing about my golden marks, she didn't look at me any differently.

"My son always told me that our scars were beautiful and that we shouldn't feel obligated to hide them," Ria said with tenderness. "And now here I am, exposing them openly for the first time, as are you, at his funeral."

I winced. "He was right, your scars are beautiful they are a part of who you are. I—" I hesitated, trying to keep myself from crying. "I didn't know your son for a long time, but I know he was rarely wrong."

This made Ria laugh. "I'm glad you never told him that! That would have given him an even bigger head, especially coming from you."

I smiled shyly. I took a sharp breath in, looking forward to going above ground. I hated being stuck in the city of nightmares.

Donavan had taken care of the unconscious boy. The lost Elite, Kian Gracing, had been found in the Undercity. Eve told me that she found him when they were searching for me. She explained how blood memories worked, that they could dig up my memories to communicate. I was touched that my friends would risk having their minds torn open to find fragments of me, but I was glad they failed. I would never want someone to seek me in such a violent way, however, if I lost one of them, I would have done the same. Being reunited with my friends gave me confidence that no power could compare to. No matter what comes next, I have Eve, Jance, and Ronan. Some people you would go through hell for, and a few you would dare to move heaven.

Kian was laying quietly on the cold ground. I watched his breathing. It was a distraction from the ghoulish noises that kept regurgitating within the Undercity. His sandy brown hair covered his forehead, I couldn't help but wonder what color his eyes were. He looked familiar, but everything did lately.

Ria touched my shoulder and ran her hand through Kian's curls. "He's been missing for so long. I feel like there are so many mysteries to solve now." She sighed and moved her hands to her sides.

I heard footsteps coming, Donavan appeared around the corner. "It is time," he said lowly.

I took a shaky breath and Ria grabbed my hand. She managed a smile of encouragement, but sadness still lingered in her brilliant brown eyes.

We ascended a stack of rocks, then the Undercity opened to the sky and I rushed forward. We walked between two hills. Sylas was there, he approached me like an old friend.

He raised his eyebrows. "You look lovely in purple," he said genuinely.

I smirked. "My favorite color."

Sylas's expression turned serious. "Shai's body did not fade to dust. But it won't last much longer."

I swallowed hard, fighting my emotions. "Thank you," I whispered.

He nodded and started to walk away.

"Sylas," I said.

He smiled as he turned back toward me.

"I'm sorry I failed you. I don't know how to save the Seers;

the children trapped in the fourth dimension. I don't know where to start looking for the one..." I let my voice fade.

Sylas's smile grew. "You did not fail. Do not think it is all over when it hasn't even begun," he said with hope behind his words. He pivoted and walked away.

I sighed, feeling weak with Shai's death weighing heavily on my mind. Then I realized it was my job to make sure he didn't die for nothing. Sylas is right, it's not over.

I caught up with Ria and Donavan. Shai's body laid in a place where no flowers were growing. They outlined him in screaming colors.

Donavan suddenly handed me a red rose and I winced, pulling my hand away I saw it had abnormally large thorns, my fingers were bleeding.

Every rose has its thorns and some of them have knives. I thought to myself.

I hesitated as I walked up to Shai. He looked beautiful like he was sleeping. Donavan started digging a hole.

When Donavan finished, he gathered his son in his arms. Bringing him by Ria, who held a straight face with tears coming down her cheeks. She kissed him on the forehead and whispered something I couldn't hear. Donavan carried him by me, this was my final farewell. I took a shaky breath and traced my fingers over his forehead to his dark spiraling curls. I locked eyes with Donavan. I didn't quite know why, but I wanted to remember Shai's eyes the most, which he had inherited from his father. I saw Shai in Donavan's eyes and I smiled.

Donavan walked back to the hole and laid Shai down

in it. Ria walked forward with her flower. I followed. Ria and Donavan threw their flowers down, I did the same. Then we covered him with the earth, which felt thick in my hands but did not stain my skin. Dirt fell off my body quicker than water, as if I couldn't be tainted. When the dirt was all pushed over, it hardened, and little spikes of grass shot up from the ground. Ria and Donavan backed away and bowed. I stood frozen, it all happened so fast. The last members of the Cassteel line walked away.

I didn't follow them. I wasn't quite ready yet. I lowered my body, putting my left foot behind my right, and spread my arms like a bird. Keeping my eyes level with the new sprouts of grass, I whispered, "I will never lose my spirit Shai Cassteel."

As I spoke I could see a stem, the start of a flower growing.

***

I stayed silent as Sylas and Eroe discussed the issue of Honoria and Jerik. I was not surprised at the bloodlust I saw in Jance's eyes about his adopted parents. He stood stiffly with his jaw clenched. Eve claimed that Honoria was responsible for the Remnant attack because the Raidens with gifts could easily reveal themselves, and she had started to gather them up quickly after the attack. I shook my head in disbelief, amazed at all that had occurred right under our noses. Eroe agreed with the hypothesis. Eve said the flowers in Honoria's room were dead, any evidence of her dark manipulation was gone. We would have to start looking for clues from scratch. She was out there somewhere, along with dozens of gifted Raidens, and we knew she still intends to pursue Jance and I. Jerik seemed to be less of a threat, he had successfully transported himself out of the Lost Paradise. However, no one knows where he ended up. Ronan expressed that Jerik was probably in the sixth dimension and Sylas believed it as well. Then again, these were all theories we still had to prove and it's going to take a long time to find the truth.

Eroe also explained to Jance, Ronan, and Eve who he was. He told my friends the truth he told me in the mind manipulation. The missing prologue to the story we were told about the creation of the Raidens. While he spoke, Jance and Eve fell silent. Ronan nodded in agreement as if he knew already. Regardless, getting the rest of Raidens to believe this was going to be next to impossible.

Jance and I shared many passing glances during the long talks. At the end of the discussion, everyone was mentally and emotionally drained. We all went our separate ways trying to find peace in the Undercity, which was like walking through fire and thinking you wouldn't get burned. Some places are not meant to be home, even if you were created in them. Where you belong is not always where you come from.

I walked the caves of the Undercity in my purple dress and my three and a half knives on my back. I wandered into Raidens, some smiled and bowed at me. While others glared and snarled. Some even gripped their weapons but they didn't dare attack. I knew what I would be up against. I was given the art of destruction and these Raidens are fragile. They trust nobody and I can't say I blame them.

No matter what they believe I am, I will rise to be the light. I didn't feel like I had to scream it from the mountaintops anymore. I acknowledge the great power within my quiet storm. Not all things call for a defense, I will only defend myself and my friends when necessary. I accept that not everyone is going to understand me, some may even vilify me. I will not entertain negativity, but I will do my best to spread the truth. Those who deny it will learn the hard way. Time is a cruel teacher and reveals all secrets. I am smart enough to know what deserves my attention and what deserves absolutely nothing. If you refuse to hear my words, I will make you feel my silence.

Rage itself does an excellent job of holding attention. I hoped that once the story was told the Raidens would at least bypass the prejudice they felt toward Raidens like me, and the Ascendants themselves. But I could see it in their eyes many were preparing to fight. My fears of the future waged in my mind. When the manipulated Raidens come to know the truth, would they be receptive? Or once they regained their strength and healed from their pain, would they attack? Would they run in fear of being manipulated again? I felt in my heart this was the finale of an old paradigm. The Undercity is full of resentful superhumans, even without special powers, these Raidens are still born to be invincible creatures. I'm worried the whole race of Raidens would unbind forever.

I sighed. My footsteps changed from patting the dirt to echoing against steel. I backed up, not wanting to go down these halls.

"You know," a voice said. "I don't want you to feel

imprisoned. If you need to go above ground—go."

I turned to see Eroe. I didn't say thank you, I didn't say anything. I ran forward, hearing my footsteps clang.

The halls were streaked with blood that would never come off. As I ran, I could hear light screams like distant cries. The voices of the past ringing against my mind, I shook them off. I lived over half my life inside my head. I was used to the voices by now.

The sunset broke the city's darkness. I leaped through the Death Meadow, my dress melting into the puddles of colors with the three and a half long knives resting against my spine. I lifted my eyes, my head spun as I tried to identify every piece of the puzzling sky. I gave up, I realized I couldn't fix that. I just looked at the rays splitting in many directions, finding beauty in something broken.

I took a breath as I gathered my facts. *I am Natalya Wells, I existed in the world, but I no longer exist there. Now I belong to the dimensions between the world, which I can somehow destroy.*

My gold scars glittered against the streams of light, the heat I couldn't feel. I cleared my mind as I took off in a run, and I loved it. At least that hadn't changed. The pace of my legs, the feeling of making my own wind as I ran through a world that had none.

I watched the sun descend in the same place it did every night, I stayed watching the image behind the glass turn dark. I bent down to pull a flower from the manipulated earth, and a new one began to sprout within seconds.

In the distance, I swore I could hear the clock ring from

Camden. My heartbeat matched every chime, and then there was silence.

My eyes glided over the plain of the Death Meadow, where the opposite side of the Divide encamped us. I ran toward it. As I came closer, I saw something standing in the way. I whipped out my long knives in preparation. I was willing to kill anything that stood in between me and the broken glass. The sudden urge, the power I could not control whispered to me.

Destroy it.

I was ready, Remnants no longer frightened me. I knew my fears and death was not one of them. I had been 'dead' before. Death was a game, and I played it well.

As I drew closer, my eyes widened, and my knives felt loose in my hands.

It was not a Remnant. The unconscious boy stood in front of the Divide. All I saw was the back of him. He stood shirtless; his body was not made of scars it was completely bare.

"Kian," I said slowly.

He turned. His face was wide set with gentle features, giving him a kind look. There were streaks of light shining through his hair like a golden aurora. His hand brushed the strands back to look at me, revealing a pair of immaculate green eyes.

My eyes were still locked on him and the voice that seemed to take over my mind was gone. I no longer felt the need to destroy.

"You don't see it?" he said. His voice was gentle with a confident edge that made me take a few steps back.

"See what?" I asked with a hint of fear.

Kian turned back. "The city made of crystal buildings, and the black mountains below the red sky."

"I only see broken glass," I faltered.

Kian's eyes were sealed on the world beyond the glass. "I can *see* it."

ACKNOWLEDGEMENTS

First, I would like to thank my mom and dad, who always believed in me and supported my dreams. For Jane, Terry, Brent, Amber, Izaac, Lyric, Bailey, and Addison. I would not have been able to accomplish this without your love and support. I am forever grateful for every single one of you. Special thanks to my grandma and grandpa, your love is truly unparalleled to anything in this world. I love you all. Thank you God, for your blessings and the amazing talent you gave me. For all the wonderful things the universe has to offer, for faith, hope, and love.

To my best friends who are more like sisters. For Jaedyn, you are a light in the darkness. You have always been by my side no matter what. You have an endless desire to work hard and always put others before yourself. I admire your relentless determination, your intelligence, and your will to always pursue the greater good, a trait I put in my characters. For Cara, you're fierce and have an amazing ability to knock out anything that gets in your way. You always seek the truth in situations and act on them bravely, an important theme throughout my novel. And for Michelle, my diamond in the rough. You have an unconquerable loyalty and always fight for the ones you love. You refuse to give up on anyone and you have a heart of gold. You have the strength to empower those around you, and it inspired my writing and your loyalty shines in all my characters. I love you girls.

For everyone that has touched my life, you all deserve thanks. For Blake, thank you for everything, all the laughs, and some of the inspiration for this book. For Christopher, you have a strength that is incomparable to anyone else I have ever met, you're a fighter, never forget that. For Ally, Kensay, and Lailah, the little sisters I always wanted. For Mike and Renee, for always treating me so kindly. For Ryan, you always look at life and see opportunities, not obstacles. For Sean and Megan, thanks for having my back and for loving my dog. For Cassandra, you always believed in my book, and you have the kindest heart in the world. For Kate, my favorite high school teacher, you have a rare determination that always inspired me. For Jenna, not only do you have an awesome name, but you have a great attitude and you never give up. For Taylor, you're fearlessly ambitious, keep being the change you want to see in the world. For Brandon, your leadership skills and positive outlook on life has helped me grow. For Matthew, thank you for being a friend to me when I needed one. For Michelle R, thank you for showing me what true perseverance is, your strength gave me courage.

Thank you to all my teacher friends. For Ashley, Jessica, Nichole, Laura, Sheila, Leah, and everyone who worked at the Child Development Center. It was an honor working alongside some amazing, hard-working women who always cared for every child and family who walked through the door. For Mark and Jennifer, your little ones, Tyson, Taylor, and Tristan, always put a smile on my face.

UNPARALLELED

A special thanks to Michele Khalil for helping me through this process. I would have never figured this out myself. Thank you for your beautiful cover design and formatting this novel for me. You've always been a strong woman, and you fought hard when times were tough. We both used our stories to empower our voices, and there is nothing more worthwhile than that. Thank you Ray, for encouraging me to put this book out there. For the incredible wisdom and advice. Thank you for buying me coffee. I will always love being called weird, like you said, it's a compliment.

I would like to thank Picasso's Coffee House. The place I call my home and where I wrote this book. For all the wonderful people who work there, I can't picture my life without you guys. Many thanks to the owner Chris, I could have never written this book without having Picasso's to escape to. For Caitie, Michael M, Amanda, Brian, Taylor, Erin, Quentin, Michal, M, Chip, Meredith, Brooke, Mindi, Yubel, Matt, Chris L, Mandi, Jennifer, Trisha, Sophie, Marcie, Michael S, Jen, Tom, Gabe, Darius, Liv, and Jessica. You guys are awesome!

For my readers, thank you for picking up this book. I hope you look at the world a little differently. I hope you embrace the strength you have, the forgiveness in your heart, and the power that lives within you. Believe in yourself and believe in your dreams. Never let anyone define who you are. Books became my escape when I needed them the most, they saved my life. I hope my book can be a guiding light for those who feel lost. For as long as these stories live, we live on.